ALSO BY SYDNEY KATT

The Shattered Alliance
Foresight is Flawless
Love Lies Bleeding

Sarcastic sexy suspense titles being added all the time

Sign up for updates at www.authorsydneykatt.com for
information about new releases

AGENTS
OF
DECEIT

Undercover Series Book 1

SYDNEY KATT

Agents of Deceit is a work of fiction. Any resemblance to actual persons, living or dead, events, or locales is entirely coincidental.

2013 Random Distraction Books Trade Paperback Edition

ISBN: 0615759467
ISBN-13: 978-0615759463

Cover art: Farah Evers
Editing: Tara M. Clapper

Printed in the United States of America

www.randomdistraction.com

987654321

For my husband.
You're still the only person I'd want by my side during the Zombie Apocalypse.

Prologue

You never forget the first time, or so they say – whoever they are. Through the course of a lifetime you may have dozens of partners, but the first one is always special. They show you the ropes and teach you everything you need to know; they watch your back. In short, your first partner is the person who keeps you from getting your ass killed.

Of course, none of that matters once the bastard runs off with your wife.

I've seen a lot in my days with the Bureau, but nothing prepared me for what I found this warm October night. This case had been wearing me thin, but I thought I had a break. The call came from my partner just after one o'clock this morning. He spotted Blackstone heading into Blaine's Rain and he was sure the deal was about to go down.

I told him not to try to take him until I got there. Jenna was sound asleep, so I hadn't bothered waking her. I didn't want to explain where I was going. I knew I would have enough to explain once this was all over, most of which she would not like. She deserved one more night's sleep before the truth was thrust upon her.

Besides, she hadn't been sleeping well.

I got to the nightclub at just before two. Blaine greeted me almost as soon as I walked past the bouncer. He was a nice guy, but I didn't have time for chitchat. Good thing he seemed preoccupied. I was able to find out that Collin had headed to the back of the club before Blaine had to help break up a fight at the door.

I fought my way through the sea of people on the crowded dance floor, scanning the room for some sign that my partner hadn't done something foolish. The shadows cast by the blacklights mixed with the smoke to create a purple haze in my field of vision. Blackstone could be long gone or standing right beside me and it would make no difference. My sharp hearing was dulled by the blaring techno music the DJ was spinning.

The bathrooms and storage rooms were clear. I was about to try Collin's cell when I heard a faint squeak from behind me. The door to the alley was open and swaying in the light breeze. A sick feeling crept into my gut and I drew my gun on instinct before heading outside.

Collin was slumped against the brick wall of the building, clutching his throat with both hands, but it wasn't helping. The blood oozed from between his fingers and dripped to a puddle on his shirt. His cell was beside him, smashed to a million pieces.

I pulled out my phone and called 911 as I knelt next to him. It was worse than I originally thought. Besides the slash to his throat, he had been stabbed in the back. The coppery odor of his blood was so pungent that I could almost taste the bitter penny and salt. Luckily, dispatch was efficient and I was able to get off the phone and back to my fading partner.

"Hang on, Collin, the ambulance will be here soon," I said, fighting to make my voice sound calm.

"Too late...for me..." Collin's voice was weak and blood sputtered from his lips as he spoke.

"Don't talk buddy. Save your strength. We'll get this bastard together."

"After Jenna...go."

Those were the last words he spoke.

I had seen death before; it wasn't new to me, but something about seeing my partner's bright blue eyes lose their shimmer and go distant as his hands fell to his lap made my blood run cold. In that instant I knew that I would never forget this image. I had never lost a partner this way before.

It was my first time.

"Sonofabitch! I'm taking you down, Blackstone. You had better pray that I get to Jenna before you do."

As the lights and sirens arrived, I jumped into my SUV and sped away.

Chapter 1

"Agent Caldwell, get your ass in here!"

I never liked the way Special Agent in Charge Sherry Banks yelled from her office instead of using the intercom system like everyone else. Come to think of it, I didn't like having to report directly to her. It wasn't that she was a woman; it was that she acted like a woman with something to prove. She loved putting her subordinates in place every chance she got.

And now it was my turn.

It was with a sense of reluctant duty I got up and walked to her office. She was on the phone when I got there, so at least she had a good excuse for not buzzing me. She motioned for me to come in and mouthed that I should shut the door. I decided to make myself comfortable though I had not been offered a seat. From the scowl on her still-tanned face I could tell that she was not hearing good news.

"Of course, sir, the next flight out. I'll be in touch."

Once she hung up the phone and turned to me, I could tell that I wasn't going to like a word that passed through her lips.

"How long will it take you to pack, Jackson?"

"Bag stays packed. Break the bad news, already. Where to?"

"The boys in Dallas need some help on a case."

"Aren't they tired of D.C. bailing them out yet?"

She shrugged. "Probably, but we need you on this one. The request for my best agent on this came straight from the top. Franklin is in deep cover so I'm sending you."

Since I'd never heard Banks pass out a compliment before I decided that was what it sounded like. It was funny to hear her speak of the director of the FBI in a formal manner. Everyone knew they had known each other since before they could walk. She probably thought her office was bugged again. It was also common knowledge that the higher up you were in our line of work, the more paranoid you became.

Maybe if I'd been more paranoid then things would have worked out different for me. Special Agent Seth Franklin had been my best friend, my partner, and my mentor when I first came to the Bureau. On some level I knew that he was the best agent my office had, it just mattered less and less to me once he'd married my wife – damn, ex-wife – over the summer. Every time Banks sung his praises, the knife in my back twisted in a little deeper.

I resigned myself to the field trip and asked, "What's the case and why me? Be straight with me."

Banks stood and walked around to the front of her desk. She sat on the edge and smoothed her sleek, burgundy hair. Unbelievable. I ask her to be straight with me and she thinks that means to flirt. She's always been flirtatious with me – and it wasn't always totally one-sided – but it was starting to get ridiculous.

Ever since Melissa ran off with my ex-partner, it felt as though I had a giant neon sign reading "vacancy" blinking over my head. Don't get me wrong, Sherry's a looker. She knew what she wanted out of life and she had a body that would get her as far as she wanted to go. Still, the Bureau was uncompromising in its policy on interoffice romance.

Of course, when you play 18 holes with FBI Director Shipley and the guy who ran the president's security detail on Friday afternoons, the rules clearly did not apply to you.

"An informant has told us that we have a freelancer planning an attack on DFW International Airport, but the timeframe is sketchy. We could be looking at anywhere from two weeks to two months."

Shit. Freelancers are the worst breed of terrorist. They have no religious or political affiliations and they fall into one of two categories. Most freelancers are glorified hit men, strictly about the payoff, but a few are just wired wrong. They get off on destruction and are almost impossible to find when in hiding. I didn't have to be told which kind I was being sent after. I never got the easy cases.

"The rest of the details we have are as sketchy as the timeline, but we know that our man will be in the area for his high school reunion when this is planned."

"That isn't a lot to go on. Am I supposed to crash the reunion and arrest him?"

"Hardly. You're going undercover, Caldwell," Banks replied with a wink.

I was more than a little puzzled by that. "Why? The Patriot Act would allow us to take him into custody and hold him for an indefinite period of time if we suspect..."

"Don't you think I know that?" she snapped. "I'm the one who wrote half of it. At least you do on occasion read the memos that I put on your desk." She fluttered one of her hands to dismiss it, pausing to inspect a non-existent chip in her flawless manicure.

"The public is getting wary of us using that power. We cannot afford to have a false arrest scandal on our hands like the CIA debacle last month. This operation has to be surgical. He had two friends in high school: Jenna Monroe and Trista Sand. The agents in Psych are sure he will contact them. They either know something, or they will know something."

Two friends in high school? He must have been a real popular guy. Shaking my head, I watched as she leaned back to retrieve four manila folders from the far side of her desk. She really did have amazing legs. The woman could send me to Siberia in the winter without a coat and I'd go with a smile if she showed a little more leg.

"Here are their dossiers. Special Agent Collin McShae will meet you at DFW International Airport. You're on American flight 654 out of Dulles. It leaves in an hour. Get going."

"One question?"

"Make it fast."

"You didn't tell me why you want me on this one."

She flashed me one of her more seductive smiles. "That's simple. Your cover is as a management consultant, fresh into town. You happen to be the only agent I have who can talk about all that accounting crap and still turn me on."

"Excuse me?" I said in relative disbelief. Though I knew she was attracted to me, this was the first time she was so blatant in her words. I didn't consider myself anything special: black hair, blue eyes, olive skin, six foot two, divorced by thirty-two – not quite every woman's dream. At least my regimen of running five miles a day and lifting weights kept me looking good enough to still attract the glances of women I'd never met.

But not this woman. Sherry could snap up anyone she wanted and it was unnerving that she'd set her sights on me. She's my boss, after all.

"Look, you're no school boy. You need to insert yourself into the lives of these women by whatever means possible." She started to dismiss me, but stopped short.

"Before I forget, read Jenna Monroe's file thoroughly. Something doesn't add up about her."

"What do you mean?" I was intrigued. Things always added up for her.

"You can read. Now, get your ass out of my office and on that plane. Oh, and when you call to check in, I'm your sister."

What a bizarre family I must have, I thought as I headed across the parking garage to my car.

As soon as we reached our cruising altitude and I had exchanged a few pleasantries with the robust man sitting next to me, I began to go through the dossiers I had been given. When I'm on assignment, I normally like to start with the file on my alias and move on to the Target File; however, Banks had piqued my curiosity. The first file I went for was the one on Monroe.

She was twenty-seven and never married. Her childhood appeared normal enough, according to the file. Monroe's parents were married up until their deaths in a church fire ten years ago. Michael Monroe was a partner in one of the country's premier law firms. It appeared that Elizabeth Monroe never worked outside of the home. I assumed she stayed home to take care of her two daughters, Jenna and Elaine, for as long as she felt they needed her before undertaking charity work for her church.

This was boring stuff so far. Maybe Banks was losing her edge if this didn't add up for her.

To help hold my attention, I removed Monroe's picture from the file. The photo was grainy, almost like we'd pulled it from a supermarket surveillance camera. Wait. She was in front of the dairy case. Apparently, we *had* taken it from the supermarket. I studied her for a minute before replacing it. She wasn't anything special, but I wouldn't run screaming from her if I saw her. She was too plain.

Not my type.

All right, time to go back to the stats. After the death of her parents, Jenna had moved in with her older sister and her husband to finish out her final semester of high school. Despite the tragedy, she finished second in her class and received a full scholarship to Harvard. Impressive. After all of this, she graduated at the top of her class at Harvard Law. She started an internship with a top Boston law firm before graduation, but she never took the Bar.

Here we go, I thought with a sense of satisfaction. This is finally going to get interesting.

Two years ago, she blew off the Bar and moved back to Dallas. She didn't even bother to put in her two weeks; she called one morning and said she was moving home. She stayed with Trista Sand for six months before both women moved to condos in North Dallas. Both were paid for in cash.

Eighteen months ago, her first book had been published and she had been on the *New York Times* Best Sellers List ever since. It seemed like a real waste of talent to me. This woman was obviously intelligent, but what did she do? Instead of helping put criminals behind bars, she spent her time writing books for children about cats.

I could see why she confused Banks. Her life most certainly did not add up. Law gets in your blood like a drug and takes control of you. You don't devote years of your life to it just to wake up one morning and say, 'Gee, I think I'll throw my career out the window and write crap for kids.' It just doesn't happen.

With the exception of that one mystery, Jenna Monroe seemed about as interesting as mud. I moved on to my alias file.

I was a consultant for Innovative Management Consulting, based out of D.C. I would have no assumed name. I would work from home, which happened to be across the hall from Monroe. Blah, blah, blah. It was always the same cover and I was sick of it.

I wanted to be transferred to the Financial Crimes Unit; they always got the good cover stories and the exciting cases. Being an agent under Banks – no pun intended – held no mystery for me anymore. My caseload was mundane at best. This assignment had to be one of two things. It was either a test to see if I could handle playing with the big boys, or it would turn out to be some kind of a hoax that would end up causing more paperwork than fieldwork.

"Good afternoon, ladies and gentlemen. This is your captain speaking. It seems we have some severe weather ahead. Everyone should return all carry-ons to the overhead compartments. We should be arriving at DFW within the hour. Due to the turbulence, I'm going to ask everyone to please remain seated and to keep your seatbelts fastened for the duration of the flight. Thank you."

Just great. Now that the person seated next to me had to put up his laptop, I knew that I would have to put up the dossiers and make small talk. I hate small talk.

Jenna Monroe filled the kettle with water and placed it on the burner. After her ten o'clock conference call with Chet Mitchell, her agent, she had promised herself she'd have a productive day. It was now after two and she hadn't completed a single thing. To make matters worse, she was out of iced tea again.

On her way back to the computer she heard a persistent knock on the condo's door. She hadn't taken the time to change out of her bathrobe and she was certain that her deep brown hair was a tangled mess, but she went to the door anyway. Her sister was the only person who ever bothered her at this time of the afternoon.

"Hi, Jen, I can't stay long."

Elaine Whitman breezed past her and flung herself down on the chair. She set her shopping bags down and threw her feet up onto the ottoman. Jenna sat on the loveseat and mentally prepared herself for whatever lecture was to come.

"I was at Macy's today and I found the most amazing dress for you. You're still a size four, right? Never mind. That was a silly question – you never gain weight. I've always been so jealous of that petite little figure. Just wait until you have kids..." Remembering what she was talking about, Elaine added, "Anyway, it's simple, it's elegant, and it's black. Perfect."

"'Laine, I don't need a dress. I don't have any place to wear it."

"Oh, really?"

"Yes, really."

"Really?" Elaine put her feet on the floor and leaned forward, a glint of mischief in her hazel eyes. "You don't have a high school reunion to attend in a few weeks?"

"I'm not going and you know that," Jenna replied.

"I know you said that, but you can't not go. You'll regret it forever if you don't."

"Somehow I doubt that."

"Look, I was talking to Trista and we both think that it's a good idea for you to go. You stay cooped up in this condo day after day, with no human contact. It isn't healthy for a young woman to be so reclusive. You have to get out there and snag a man before you lose your looks. You don't want to end up like Aunt Iris, do you?"

"That is exactly what I want, Elaine."

"Dear, I think we both know that's a lie."

"Is not. In fact, I used to dream of being just like Auntie Iris when I was a little girl."

"Jenna..."

"Nope. You had your dolls and made Sissy Tomkin's little brother play house with you and I dreamt of being the crazy, reclusive cat lady that made all the neighbor kids too scared to show up at her door on Halloween."

"Your fans will be devastated."

"Then they shouldn't show up on my doorstep to try making me do something I have said, repeatedly, that I will not do."

Elaine put up her hands in defense. "Okay, fine. I can't talk to you when you get snippety like this. You know that I worry about you. I just have your best interests at heart." She stood, making a point to leave the shopping bags when she crossed the room to the door. "I have to run if I plan to pick up Lana from school on time. About the reunion thing, please just think about it. It's been two years, Jenna. You can't torture yourself forever. You have to move on."

Elaine opened the door and turned back. "And, Jen, for goodness sakes...get out of the bathrobe once in a while and wash your face. Just because your skin looks like it's cut from porcelain now, doesn't mean that it will forever. You need a beauty regimen. Looks take work."

Jenna stayed on the loveseat for a long time after her sister left. She knew that Elaine meant well, but she heard the speech often enough that she could recite it herself. Elaine couldn't understand what she was going through; she was certainly in no position to be giving advice.

It was common knowledge that Elaine's marriage was always on the rocks. She had married a pilot for American Airlines when Jenna was still in high school and he spent a good deal of each month away on business. On top of the strain of having a long distance marriage, there were also all of their financial problems.

Despite the fact that Daniel Whitman made more money than most families needed in a year, they were up to their eyeballs in debt. Jenna always pretended that she didn't know anything, but it was obvious that they lived well beyond their means. They lived in a million dollar home in the ritziest country club estates in the posh city of Frisco and Lana attended the finest private elementary school in the area.

Daniel often possessed the nerve to tell her that she was wasting her money on her condo in North Dallas. While she had more than enough of her inheritance left to purchase whatever home she chose, Jenna liked the freedom of having a condo association to take care of whatever repairs and maintenance she may need. Besides, somebody needed to put some cash aside for Lana's college fund, even if it did cause more conflict between Jenna and her brother-in-law.

The whistle of the kettle brought Jenna back from her reverie.

"Okay," she said to herself as she stood. "First, let's get the iced tea brewing and figure out what to do with this dress. Then I'll kill Trista for this when she gets home. I hate it when she conspires with my sister against me. Why should they decide when I'm ready? They weren't there. They don't know. I thought this was my life. I'll sit around in my bathrobe all day long if I want."

Jenna realized that she had just become one of those women who lived alone and ranted to her cat. She shook her head and hurried into the kitchen. Maybe she shouldn't be joking about turning into the crazy cat lady...

Chapter 2

The pilot hadn't been kidding about the weather; it was raining cats and dogs in Dallas when the plane landed. What I had not expected was the damned heat. As soon as I got off of the plane, I felt a thick curtain of hot and sticky air hit me in the face. I always thought rain cooled things down, especially at the end of September, but I was wrong.

Very wrong.

This had to be what hell was like.

Luckily, I didn't have a lot of luggage to haul through the airport. I always kept a suitcase packed and in my car, just in case. I was also glad that my new partner would be meeting me here. I had heard horrible things about Dallas traffic and I was not looking forward to getting out there in it while it was raining.

My first impression of Special Agent Collin McShae was not a good one. He was leaning against the wall in front of the main security checkpoint wearing rumpled khaki shorts and a faded green golf shirt. Water droplets were falling from his red hair as his eyes darted around, following the path of every attractive woman nearby. In his hand was a torn half sheet of poster board with my last name scribbled on it in what could have been the handwriting of either a little kid or a serial killer. Clearly, he was not the most seasoned agent Dallas had to offer.

If he was then God help us all.

I didn't bother to hide my exasperation with him when I walked up.

"What the hell are you doing?"

He narrowed his bright blue eyes at me. "Caldwell?"

"You're supposed to know who I am."

"I didn't know what you looked like and I didn't want to walk up to a complete stranger and start chattin' him up about the case if it wasn't you. So instead..."

"Stop talking. I don't want to talk in the open like this. Where are you parked?"

I could hear him muttering to himself about me as he led me to the parking garage. I swear I must have followed him for fifteen minutes before he figured out where he had left his car. At least the parking at DFW was covered.

Once inside his red Ford pick-up, I expected him to snap at me for the way I spoke to him. He did not. We drove for another ten minutes before I broke the silence.

"Sorry I snapped. I just figured you would have pulled my file to know what I looked like before you came to pick me up."

"I didn't have time. I get called in on my day off, walk into the office, was given your name and told to pick you up at the entrance to terminal A."

I could tell he shared my exasperation.

"You never know who might be watching," I began. "Tell me, how would it look if you see a guy holding up a sign at the airport one day and the next day he begins to introduce this guy as his best friend from college?

You have to admit that it would make you suspicious, wouldn't it?"

"I get it Caldwell, I fucked up. Can we please drop it now and talk about the case?"

He didn't bother to wait for my answer.

"I don't know what your office told you about Blackstone, so I'll fill you in on what we know so far. We have an informant down in Houston who sent us a tip about a month ago that one of the terrorist groups had approached him about freelancing for them. They, of course, are all on our watch list and they need someone who is not. They want someone average looking, who won't raise suspicion going through airport security and Blackstone doesn't fit the profile for any of this. He's a biochemist for a pharmaceutical company, for chrissakes. He probably doesn't know the first thing about building bombs."

"Maybe not, but any man who has spent a great deal of time studying the way the human body reacts to different chemical agents is definitely a formidable adversary," I retorted.

I was not happy with the way my new partner was underestimating the destruction that this Blackstone guy could cause. This partnership was clearly not getting off to the best start. We drove the rest of the way to FBI Headquarters in downtown Dallas in silence.

Chad Blackstone shuffled papers around on his desk and ran his fingers through his unkept white-blonde hair, making more of a mess of it than it had been before. He had already finished the final reports on all of the clinical trials he'd worked on for the past several months. All of the studies that were still in progress had been turned over to the Clinical Research Associate who would handle the case from this point forward.

Friday would be his final day with the Houston office of Lone Star Medical. At first the transfer to the Arlington office had been unwelcome; moving back to the area he had grown up, being around all of the people who had tormented him, felt like a punishment. Now it was a blessing. Smiling at the people who would pay dearly for their sins...that made all of his sacrifices worthwhile.

All of his possessions were already sealed in boxes, waiting for the movers to arrive first thing on Saturday. He kept out only what he would need for the next few days and an overnight bag. The company had taken care of all of the details for him, including the matter of the bill. Chad enjoyed that his employer would be paying for him to stay in corporate housing on the Fort Worth/Arlington border until he found a comparable home to the one he was now renting. He was also getting three paid weeks to get 'acquainted with his new surroundings.'

Three weeks would be more than enough time for Chad to carry out his revenge. His high school reunion was two weeks from Saturday, which gave him ample time to set everything in motion. It would also provide adequate time for his plans with Jenna. Even without the new revenge scenario, he was enthusiastic about what they had planned.

Chad tried to suppress the fiendish glint in his cold, grey eyes when he thought about the event that had changed his life four short weeks ago. He was at work late the night he found out about his transfer; eleven thirty-six, to be exact. Two shadowy figures had approached him in the parking lot. They claimed that a mutual friend with sympathies similar to their own had suggested that they speak with him about their cause.

They wanted a bomb that could pass through airport security undetected.

He had, of course, told them that he could not be of any help. He was just a biochemist and did not feel that he had the specialized knowledge needed to construct such a device. It had been a risky move on his part. If they decided that he was a liability to them if left alive then he would have been powerless to stop them. They looked like the kind of guys who spent all of their time building muscle. Since the only muscle Chad worked was his brain and he had a physique that made that abundantly clear, his problem was obvious and immediate.

After a tense moment that Chad had known would be his last, they told him that they respected that. They also told him that they were confident that he was smart enough to know that telling anyone about this visit would mean the end of his life. As though he had a choice. Did they really think anyone would have believed him if he was dumb enough to talk?

Shaken, Chad had driven home slowly that night. He could not imagine which of the few friends he had would believe that he was devious enough to build a bomb. It was then that a rush of adrenaline shot through his body, causing his heart to palpitate with wild abandon. Somebody thought that he was clever, not devious, enough to do something of this magnitude.

At that instant the idea was born. There was enough money in his hidden reserves to fund this operation. After that, he could trade on this to get future jobs. Why hadn't he thought of this sort of thing sooner? Chad was confident that he'd be able to pull in enough from one well selected job to equal what he made in an entire year running clinical trials. Of course the threat of potential jail time existed for him to overcome, but he hardly concerned himself about that. With his superior intellect, there would be no stopping him once he set his eyes on the prize.

Step one: put this plan into action. Step two: rendezvous with Jenna to complete the plan. And step three: do whatever he wanted. The world would be his playground and anyone who got in his way would regret making that mistake.

Just after six o'clock, Jenna heard the familiar squeak of the access door to the condo and knew that Trista had arrived home from work. She allowed her a few minutes to check the mail and get into her condo before she went downstairs and barged into her friend's home. Trista didn't bother to turn around before she spoke.

"You can be mad at me all you want to, Jenna," Trista began as she sorted her mail over the garbage. "You never listen to me anymore. I figured that if I enlisted the help of your sister, you might reconsider the whole reunion thing."

"I don't like being attacked from both sides," Jenna snapped, a hint of resentment present in her voice.

Trista spun around, causing her chin-length golden hair to fly in front of her turquoise eyes. The muscle in her jaw worked for a moment, her attempt to remain calm, but after an instant she snapped.

"I haven't done anything wrong here. I'm trying to get you to go out with a group of people who you enjoyed spending time with once upon a time. I'm not trying to fix you up with some random guy off of the street."

Jenna could tell that her friend was hurt and she relented. "Okay, I'll think about it."

"Good," Trista said as she tucked a strand of hair behind her ear. "Did you hear that they rented the unit across the hall from you today?"

"No. Is it another elderly couple?"

Trista shook her head. "I don't think so. I wasn't able to get a lot of details because I wasn't talking to the guy in the management office who's got the hots for me, but I do know that all of the arrangements have been made over the phone."

"That seems a little odd. I don't know many people who rent a condo without bothering to look at it first."

"It happens," Trista called to her from the bedroom.

Jenna made herself comfortable on the floral couch while she waited for Trista to finish changing. Since they had been in high school together, Trista had never been one to stay dressed longer than she absolutely had to. Jenna remembered how she used to drop by on weekend afternoons and still find Trista sitting around in her pajamas.

She was shocked when Trista emerged from her room dressed in faded blue jeans and a t-shirt that hung lifeless on her lean body. Jenna's tone told her as much.

"Going somewhere, Trist?"

"Dinner. You're welcome to come if you want to, but I doubt you will."

"Why do you say that?"

"It's a working dinner. Maureen will be there and I know that you don't like her much."

Jenna couldn't refute that. It wasn't that she didn't like Trista's boss; it was that Maureen Jenkins had the annoying habit of always hounding her to take a few refresher courses in law at SMU. She couldn't seem to get it into her head that Jenna didn't want to take the Bar and join her law firm. She avoided social situations involving Maureen as much as possible.

There are only so many times that I can stand explaining myself, Jenna thought to herself. Out loud she said, "Yeah, I think I'll pass this time, if you don't mind."

Trista shrugged. "I won't be good company anyway. This new case is high profile and is going to require that I spend a lot of time looking for precedents at the law library. Besides, you know how overbearing Maureen can be when she wants to impress a new client. Come to think of it," Trista said, confused, "she still hasn't mentioned the client's name to me. It must be a bigger deal than I realize."

It ended up being an extremely long day. Because we didn't get to headquarters until late in the afternoon, I wasn't able to sign the rental paperwork to take possession of the keys to the condo. I wasn't wild about the idea of staying the night in a motel, but the idea of staying with McShae was even less attractive to me. I could only imagine what his place would be like: beer cans and pizza boxes on the floor; women's panties in couch cushions.

Come to think of it, that sounded like exactly what my apartment had been like before I hooked up with my ex-wife.

After being issued my black Chevy Blazer, McShae talked me into following him to Friday's for dinner. The rain had slowed to a trickle, but even with the reprieve it still took us well over an hour to get to the restaurant. The people down here had no idea how to drive. It wouldn't surprise me if half of them didn't even have a license.

By half-past nine we had finished our meals and were talking about the case over a few frothy beers.

"Trista already has a boyfriend, so she won't be the angle to work. Her boyfriend owns a local club. It's a real happening place to be," McShae said expertly.

I set down my beer. "Are you aware that the seventies have been over for decades?"

He took a swig of his beer and continued, finding no humor in my sarcasm.

"It's called Blaine's Rain. You should be able to find Trista there at least four nights a week."

"Party girl?"

"Not really. She seems to spend most of her time there sipping on the same club soda or glad-handing guests with Blaine. Anyway, she's a waste of time. She's friendly and all, but I don't think you'll be able to get into her personal life fast enough."

"That leaves me with this Jenna chick, right?"

"Unless you want to turn your charms on Blackstone directly, I'd say so."

"What kind of intel do we have on her? I need something to go on besides living across the hall."

McShae set down his beer and leaned forward with a flash of camaraderie.

"This will not be an easy one, Caldwell. She doesn't leave the condo much. She has not been observed with a boyfriend of any sort, so at least that gives us an angle to work. She does her grocery shopping every Thursday morning around eleven and she has dinner with her sister's family every Sunday evening. Other than that, she hasn't been observed out of the house unless she is with her sister or Trista."

"So basically," I began, "I have my work cut out for me."

"Pretty much. Is that going to pose a problem for you? We can always place me in the condo, but I'm afraid my superiors don't have much faith in my undercover abilities. They don't think that I have the kind of personality that makes women want to tell all."

Why didn't that surprise me? "I'm not worried about it."

"Well, I'm glad that you've got this all figured out. You can expect to hear from me at least once a day. I'll help you 'move in' tomorrow morning."

Great, I'm stuck with a partner who likes to use finger quotes when he talks.

"After that, I'll check in by phone to check on your progress and give you an update on what we've uncovered about Blackstone that day. I'll pop by as needed to add credibility to your cover story. I'm your best friend from college who got you your job with the consulting firm. Remember, if I'm your friend, you have to at least pretend that you like me," McShae said.

"Which office is in charge on this one, McShae?" I had been dying to know since before my arrival in Dallas.

"Technically, my office is because most of the manpower is from here. However; because of your boss's, um, affiliation with the director, your office will have jurisdiction on this one. You'll report to D.C. and I'll handle the contact here."

At least I didn't have to report to him.

"What time can I sign the lease and start to move in?"

"Eight a.m. sharp. The moving van pulls up at a quarter of nine."

Let the games begin.

Chapter 3

As promised, McShae had pulled up in the moving van as I was touring the condo for the first time. It was more than adequate for the purpose it was to serve: two bedrooms, one bath, fireplace, and a wet bar for entertaining. I did feel that it was pricey, thirteen hundred dollars a month for what I was getting, but I wasn't the one footing the bill.

After spending the next two hours lugging furniture up the interior stairs and setting up the rooms, we were left with boxes of personal items. By that I of course mean the family pictures and other memorabilia that the boys in design had worked up the previous evening. I hadn't seen them yet, but I knew I was sure to find several pictures of my beloved sister, Sherry.

I finally let myself wander around to get a feel for the layout, which was difficult. As Melissa would say, it had no sense of flow or feng something or the other. Scrutinizing the less than adequate kitchen, I realized that having bad qi was going to be the least of my problems with this place.

I had to admit that the furniture looked pretty damn good. It was the exact stuff that I would have chosen, had I been given a choice in matter. The living room was filled with two hunter green leather sofas and a matching recliner, a big TV in the entertainment center and tasteful pale green ceramic lamps on top of the walnut tables. There were a few well-placed family photos mixed around with the Monet prints.

The master bedroom was black lacquer and brass. It was almost as though they read my mind and discovered my ex-wife forbid that sort of furniture, no matter how much I liked it. I thought the mirrored headboard was a little too bachelor's pad for my taste, but I was the only one who would be seeing it, so I let it go.

The second bedroom would be my office. It was a standard set-up: L-shaped computer desk with a hutch, file cabinets with special locks, and a floor lamp fitted with a hidden camera in the knob. My case files, as well as any evidence collected, would be kept in the filing cabinets and I had enough fake files to line the front in case I needed to explain what I did or look busy at a moment's notice.

We broke for lunch around noon. Collin knew the area like the back of his hand. It turned out I lived minutes away from whatever food I wanted, which was good. I was an above average chef, but I hadn't done much cooking since Melissa left. It wasn't as much fun to spend all of the time in the kitchen to cook for one. Besides, something about the leftovers was depressing.

"So Caldwell, how long have you been with the Bureau anyways?"

"Six years." I didn't bother to look up from my sub sandwich. Food was the top priority for me, not making a new best friend. "How 'bout you?"

"Six months," he answered with pride in his voice.

Dammit! I knew he was still green. No wonder I had to fly all the way out here. If I hadn't, this operation would be doomed from the start with him at the helm. I just hoped the support team on this one was more experienced.

Out loud I said, "Six months, huh? What area did you come from?"

"Law enforcement, of course. I was a lieutenant with the Dallas PD. Where else would I have come from?"

"There are other specializations that people can come from, you know."

I watched a smirk come across his face. "Oh, is that a fact? Where did you come from?"

"I have my Masters in Accounting. I was an auditor for a top D.C. bank when the Bureau recruited me."

"How the hell does gawking at perky tellers all day lead to a career in intelligence?"

It figured that he would look at it that way. Only half my day was spent that way. The rest of it was spent trying to get them into the safe deposit box viewing rooms with me during their breaks – the one place in a bank that didn't have surveillance. Good times. "Who do you think handles the financing for all of the operations that are underway?"

He shrugged. "I don't know. I thought that all of the departments in the Bureau were interesting and... Oh, sorry."

"It's okay. I hate what I've been doing lately. I keep waiting for an opening in Financial Crimes to come up."

"Financial Crimes? You mean bank robbery, right? Why would you want to get into that?" McShae asked.

"My background is in banking, so it's a natural progression for me."

"Okay."

I could tell what he was thinking by the glint in his eyes. I cut him off before he could say it.

"Look, McShae, I don't think that I'm going to learn how to surf to catch the bad guys. I know that it wouldn't be anything like that movie."

"Good. You're no Keanu Reeves," he quipped.

"Well, let's hope that I'm enough like him to get to the girl and catch the bad guy."

McShae shook his head. "You're one lucky bastard. The girl was the main reason I wanted to be undercover on this one."

"Really?" I couldn't figure out why he'd want her. "I don't get it. She seems bland to me."

His eyes sparkled. "Yeah, but the quiet ones are the freakiest in bed."

He had a point. "That may be the case. I just really don't want to pretend to care about cat books to get to her."

"She might have something else to say. Anyway, we'd better go over your cover one more time," his voice grew serious. "It's unlikely you'll be in the condo for long before you meet Trista or Jenna. You can't slip or we're finished. Jenna Monroe is a smart woman, even though she traded in her law books for picture books. If she senses something isn't right about you, any chance of getting into her life will be gone."

"McShae, I've got this down cold. I'm a management consultant for Innovative Management Consulting. I've been brought in because LifeTek, Inc. has made a hostile takeover of McConnell Systems. My job is to go over the books, look at current processes and make my recommendations about staffing to LifeTek."

"Where are you from?"

"Virginia. I lived there with my parents until I went to the University of Maryland. Right before graduation, I was recruited by Innovative."

"You sound like you're reading your resume. Just say you went to UMBC unless you want to sound like a robot."

"Whatever."

"Have you ever been married?"

"Yes, shit, I mean no." I shot him a quizzical look. "Does that even matter?"

"Only if you forget which version you've been selling. I think we need to spend more time on this."

I hated that he was right.

Jenna sat in front of her computer, staring into the empty screen. Another day come and gone and she had nothing to show for it. The problem wasn't that she was out of ideas; it was that she had too many swimming in her head. Her deadline was fast approaching and she didn't even have a title yet.

Where was Trista when she needed her? She was always good at helping her focus, except when she was distracting her. Jenna could use her for either one of those right now. It didn't matter which.

It was no use. She gave up and shut off the computer. When Jenna went into the kitchen for a drink, she was shocked to find it was already past five o'clock. While she knew she'd been staring at the blinking cursor on the screen for quite a while; she hadn't imagined it was almost eight hours.

"Take-out it is," Jenna muttered to herself as she thought of the frozen package of chicken she'd neglected to remove from the freezer.

"Jen! Jenna, where are you!"

"Kitchen, Trist," she called to the direction of the slamming door.

"What do you think you're doing?" Trista looked out of breath.

"I was trying to decide between pizza and Chinese food. I lost track of time and forgot to..."

"That's great, but stop talking for a sec," Trista cut in, doubling over while trying to catch her breath. "I can't believe that you look like that."

"Excuse me?"

"You have no idea what's going on outside, do you?"

"Someone sprinkled you with crazy dust?"

"Cute, Jen, real cute. Do you remember the new tenant I told you about?"

"It was just yesterday. What about him?"

"He moved in today, he's fully hot, and you have no idea what I'm talking about. I can't believe that you were so lost in your writing that you didn't hear a hottie moving in across the hall. You should have offered him a glass of iced tea by now. I mean, really, it is a scorcher out there."

"What do you want me to do about it now? Should I go over there, iced tea in hand, and offer to help him unpack?"

"I know you're kidding, but that would be really good if he was home."

"If he isn't even there right now, what are you griping at me for?"

"He's in my living room."

"What!"

Trista shrugged. "I thought it would be nice to get to know my new upstairs neighbor."

"What about Blaine?" Jenna couldn't hide her shock.

"For the sake of our friendship, I'm going to pretend that I don't know what you mean by that. I want you to come over and meet this guy. His name is Jackson."

"I thought you said you weren't going to set me up with some random guy off the street. You know that I'm not ready for this sort of thing."

"What's not to be ready for? Look, all you have to do is come over and have a drink with us. Just be hospitable for a while and you can come back over here and be a hermit again afterwards. Deal?"

Jenna rubbed her face with her hands. She knew that Trista wasn't going to let this thing go until she gave in and went over there. Maybe when she saw how uncomfortable Jenna was with all of this she would back down.

"Deal," Jenna reluctantly answered. "Let me wash my face and I'll be right over."

"Good idea. You won't regret this." Trista turned to leave, but stopped short at the door. "While you're at it, Jen, why don't you put on a little mascara and one of those cute sundresses?"

Trista left before Jenna could answer.

Jenna stood staring at the door in silence for a moment after Trista left. Finally, she walked into her room and opened the top middle drawer of the dresser. She removed a snapshot with gentle fingers, careful not to bend it.

"Dammit Tony, I don't know if I can do this." Shaking her head, "The plan never should have changed."

I had to admit as I sat on the sofa in Trista Sand's condo, she had a nice place. The furniture was too pink and girly for my taste, but the floral pattern probably suited her well. From what I could see, the layout was the same as my own condo. I stored that tidbit away for future reference; you never knew when you might need to know the inner workings of somebody's home. If I had to guess, Monroe's would be a mirror image.

Even though I knew I would have to find a way into their lives, I hadn't expected to be invited into it. Especially not so quickly. Trista came home as I was affixing my name onto the mailbox. She introduced herself and asked me if I wanted to come in for a drink. After handing me a tall glass of lemonade, she excused herself and fled the condo. Since I could hear her running up the stairs, I assumed subtlety was not her best trait.

I could also assume she was going to get her friend so they could grill me together. That was a good thing since I was supposed to focus my attention on Monroe, but it would have been easier if Trista didn't already have a boyfriend. She was really more my type. By the end of the weekend, she'd have me staying over. Maybe I'd get lucky and she'd have a fight with her boyfriend so I could offer a shoulder to cry on. That always suited me well in the past.

When I was beginning to wonder if I was going to sit in the den alone all night; Trista appeared at the door. "Sorry about that. You must think I'm absolutely awful."

"No, I understand. You just got home when you saw me. You probably have other things to do," I replied.

"Don't be silly. It's just I had dinner plans with my friend Jenna and I wanted to let her know I was home. She has the condo across the hall from you. You'll get to meet her soon. She'll be coming down in a few minutes."

When Trista flashed me a coy smile, I could tell she was lying. Dinner plans, my ass. It's been a while since I did the dating scene, but I could smell a set-up a mile away. It was funny, though. She didn't have any idea how much she was helping me out.

I decided it might be fun to test her lie, so I stood and said, "It was nice to meet you, but I should go. I don't want to interfere with your plans."

I watched as a look of panic flashed through her turquoise eyes. "I wasn't trying to give you the impression I was trying to get rid of you. You should come with us. It'll give you the chance to get to know the area."

"I don't want to be a third wheel," I insisted.

"My boyfriend is meeting us at the restaurant. It wouldn't be an imposition at all," she assured me.

"What won't be an imposition?"

I turned to face the person who'd spoken. The woman standing before me was far more beautiful than her picture in the dossier made her appear. It was official; I withdraw my idea of working on Trista. Her long chocolate brown hair was pulled back, but a few strands had come loose and were framing her face. It was obvious she wasn't wearing much make-up, but her complexion was still creamy and smooth. The description in the file had also been lacking when it came to her figure.

I hadn't even imagined from her height and weight that she would be as curvy as she was. It was a lucky thing for me that I had long ago learned how to study a person without obviously looking them up and down. Otherwise, I'm sure I would have got smacked. Shapely legs leading to smooth hips, a slender waist, voluptuous chest...I had to stop this line of thought before it got any more out of hand. Okay, Jackson, focus on something else...look at her eyes or something. Crap, that was a bad decision...just look at those eyes...I was a sucker for beautiful brown eyes.

My ex had gorgeous eyes.

Out loud I said, "Hi, I'm Jackson Caldwell. I just moved in upstairs."

I extended my hand out of habit and was surprised when she took it. She had a good grip – something on which I definitely couldn't allow myself to dwell. Most women tended to let their hand fold into yours. I hated it when women did that and I was glad Jenna was different.

Trista walked from behind me to close the door and said, "I was telling Jackson about our dinner plans. I hope you don't mind, Jenna."

"Dinner plans, Trist?"

I could tell that Jenna didn't know a thing about any dinner plans. She didn't seem too happy about it, either. If Trista noticed, she ignored it and walked into the kitchen. After clattering around in there, she walked back into the den and handed Jenna a glass of lemonade.

"You know, Jenna? The plans we made to go to dinner with Blaine? I thought it would be nice if we asked Jackson to come along with us."

Jenna looked shaken, but quickly regained her composure. Sipping at her drink she said, "Oh, that dinner."

Trista ignored her again and continued speaking. I was getting the impression that she did that a lot. "I was letting him know that we would love to have him come out with us so he can start learning the lay of the land."

From that I took my cue. I didn't want Jenna to think that I was overeager. I've always been able to read a woman like a book, and the opening line of *this* book said that tactic would be rejected. I needed to appear aloof. That always worked for me when I was still single and playing the field. Maybe I should go back to that since I'd been single for quite a while.

"Really," I said as I walked to the door, "I have quite a bit of unpacking to do and I should let the two of you get going. Like I said, I don't want to intrude."

"You won't be intruding, Jackson. I always have to be the third wheel at dinner. Please come with us."

"Let me go change. I'll be right back."

I was surprised by the response I got. The plan worked; the request came from Jenna.

Chapter 4

As soon as Jackson closed the door behind him, Jenna turned on her friend. As usual, Trista ignored her while she called Blaine to inform him of their new plans. Jenna resigned herself to the setup and went upstairs to put on a touch more makeup.

In the car, Trista had insisted that she sit in the back and that Jackson drive. Jenna had given him the directions to the restaurant while Trista kept up a steady stream of chatter. No one was better at small talk than Trista.

Jenna did her best to hide her unease when they arrived at the restaurant and found Blaine already seated at a booth instead of a table, clearly on orders from Trista. Relief flooded through her when no one else noticed. The conversation started without hesitation.

"Hello, I'm Blaine Rainier. I heard you moved in the condo above Trista."

"Jackson Caldwell. It's good to meet you," he answered with a nod.

Jenna watched the two men shake hands while they let the women take their seats. It always struck her as odd that Blaine was the man with whom her friend decided to get serious. He had light brown hair, green eyes and didn't look a day over thirty-five, despite that he was about to turn forty. While she didn't know exactly how tall he was, Jenna reasoned he couldn't be much taller than five foot six since he didn't seem to be all that much taller than she. Jenna always thought he was nice and it was obvious he truly cared for Trista, but her friend had never been the sort to make the safe bet with her heart. That was always Jenna's specialty.

Sort of.

After they all placed their drink orders Jackson said, "I appreciate all of you being so nice to me. Besides the people I work for, I only know one other person in the area."

"That's my Trista." Blaine put an affectionate arm around her shoulders.

"So Jackson, what brought you into the area?" Trista asked after the drinks came and everyone ordered their meal.

"I'm a consultant with Innovative Management Consulting. I got transferred in from D.C."

"That must be a change," Trista said.

"It's not too bad. The weather is the main difference, but I can do my job from anywhere with a computer and a modem."

"Do you work from home, too?" Blaine asked.

"Most of the time in the beginning of a new assignment I do. Who else works from home?"

"Jenna does," Trista volunteered.

"Really? What do you do, Jenna?" Jackson turned to face her.

Jenna took a sip of her iced tea before she responded. "I write children's books."

"Why children's books?" Jackson asked. That he asked the question didn't surprise her in the slightest. She got it all of the time.

"They're easier to write than full-fledged novels. The plots are less complex and you only effectively write a fraction of the material of adult fiction. Plus, the demand is there."

"That sounds interesting."

"It isn't." Jenna was ready to have the attention off of her. Truth be told, Jackson's attention was making her nervous. "If you want excitement, you should talk to Blaine. He owns a night club not far from here."

"Really?" Jackson sounded interested.

"My place is called Blaine's Rain. I know it isn't very original, what with my last name being Rainier and all, but it seems to be popular with the twenty-something crowd. You should come by and check it out sometime. Lots of single women come out."

To Jenna, it looked as though that comment made Jackson uncomfortable.

"I think I will come by, but I don't really enjoy the dating scene."

"It must bother your girlfriend, huh?"

Jenna could have kicked Trista for her obviousness.

"I suppose it would if I had one."

Trista's jaw dropped in feigned surprise before she asked, "How is it no one has snagged a polite guy like you yet?"

"Not interested, I guess," Jackson replied.

"I can't imagine that would be the reason. Why don't you like the dating scene?" Trista continued.

Jenna was fuming now. The guy wanted to be left alone about dating. She could more than relate.

"I don't know. There's something about going out to some bar to pick up women that seems cheap. No offense, Blaine."

"None taken, but how do you expect to meet anyone if you aren't putting yourself out there?"

"It's happened before. I'm sure it can happen again," Jackson answered as dinner arrived.

Jenna was grateful for the silence that followed. She was so angry with Trista she could hardly remain polite. She agreed to come over and meet her new neighbor, but she somehow let herself get saddled into a double date. If that hadn't been the case she would almost be enjoying herself.

She had to admit that Jackson was handsome, but not in that pretty-boy way. At the moment, his black hair was carefully gelled into place, but when she first met him it was wavy and tousled from the move. His eyes were a clear blue that appeared both serious and boyish at the same time. His smile was easy and disarming, revealing the hint of a dimple. Trista hadn't been kidding earlier when she'd told Jenna she was missing a hottie moving in across the hall. She didn't remember the last time she'd met a man with a desk job that looked as good as he did.

Of course, she couldn't remember the last time that she'd noticed a man. Why had Trista insisted on dragging her out with this one? It wasn't a good idea at all. Especially since Jenna estimated his height to be just over six foot.

Jenna had always found herself attracted to tall men with rugged good looks.

"Trista, what is it you do?" Jackson asked halfway through the meal.

"I work for a law firm."

"You're a lawyer?"

"Hardly," Trista laughed. "I'm not smart enough for law school. I'm just an assistant. Jenna's the brain at this table."

Jenna could feel her face grow warm. "Trista's being nice."

"Stop being modest. Jenna was Salutatorian of our high school."

"Trista," Jenna hissed.

"What? You should be proud of what you accomplished. She went to Harvard."

Jenna kicked her under the table, but it was too late.

"You went to Harvard?"

She hated that Jackson sounded impressed. "It's no big deal, really." She tried to make her voice sound nonchalant, but knew she failed.

"How can you say that? Harvard is an excellent school. What were you there to study?" Now Jackson seemed too interested; too impressed by her.

Jenna gave Trista a look to keep silent before responding, "Law. I was going to be a lawyer, but it didn't work out. So, Jackson, what does a management consultant do?"

"Are you familiar with LifeTek, Inc.?"

"They make some kind of medical equipment, don't they?" Blaine ventured.

"That's right," Jackson continued. "They make heart monitors and pacemakers, mainly. They've taken over McConnell Systems, a major competitor, and they need someone to go through their books and make recommendations about their staffing situation."

"How do you do all of that?" Trista asked.

"It's not interesting. I go over the books and procedures from home before I stop by the business unannounced. I observe what they're like before they know who I am and I make my recommendations about staffing and finances. The goal is to make the transition as smooth as possible for both companies and their employees."

"How did you end up with a job like that? That sounds damn higher level to me." Blaine asked, signaling for the check.

"I have my Masters in Accounting. When you think about it, all I'm doing is playing with numbers all day. Hey, how much was my part of the bill?"

"Don't worry about it. You can get it next time we're all out together." Jenna picked up on the note of finality in Blaine's voice. She hoped that Jackson wouldn't press the issue. She hated when men got into testosterone-fueled fights.

"That sounds fair enough," Jackson conceded.

"So is everyone up for some fun at the club?" Trista asked with a gleam of mischief in her eyes.

"Um, Trist, I'm a little tired. Would you mind dropping me off on the way?"

"I can take you home, Jenna. I'm beat from all of the moving and, well, let's face it, you're on my way home," Jackson offered.

Jenna tossed a dirty look at Trista. She hated the position her friend put her in. She didn't want to seem ungrateful to Jackson, but she didn't like the idea of being alone with him. He seemed like a nice enough man, one that she might have wanted to pursue a relationship with under other circumstances, but this was how it was now. Besides, she'd just met him.

"Thank you, Jackson. That would be great."

After saying goodnight to Trista and Blaine, Jenna followed me out to the car in relative silence. She closed her door and turned to stare out the passenger side window. I started the car, but didn't put it into gear right away.

"Jenna, there's something I think you should know."

She turned to face me. "What's that?"

"I didn't have anything to do with this. I thought you should know that."

"What do you mean, Jackson?"

"Tonight was an obvious set-up and I wanted you to know I didn't have a hand in it."

"I never assumed you did. I know it was all Trista's doing. I was hoping it was only obvious to me because I know her so well."

"She isn't exactly the most subtle person in the world, is she?"

"She isn't, but at least I know she means well," Jenna replied.

"I know what you mean. People have been trying to fix me up like crazy ever since Melissa..."

I put the car in gear and hoped she didn't pick up on that. I didn't know how I was going to get myself out of this one. I wasn't supposed to have been married, but maybe she didn't notice.

"Melissa?"

Shit! I couldn't think of anything to say at first, then it all fell nicely into place.

"I didn't mean to bring her up; that slipped out. She was my wife. She died eighteen months ago. I wish I hadn't said anything. People always seem to treat me different after they find out I'm a widower."

Jenna fell silent. It was good I remembered the directions. I let her stare out the window while I drove back to the condo. The way I saw it, it was only half a lie. Melissa had been dead to me ever since she'd run off. And I'd had a few great dreams she really was dead. Franklin too. It was always a disappointment to wake up from those.

Once I parked in front of the condo, Jenna turned to me and broke the silence. "I'm sorry about tonight."

"What do you have to be sorry about?" I asked.

"Well, you know."

I really didn't know what she was talking about. "I'm not following you, Jenna."

"I'm sure you were looking forward to getting away from all of the pressure to move on when you moved here. I'm sorry Trista interfered."

"Don't be."

"I don't understand. I would want to be left alone," she said.

"For a long time, I did want that, but you begin to learn how to deal with things a little better every day. It's like the way I wanted to hold on to all of her clothes and keep all of the pictures of us around; almost like I thought it would make her less gone. I learned all it did was keep me in a constant state of grief. It was hard, but I felt better once I packed up her things and stopped looking at our wedding album every day."

I sounded so sappy to my own ears that I wanted to kick my own ass. It had better be true that women went for this sort of crap.

Jenna appeared thoughtful. "I never thought about it that way, I guess. I still am sorry about Trista, though."

"You shouldn't be," I said with a smile. "I had a good time tonight."

"You enjoyed being grilled by a table full of strangers?"

"People are only strangers until you get to know them."

"True."

"And everyone at that table wasn't grilling me. You were quiet most of the night."

"I'm a quiet person," Jenna said softly.

"It's too bad," I said as I opened my door. I was starting to feel more confident in the role I was playing. It was fun to be the old me again.

Jenna climbed out of my SUV and asked, "What is?"

"You were the person at the table that I wanted to be grilled by. I wouldn't mind getting to know you better." Much better.

Jenna stopped short at the access door to the condo and stared at me in shock. Perhaps I had been too up front in my approach. The look on her face didn't seem to be one of amusement. Her voice was coarse when she spoke.

"Listen, I'm sorry if I've given you the wrong impression here. This was not a date; it was people getting together for dinner. That's all. Thank you for the ride home, but I think you had better go now."

"Go where?" I asked, looking around. "I live here and even if this had been a date, I wouldn't have felt it appropriate to follow you up to your place without an invitation." Unless I thought I could get one in the time it took to get to her door, that is. "The problem is that, unless you expect me to go around back and break a window to get in, I have to follow you up."

"I didn't...you...ah...goodnight."

With that, Jenna turned and walked up the stairs to her condo. I followed her up at a respectable distance. When we were both at our respective doors, I turned to her and said, "It was a pleasure to meet you. Goodnight, Jenna."

As soon as I closed the door I went for the phone. I hadn't had time to set up the low-tech answering machine yet and I knew McShae had tried to call me a dozen times already. Besides, I felt like throwing the evening's success in his face. He'd bet me twenty bucks before he left that I wouldn't have any luck for a few days.

The phone barely had the chance to ring before McShae picked up.

"Talk to me, Caldwell."

"Caller ID?"

"Cut the humor. I've been trying to get hold of you all night. Your boss has called me three times wanting to know where you are. Do you have any idea how bad it makes me look that I have no idea what my partner is doing? Why do you have a cell phone if you don't answer it?"

This was like being married all over again. "Calm down, McShae, I was working. I went to dinner with Jenna, Trista and Blaine. You owe me twenty bucks."

I knew he heard the gloating tone in my voice, but he didn't give me the satisfaction of reacting to it. "How did you pull that off?"

"Trista's determined to get Jenna a boyfriend. I was out front when she came home from work."

"Did you find anything out yet?" he asked.

"Why, yes. Over dinner, they just happened to mention they have a friend who's a terrorist. By the time dessert arrived I had full details about his master plan."

"You're kidding, right?"

I could imagine his eyes growing wide when he said that. "Do you really think the FBI would have taken the time to furnish an apartment if it was going to be that easy? The only thing I know that wasn't in the dossiers is that Jenna is a nut. She seems almost interested one minute and the next she flips out about how this wasn't a date."

McShae was silent.

"What?"

"What did you say to her? I mean word for word what did you say to her?"

I recounted the evening to him. McShae was quiet up until the very end and he said, "Looks like it was your turn to fuck up, Caldwell."

"What did I do?"

"You can't come on to women like that nowadays. They get caught up in their feminist thing and shut you down. You have to..."

"Why am I taking dating advice from you?" I snapped.

"Because I'm still out there in it. You've been off the market for too long and frankly, you need some help with your game. That whole straightforward thing you have going isn't working anymore."

"You don't know what you're talking about."

"Oh?" Collin replied, sarcasm dripping from the word. "Since I had some free time on my hands this evening while I was hitting redial, I pulled your file, Caldwell. Then I made a few calls about you. I know you haven't been on a real date since your marriage went sour. That also explains why you've gone out of your way to be such a dick to me. I'm not your last partner." After a pause, "I also know this is the first field assignment you've had since that whole mess. Oh, and by the way, I saved your ass with your boss tonight."

"Oh yeah, what did Banks want?" I asked to change the subject.

"You never checked in. She hasn't heard from you since you left D.C."

"And?"

"You're undercover; you're supposed to check in as soon as you're in position and at least every 48 hours after that."

"What did you tell her?"

"I lied and told her that you were staking out Blaine's club last night and that you were with the mark tonight. I didn't actually think I was right about the second one."

"Does she want me to check in tonight still?"

"It's almost midnight there and I think I was able to pacify her. For now, anyway. Just make sure you check in on Friday and don't miss anymore."

"Okay."

"I'm serious. If you don't want to get stuck behind a desk for the rest of your career, don't piss her off."

"Don't you think I already know that? Drop it already."

I was getting sick of his mouth. What gave him the right to check up on me anyway? I was the ranking agent on this assignment. He was lucky to even be with the Bureau.

"Okay then, what's your next move?"

"I haven't thought about it. Since you're the expert on women, do you think it would be too forward to go over there tomorrow and apologize for my behavior?"

"Very funny, but yes. If you make a special trip to her door with some rehearsed apology, she will see right through you," McShae replied.

"What then? Do I sit around and wait for Trista to fix us up again?"

"Sure. We've got that kind of time. Look, tomorrow is Thursday. Go to the grocery store and 'accidentally' bump into her. Work the apology into the conversation."

I was skeptical because it was a rookie plan. I was annoyed because I was visualizing the finger quotes. "Do you really think that will work? Won't it just seem like I followed her?"

"It'll work. Just make sure you leave for the store first and you won't have a problem."

"Even if she doesn't think I'm a stalker, we'll still have a problem with her. You don't have to deal with her, McShae."

He sighed. "Fine. You lay the groundwork and get me an introduction. I have no doubt I can get what I need from her."

"Whoa. I never said I couldn't handle this." It took everything in me to keep the annoyance from my tone.

"Whatever, Caldwell. The way you're talking it sounds like you've already thrown in the towel. No one will blame you for this. You've been out of the field too long to effectively deal with a mark."

Now he'd crossed a line. "McShae, I guarantee that we'll get what we need from her."

"I smell another wager."

I grinned. "A hundred bucks says that not only will she tell me everything I want to know, but she'll fall for me in the process."

"This will be the easiest c-note I've ever made."

We'd just have to see about that.

Jenna wanted to climb into bed and forget about the night as soon as she got home, but knew she couldn't. She was gone much longer than she'd originally anticipated and her three-year-old grey cat let her know she was late once the door opened. He was accustomed to having his dinner promptly at seven every evening and made his displeasure known by biting her on her right calf.

"Okay, Buddy, I know I'm late. Let's go get something to eat."

Once she put his canned food onto a plate, he began to purr to show she was forgiven. Under ordinary circumstances, Jenna would search for her calico kitten, Chloe, but she was ready for her day to be over. Chloe would have to wait.

She changed into her pajamas and washed her face. The thought of curling up in bed with a good book crossed her mind, but was dismissed straight away. Jenna crawled under the covers and hoped sleep would come quickly so she wouldn't have to replay her evening on an endless loop.

"Meowwwwwwww!"

Chloe had other plans for her. Jenna shook her head in frustration. She would almost swear that cat knew when she was trying to get some sleep. She had no use for Jenna the rest of the day.

"Chloe." Jenna called out into the darkness, knowing full well her feline friend was on the floor beside the bed, looking up at her with those big yellow eyes.

"Meooowwww!"

"Come here, little girl."

"Meow."

"Get up here or shut up."

On cue, Chloe jumped up and bumped heads with her. She stayed in bed purring for about five minutes before she leapt off the bed to chase Buddy down the hallway. Jenna, now fully awake, cursed the playful kitten phase in silence and stared at the inside of her eyelids.

As she lay there, Jackson's words tumbled through her head. She hated to admit it, but he was right. She was sure he hadn't realized he was giving her advice she needed to hear. Jenna had been living with a ghost for the last two years.

Oddly enough, that hadn't bothered her until tonight. It was only once she opened herself up to the possibility of meeting someone else that what she was doing dawned on her. It also made her bed feel extra empty tonight. A strong, handsome man next to her would take the edge off her insomnia. Where that thought came from was a mystery, an accurate assessment, but still a mystery.

Granted, after the way she flaked out on him, Jenna wouldn't be surprised if she'd slammed the door on that possibility. At this point, he probably thought that she was insane, or at the very least, way too high maintenance to pursue. Either way, she didn't know how to smooth things over.

Jenna resisted the urge to get dressed and go across the hall to talk to him. It was just as well because she didn't want to give him the wrong impression. He'd made his interest in her known and she was beginning to think she might feel the same. No, going over there now wasn't an option. Her mind was conjuring all sorts of scenarios that were wildly inappropriate based on the length of time she'd known this guy. Going across the hall would be like giving him the green light to make a move on her.

That thought conjured more images, all racing through her mind with fiery intensity. This was ridiculous. She was fantasizing about a man she'd known for a few short hours. At this rate, Jenna realized she may as well head over there because there was no way she'd be able to get any sleep. But she couldn't do that; the voice in the back of her head wouldn't let her.

"Don't be mad, Tony. I think it's time for me to move on," she whispered, hoping sleep would soon take her so she wouldn't have to dwell on the man thirty seconds away.

Chapter 5

I knew the stockers at the Tom Thumb thought I was nuts. I hadn't remembered at what time Jenna would be doing her shopping and I was not going to let McShae know that, so I got up at eight o'clock and headed over. As it was already a quarter past eleven and Jenna was nowhere in sight, it would seem she was a late sleeper.

I decided she wasn't going to show after all, so I headed to the checkout lanes. It was as I got in line I realized that, despite all of my fake shopping, I still failed to pick up the few items I would legitimately need. With reluctance, I turned the cart around and headed back to the dairy section. I was reaching for the milk when I heard a voice speaking to me from behind.

"Are you following me?"

I didn't have to turn to know who it was.

"No, I think you're following me, Jenna."

"How could I have known you would be here?"

"I don't know," I said turning around and flashing her a smile, "but your basket is empty."

She looked puzzled by my statement. "What does that have to do with anything?"

"It proves my point. I got here first. Naturally, you must be following me."

It worked. Jenna cracked a smile before speaking again.

"At least my basket isn't filled with junk." She eyed the contents of my cart. "You have enough frozen dinners to fill up both our freezers. Can you even cook?"

"I'm insulted. I happen to be an excellent chef."

I held the glass door open for Jenna as she reached in for a gallon of milk. None of that low fat shit women seem to always buy, but whole milk. At least I knew she wasn't on the never-ending diet my ex had been on. She put the milk in her basket and leaned against it before she replied, "I'm not trying to pick on you. I'm sure you can thaw out one mean lasagna."

When Jenna started to push her cart away, I followed. "You shouldn't knock my skills until you've tried them."

"Oh, I'm sure your skills are impressive. Wouldn't want to damage the fragile male ego."

Was she coming onto me? "Only one way to find out for sure, Jenna. You could put my skills to the test."

Her teeth scraped over her lower lip in the most alluring manner. "Frozen lasagna, Jackson? I've had that before. It isn't really my thing."

"I've only been doing the frozen dinner thing since I've been alone. It's depressing to put together an elegant meal for one. All the leftovers in the fridge are a reminder you're alone. Not to mention all the dirty dishes."

"So you're saying you can cook?"

I smiled as I followed her down the bread aisle. "I'll tell you what; I can prove it to you. Come over for dinner tomorrow night."

Jenna lowered her eyelashes. "I don't know." Seemed a little late to play shy now.

"Come on, Jenna. It'll give me a chance to eat something other than fast food and frozen dinners."

"I should really spend the time working on my book. I'm under a deadline."

"I'm not asking you to spend the entire weekend with me." Not yet, anyway. "It'll just be a couple of hours so you can get to know your new neighbor and I can keep my culinary skills from getting rusty."

"Okay, I'll come on one condition."

"What's that?"

"No fish of any sort," Jenna said with a firm voice.

"What about shrimp?"

"Nothing that lives in the water."

"Well, Jenna, you have yourself a deal. I'd better do some real shopping now and put some of these frozen boxes back."

Taking McShae's money was going to be too easy.

Chad smiled at a group of his colleagues gathered by the water cooler, talking in hushed tones. He knew they were making the final arrangements for his *surprise* farewell party the next day. Of course, he knew nothing about it. He was little more than the simple fool who sat at his desk and figured out how to make the company rich all day. It wasn't as though he could ever figure out they would use any excuse to serve cake.

It was pathetic, really; they thought he wouldn't see through their ruse. The common man didn't have a chance when they were up against a man whose IQ was so clearly off the charts. He didn't have to take a test to know it for a fact. For that matter, Chad didn't think anyone he knew would be able to match wits with him.

He put away the busy work he was given to fill his last days. It was only four, but he doubted anyone would care if he cut out early. After a few pleasantries with the conspirators in the corner, Chad headed to the lab. He wanted to talk to his friend Alex before he left for the day. He was the single person Chad told about his encounter with destiny.

He passed a pair of official looking men in black suits as he neared the labs. They'd been having site visits from the big shots up at corporate all week so he didn't think anything of it. When Chad got to Alex, he seemed shaken.

"Dude, what are you doing here?"

"I was cutting out early and I thought you might want to get out of here too."

"I've got a lot of work to get done here. I should probably stay. Rain check?"

"You realize that I leave in a few days, right?"

"Yeah, but I have a lot of work to get done, man, and I have to finish it."

Chad was suspicious. He walked over to the door and pushed it closed until he heard the faint click. He knew all of the doors to laboratories were self-locking.

He also knew all the other chemists chose to work the early alternate shift the company offered. They all left over an hour ago and wouldn't return until early Monday morning. Some things were just too easy – even for him.

"What are you doing, dude?"

Anger flashed in Chad's eyes before he turned to face his so-called friend.

"Who were the suits, Alex?"

"You know how it is..." Alex looked everywhere but at Chad, "We've had corporate on our ass all week and..."

"Don't toy with me." Chad took a menacing step forward.

"Dude, they already knew. I swear they didn't find out from me. I only told them what they already knew. I swear to you."

"Who knows?" Chad asked firmly.

"The FBI."

"You spoke to the FBI. About me."

"I had to. My kid sister is screwing some big shot drug dealer they've been monitoring. They told me they could bust him when she was with him, so pumped full of amphetamines that she'd never get out of prison, or they could bust him when she was gone and get her treatment. They said the choice was mine."

"I thought we were friends, Alex."

"We are, but Christ, she's my kid sister." Alex stood and stepped back, the very picture of a scientist trying to escape from a schoolyard bully. "She's barely out of school."

Chad shoved him against the wall. "Do you think that I give a damn about your druggie slut of a sister?"

Alex shoved Chad back. "Don't you ever talk about Maggie that way again or I'll..."

"Or you'll what? She's a cheap slut and you know it. Shit, she fucked me in the bathroom at your birthday party last month."

"Fuck you!" Alex took a swing at Chad, but missed. "I hope the feds catch you, you twisted prick! I bet they haven't gone far. All I have to do is make the call and they'll haul your sorry ass off!"

Chad calmly walked over to the desk and picked up the phone. "Do it. Come on. Do it. You don't have the fucking guts. Do it!"

Alex walked up and snatched the receiver out of his hands. "You should have kept your filthy hands off Maggie. We were supposed to be friends."

"Whatever; she begged me for it." Chad knew that was a lie. She'd actually been in too deep of a chemical-induced haze to understand what was going on, but he wasn't about to let Alex know that. Playing with his mind was too enjoyable. "Your sister's into some kinky shit. Hey, I bet she'd do you if you asked."

"That's enough." Alex pulled a business card out of his shirt pocket. "You only had a chance with her because of the drugs. She's disgusted by you. She told me that once, back when she was clean, before she got mixed up with that dealing bastard. She thinks you're fucking scum. She thinks that you're nothing but a sniveling little coward who's never been with a woman for free." He glanced up to meet his eyes. "I think she's right."

Alex looked down at the telephone to dial. Effortlessly, Chad picked up the base of the phone and slammed it across Alex's temple. He crumpled to the ground, blood pooling on the pristine laboratory floor. Calm now, Chad retrieved the door key from the desk and picked up the business card. If only Agent Bradley knew he'd just cost a man his life.

A smile played at the corner of Chad's crooked mouth as he walked across the parking garage to his car. The adrenaline was still pumping through his veins as he headed home. He'd never realized how satisfying it could be to end a man's life with his bare hands. Perhaps that was why people lifted weights...

A few minutes past six o'clock that night, Jenna heard a light knock at her door. She discovered Trista in tears when she opened it.

"It's Blaine," Trista sobbed as she was led her into the living room and handed her a box of tissues.

"What's wrong with Blaine?" Jenna was concerned. Trista had never been one to cry over every little thing. Something had to be seriously wrong for her to be too upset to speak. She went to the kitchen to retrieve a bottle of water for her friend.

"Thanks, Jen. I don't know what to do. I want to believe Blaine, but I just don't know."

"Start at the beginning, Trist. I'm not sure what you're talking about yet."

She took a few deep breaths and a long sip of water before she could find her voice over the lump in her throat. "You remember the case I told you about a few days ago, right? The really high profile one."

"I remember you said there was a new case you would have to devote a lot of time to, but you didn't give me any specifics."

"I didn't have them, not until this afternoon." She paused long enough to take another steadying breath. "There's a prostitution scandal. There's a lot of evidence against a nightclub. The prosecution says this club is pimpin' girls out the back. They even have some of the hookers ready to testify. It looks bad for the client. I mean really bad. He looks guilty as sin."

"What does any of this have to do with Blaine?" Jenna asked.

"It's Blaine's Rain."

"Oh, Trista...I'm sorry."

"Yeah, me too. Maureen didn't want me to know all the details. She purposefully kept me from knowing which club we were dealing with until this afternoon. I don't think she would have told me, but Blaine was in her office when I got back from lunch. I think they were both trying to protect me."

Trista looked more hurt than angry.

"You can't believe he's guilty of something like that. He's not a criminal. Besides, you're down there half the week. There's no way he would be able to hide something like that from you."

"There's so much evidence against him," Trista sobbed.

Jenna gave Trista a consoling hug. "Look, we both know he isn't capable of this. Cheating on his taxes...maybe, but not this. Someone has to be trying to frame him."

"I already thought about that, but Maureen and I don't know how to prove it." Trista looked Jenna squarely in the eye. "If it wasn't Blaine, I would never ask you this. Please help us with this case, Jenna. I know how you feel about this, but I need someone to work with that cares about him, not just the fee he's paying. Please."

"I'll do anything I can to help. When do we need to start?"

"I'd say right now except Maureen had a dinner she couldn't get out of tonight. Besides, we won't have all the files from the DA until tomorrow. Do you want us to meet over here?"

"Um, tomorrow?"

"Is there a problem with that?"

"No, tomorrow's good. Do you want to get something to eat or see a movie or something tonight to take your mind off of things?"

"No. I think I'm going to go take a bath with Ben and Jerry, maybe a Melatonin chaser. You know, get to bed early tonight."

Trista stood and headed towards the door.

"I'm here if you need anything, Trist. Love you."

"Thanks. Love you, too."

Once Jenna heard the door to Trista's apartment shut she decided to go and see Jackson. She hadn't wanted Trista to know she had plans with him for the following night. If she'd known, she would have insisted she go instead of helping her. It was better this way.

Now she just had to tell Jackson.

I was pleasantly surprised to see Jenna at my door. "I hope it isn't already tomorrow night. I haven't even started to thaw anything yet."

"Can I come inside for a minute?"

I could tell by the worried look in her almond-shaped eyes something was up. "Of course. Is everything okay?"

"No." She walked inside and sat before continuing. "I'm afraid I can't have dinner with you tomorrow night."

Great. Right when I start to make some headway with her, she takes a giant step backwards. It was time to turn up the charm if I was going to win my bet.

Erm...better make that close the case. Fuck it. Close the case and win the bet...

"Hey, I came on a little stronger than I should have last night, but I can assure you I'm not always like that. Some people actually think that I'm a nice guy."

Jenna shook her head and made a dismissive gesture with her hand. "It isn't that. I know I overreacted."

O-kay. I sat next to her on the couch. "What then?"

"Blaine's in some trouble with the law. Trista's boss is defending him, but it looks like the prosecutor's office already has a strong case against him. Trista asked me if I would help her out tomorrow. You know, brainstorm and try to come up with a defense."

Of course, the whore thing. I'd almost forgotten that Collin told me about that earlier in the day. I feigned surprise.

"Blaine's in trouble with the law? I know I just met the guy, but he seems strait-laced to me. What did he do?"

"I don't think that he did anything, but I haven't seen the evidence yet," Jenna said and shook her head. "Allegedly, he's been running a prostitution ring out of his club. All I know is some of the girls are prepared to testify against him."

"That doesn't sound good. Are you sure he's innocent?"

She sighed and slouched back into the couch. "No, but he has to be, for Trista's sake. She loves him too much. It would break her heart if he was a criminal. She deserves better than that."

"Is there anything I can do to help?" As soon as I said it I realized Jackson the FBI Agent could help; however, Jackson the Consultant was only good if she needed her books audited. At least it got a smile out of her. Damn, she had a sexy mouth. It was the kind of mouth that gave a man ideas.

Perfect, I'm trying to convince her I'm not a cad while running my own personal little porno in my head. Thank God the woman couldn't read minds or she'd be running away to the theme music of bow-chicka-bow-wow.

"You could understand and give me a rain check on dinner."

"Of course." Chicka-bow-wowwwww. Ugh. Now porn music was stuck in head. "I can cook anytime."

She bit her lip. "Good. I can't wait to see you in action. Um, you know, in the kitchen." She stood abruptly, turning several shades of red. "I've got to go. I've got, um, stuff I need to..." She pointed at the door. "I'll just let myself out."

I allowed myself to smile once she left. Either she was warming up to me or she had split personalities and this one had the hots for me. Either way, she was starting to feel like she could trust me. The craziest thing about this whole situation was, under other circumstances, I would have considered pursuing something with Jenna. In this situation, it didn't feel right. This had to be about the case and the bet, nothing more. I couldn't let myself feel anything for her, porno soundtrack notwithstanding.

But I could try to help her out.

After I made sure the door was locked, I went into the office where we set up my secure phone line. I couldn't have picked a better condo from which to perform surveillance, putting the office in the farthest location from the door was a stroke of architectural genius. The phone rang once before it was answered.

"Get a team together first thing in the morning. I want to know exactly what Blaine Rainier has been up to."

Chapter 6

Jenna spent all of Friday at her computer, her mind on fire with ideas. She was barely able to shut off her mind long enough to sleep the previous night. It was as though the moment she stopped denying her attraction to Jackson, her writer's block vanished.

Too bad she couldn't put what she was thinking into a book for kids...

By the time Trista and Maureen arrived at half past five, Jenna had typed fifty pages of her first real novel. Though long since forgotten, she could now remember writing love stories of angst and woe when she was in high school – just not exactly to this precise level of spice. All her years of writing essays and legal briefs sucked the joy out of writing; the time spent on the simple prose of children's books made her forget the pleasures of constructing a sentence so rich with meaning the reader might be compelled to read the passage again and again to uncover its hidden beauty. So lost was she in reacquainting herself with these old friends that she forgot they were even coming over until the unlocked front door opened and Trista let herself in. Truth be told, after all the steamy tension she was weaving into those opening passages, she was half-hoping Jackson would stop by for...well, anything.

"So how's the Curious Kitty today, Jen?"

Jenna smiled at the way her friend asked about her children's book character and shut off the computer. "I wouldn't know. I decided to try my hand at a real novel."

"What happened to children's books being easier to write?"

"Let's just say that I got some inspiration. Okay, now where should we start?"

Maureen closed the condo door and handed Jenna a stack of file folders. "Read over these first. That should bring you up to speed the quickest. Also, see what you think of the prostitutes' statements."

Jenna cleared off her desk, though it didn't stay clean for long. She spread out the contents of the first folder and pulled several packets of sticky tabs out of her drawer. Even though it had been a few years since she'd worked a case, she still remembered how to attack a case file. By seven o'clock, her head was spinning with details of the case and she was out of sticky notes.

It wasn't looking good for Blaine.

Maureen stood and stretched with a loud yawn. "Whatcha think, lady?"

Jenna took off her reading glasses and set them on the stack of papers. "I don't know. They don't have much of a case, evidence-wise." She stopped to rub her temples. "But cases are won with circumstantial evidence all the time."

"Dammit, Jenna! Don't you think we know that?"

"Trist, I just..."

"I need some air," Trista cut her off and headed onto the back porch.

After she was out of earshot, Jenna asked, "Has she been like this all day?"

"Yep." Maureen flopped down onto the couch. "This has got to be tough on her, but Jenna, she made me keep her on the case. I offered to pass this onto another partner at my firm, but she insisted that we take it. Damn, she's stubborn."

"Get used to it, Maureen. She's been like that for as long as I've known her."

"But why would she do this to herself? There are a lot of unflattering details in there I wouldn't want to read about my boyfriend, if I had one. If it turns out he's guilty, we're gonna find it and she'll know beyond a shadow of a doubt."

"We can't think that way right now." Jenna stood and brought the file filled with depositions over to the couch where Maureen was sitting. "One of these statements isn't adding up. Actually, most of them don't add up. They're all contradicting each other."

"I noticed that, but I didn't think anything of it. Hookers aren't usually known for their attention to detail. Besides, even if there are holes in their stories, it won't help our case. These women blow men for money; there isn't much I can say that will make them seem less credible to the jury."

Jenna rifled through the file until she found what she was looking for. "Keep in mind everything that you just told me and read this one."

Maureen's eyes narrowed as she read. "I think I see where you're going with this, but tell me anyway. I like going along for the ride when your mind gets going."

"This one has too much detail. This girl is giving dates, times, names...she's saying too much. I worked prostitution cases in Boston, and I can tell you right now that this girl is no hooker."

"Explain."

"Language. Her grammar is just a little bit too perfect. This operation isn't described as a high class escort service, but a back alley kind of thing. This girl doesn't fit."

"So she's some spoiled rich kid who couldn't hack it in business school and got cut off by her parents to teach her a lesson. What of it?"

"Okay, fine, that's just a gut reaction right now. Let me interview her for five minutes and I can prove I'm right. We'll revisit that point later. Look at the specific dates she's named as the times she spoke with Blaine about it."

"What did I miss?" Trista asked, closing the screen door behind her.

"I'm about to point out how I know Blaine is innocent of this."

Trista arched an eyebrow, but remained silent.

"This one girl names specific dates, one in particular, she spoke with Blaine about a job. When she was asked if she was sure about the date she says, and I quote, 'Of course I am certain. A girl does not often forget her birthday."

Trista shook her head in frustration. "I don't get it."

Maureen tossed the file at her. "Reread the beginning of that deposition."

They watched as Trista's face turned a deep crimson. When she spoke, her voice was measured. "Asshole. Let's take a field trip down to the club. I need to talk to Blaine right now."

"That's it? That can't seriously be all your man got in two days."

I was not pleased with what McShae was telling me. He'd had an agent in Houston for two days and we still had nothing. "I thought you said you were sending someone who knew his job from his..."

"Agent Bradley is one of our top agents," McShae said. His voice was measured and calm when he spoke, but his eyes were ablaze with anger. I guess redheads really did have bad tempers. Too bad for me this one didn't have the hot body to go along with it. That would have made putting up with his mouth worthwhile.

He was lucky we were sitting in my dining room instead of Headquarters or I would be raising hell with his supervisor over this supreme waste of time we didn't have.

"That scares me, McShae. Tell me something good."

"Look, Caldwell, you said that you wanted discretion. You didn't want Blackstone to know that we're on to him and he doesn't."

"Well, McShae, I'm so sorry. You're right." I could see he noticed the sarcasm dripping from my words. "I'm so pleased that he isn't on to us, especially since we know nothing more than we did before Bradley started."

"We now have confirmation that Blackstone was approached," he offered.

I shook my head in disgust. "We also now know he turned them down, but he has something else brewing. Instead of one band of psychos to worry about, I have two. Oh, and I don't know what either of their plans are!"

"You don't have to yell. Jenna will hear you. These walls aren't that thick."

"Don't change the subject. I want Bradley back in Houston first thing Monday morning. Blackstone won't be there, so we won't need discretion. I want him to talk with every person Blackstone has ever worked with. I want to know how this sonofabitch takes his coffee."

"Done. Agent Bradley is supposed to be there Monday to follow up with this chemist that seems to know Blackstone pretty well."

"Why the hell don't we have that guy in interrogation right now? Did Bradley have big weekend plans or something more pressing than catching a terrorist?"

"I don't appreciate your tone, Caldwell. I told him to back off. This Alex guy is tight with Blackstone. We're following up with him on Monday to give him a chance to find out all he can before Blackstone heads up our way."

His argument had logic behind it, but it was still a rookie mistake. A lot could happen over the weekend to change this guy's mind. The chances of him finding out more than he already knew were slim. The payout simply did not outweigh the risk in this instance.

"Or you've just given this guy a few days to tell Blackstone we're onto him so he can be ready for us when he gets here."

McShae sighed. "It was my call to make."

"And it will be your ass when this backfires on you. This is my op. Got that? If you do anything like that again without running it by me first, I will have you removed from this operation. Is that clear?"

"Yeah, Caldwell, it's clear as water. I'm not going to get into a pissing contest with you on this."

I decided to let that one slide. It was almost eight o'clock and I was starving. The incompetence in the Dallas office was wearing on me. I'd been with a team of researchers, investigators, you name it, all day and I had nothing to show for it. I thought it was clear we needed to find out what Blaine was up to, if anything. Apparently in Texas, when you say to put a rush on something, it means to toss it to the bottom of your inbox and do it whenever you feel like it.

Why didn't anyone understand the more time Jenna spent working on her case, the less time I had to find out what she knew about mine?

"Look, I'm starving and it isn't as satisfying to gripe at you while my stomach growls," I said, willing to let him off the hook for the sake of stopping the rumbling.

I could tell McShae was grateful for the subject change. "I say we head to Blaine's club. I'm sure they have some sort of food we could eat."

I couldn't conceal the smirk caused by his statement. "I hardly think going clubbing is going to make..."

"No, it's recon," he interrupted. "We can see what's going on down there first-hand. Besides, it's Friday night and you need to unwind."

I knew he was going to press this until I relented.

"Fine, you win. Just let me grab my wallet."

"Oh, and just so you know, you only have one psycho to worry about. Homeland Security wants us to focus on Blackstone. They've given the CIA jurisdiction over the terrorist group until our case is over."

Finally, some good news.

Trista was inconsolable during the short ride to the club. Jenna knew as soon as she read the statement that the date in question was Trista and Blaine's anniversary. Maureen remained quiet as she drove, which was out of character for her. Normally, Jenna would welcome a silent Maureen, but right now she could use a steady stream of chatter.

Once the car came to a stop, Trista jumped out and stormed passed the bouncer without so much as a nod. Jenna and Maureen sat in the car for a moment, looking after her before either of them spoke.

"I hope to God that he's innocent," Maureen said quietly.

"Me too. Maybe he has a good reason why he made so many calls to the club that night."

Jenna was referring to his cell phone bill for that night. Once a specific date was mentioned, Jenna began to highlight the calls to and from the club on his cell phone bill. There were over a dozen.

"It won't matter, Jenna. She won't believe him without proof."

"She might. Trista puts on this tough girl act, but that's all it is. She has a real soft spot for him. I think we could find the most damning evidence and she would try not to believe it. Should we head in? I don't want to leave her in there by herself if she can't find him."

Maureen nodded in agreement. Jenna got out of the car with reluctance. She didn't really enjoy the whole club scene and came with Trista often enough to appease her. That was it. Something about the way people interacted at clubs was unsettling to her. While she didn't know exactly why that was, Jenna could imagine it had something to do with the women who frequented these kinds of places. Everyone expected men to cruise bars looking for one-nighters, but she couldn't understand women who did the same.

Trista was nowhere to be found, so Jenna followed Maureen to the bar. Once Maureen had her martini in hand, she turned her attention to the crowded dance floor. Maureen was one of those women Jenna didn't understand; always on the prowl.

"Hey, lady, you've got to turn around and check out the two guys heading our way. I'd do 'em both, but this one guy has the most amazing bedroom eyes I've ever seen. Too bad those sexy things are staring at your back instead of my front. Act natural. Here they come."

Jenna let out an exaggerated sigh. They hadn't even been there for ten minutes and she was already going to have to give some loser the brush off. She turned around ready to attack, but her scathing remark died before it even reached her lips.

"What's a pretty girl like you doing in a place like this?"

"Please tell me that you didn't just say that," Jenna snapped, keeping a playful lilt to her tone.

"I thought it seemed fitting," Jackson replied.

"So, y'all know each other?"

Jenna could tell Maureen was fishing for an introduction.

"Maureen, this is my new neighbor, Jackson Caldwell. Jackson, this is Trista's boss, Maureen Jenkins."

"It's a pleasure to meet you, Maureen."

"No, trust me, the pleasure is entirely mine," Maureen purred. "Who's your shadow?"

"This is my friend Collin McShae. He's..."

Maureen interrupted. "McShae? That's Irish, is it not?"

"It is."

Jenna watched as Maureen switched into attack mode. "I absolutely love everything Irish. Do you dance, Collin?"

Without waiting for a response, Maureen pulled Collin onto the dance floor. Jenna didn't know if she should feel sorry for Collin or not. However, she did know it bothered her that she ran into Jackson here. The fact that it bothered her bothered her even more. She'd known the guy for a whopping two days. She hardly had cause to be jealous.

Hardly? This was bad. She had zero cause to be jealous.

"Your friend seems nice."

Jenna smiled. It was obvious Jackson was only being nice. "That's one way to put it."

"I was being tactful. So anyway, you never answered my question."

"I didn't know you actually wanted an answer. I thought it was just a line."

He grinned. "Did it work?"

Jenna smiled slyly. "No."

"Then it was a real question."

"We found out some stuff that really bothered Trist when we were going through the depositions. She needed to talk to him face to face, so we're kind of here by default."

"I think you mean you're here by default." He nodded towards the dance floor. "Maureen seems like she's in her element."

"So does your friend, what was his name, Cole?"

"Collin. He does seem at home out there."

Jenna motioned to the bartender that she needed another club soda. She took a sip before she spoke again. She hated to admit it to herself, but her mouth had gone dry the instant she saw him. She was twenty-seven years old and she felt like she was in high school all over again.

"So, Jackson, what were you starting to say about him before Maureen dragged him off?"

"I was just going to say that I had known him since I was in college. I think he could tell I needed a change of scenery and got me the assignment out here. He's the reason I relocated."

Jenna made a mental note to thank Collin for that. Aloud she said, "Friends have a way of deciding what's best for you without letting you in on it first."

"Yeah, but sometimes they're right," Jackson replied.

"I suppose."

"In this case, they were definitely not right." Jackson made a sweeping motion with his hand as he spoke before he expanded on his statement. "When I told you the other night I wasn't a fan of the club scene, I wasn't just saying that. Collin thought I needed to get out and stop going through my files. Apparently, he's one of those people who think work stops on Friday at five." He paused and flashed Jenna a warm smile. "Annoying, isn't it?"

Jenna nodded her agreement. "He clearly works in an office, not at home."

"That he does."

Jenna noticed a distinct change in his tone from the joking one of a moment before.

"Is something wrong, Jackson?"

"No offense to Blaine, but I can't concentrate on a conversation in here. I can't hear myself think, much less you talking. I know it's starting to get late and I haven't eaten yet. Do you want to get out of here?"

Jenna was torn. Yes, she did want to leave - especially with Jackson. She hadn't eaten either, but that wasn't the reason. However, her better judgment wouldn't let her leave a friend.

"I'd like to, but Trista was so upset when we got here. From the looks of those two," Jenna nodded to a darkened corner of the dance floor where Collin and Maureen seemed to be hitting it off famously, "I don't think Maureen will be here much longer. I don't want to leave Trista here by herself if she's upset and she doesn't get the answers she wants."

"I don't think that's something you have to worry about."

"Why do you say that?" Jenna asked, turning her head to follow Jackson's gaze. Blaine and Trista were on the other side of the horseshoe-shaped bar gazing into one another's eyes, love etched on their faces.

"Okay, Jackson, crisis averted. Let's go."

Chapter 7

It was slightly after three on Saturday morning when a shadowy figure entered the lab. He didn't worry about being identified by the cameras. The baseball cap Alex left in his car a few weeks ago was pulled down far enough that the bill kept his face in shadows. Chad wasn't worried about the security logs, either. He'd been smart enough to take Alex's keys and badge when he left earlier.

Once inside the lab he worked efficiently, pausing long enough to kneel down next to his former friend. As expected, he was still unconscious and his breathing was labored. Chad knew he would be dead before morning if he chose to leave him there. As appealing as it was to let the feds know he'd done this because of their interference, it was a risk he couldn't take.

Chad realized his carelessness the previous day during his *surprise* going away party. Because he hadn't been expecting his friend to narc him out he hadn't been prepared for what happened. No gloved hands, no careful wipe down of the room to ensure that a rogue hair wouldn't betray him. Careless and stupid is what he was. If one single speck of DNA evidence linked him to Alex's death, the game would end here and he couldn't allow that to happen.

It had yet to even begin.

Chad hastily undid the ties that bound Alex to the heavy workstation, a precaution he took just in case the injury hadn't been as fatal as he hoped. He wanted the bastard to pay with a slow, agonizing death; however, if he miscalculated the head trauma he could simply get up and walk out of the lab.

"Right to the feds, you sonofabitch," he said aloud.

Angry now, he turned on all of the gas jets and partially plugged in a piece of equipment that was thrown in the trash after causing sparks earlier in the week. Luckily, the cleaning staff was never permitted into the labs unless a service call was placed with them and a security officer was with them the entire time. The company would never know its need to keep things confidential was helping him out immensely.

Chad tossed Alex's keys and badge onto his desk and fled the room. His last problem was solved for him the moment he saw an approaching security officer, one who was known for leaving his security badge on his desk.

"I'm so glad I found you, Sal. I can't get Alex to come out of the lab. I don't have a key to get in there and I think I smell gas."

Sal let loose a string of profanity while he searched his keys for the master lab key. "I'll get Alex out of there. You call 911."

"Done," Chad said as he started towards the guard's station.

"Alex is lucky to have a friend like you, Chad," Sal called to him as he raced to what he couldn't know would be his death.

The building's doors were designed not to open without the employee badging-out. Chad knew the entrance/exit logs were stored on a server at an offsite location. He couldn't use his own without linking him to the scene and it would raise too many suspicions if he used Alex's. He was, after all, about to die in a laboratory explosion.

Chad grabbed the badge off of the corner of the desk and sprinted to the nearest door. Electricity and gas were volatile elements; almost impossible to predict. He stopped momentarily outside the door and badged back in before dropping it to the ground.

Sal was a good man. He deserved to die a hero.

"The entire building?"

My anger at being awoken at five o'clock on a Saturday morning was now replaced by fury. Collin handed me a Styrofoam cup of cheap coffee he must have picked up on his way over and walked into my apartment. It tasted like dirt, but I still took several grateful gulps after I closed the door behind him. The caffeine would help clear the last of the haze from my mind.

Collin waited for me to sit down on the sofa across from him before he answered me. It amused me that he wanted me to be sitting down for his news. For Christ's sake, I wasn't a woman.

"There was an explosion in one of the labs just before four this morning. The place was gone before the fire department even got the call. It had to be a gas leak. From what I hear, the place was ash within ten minutes."

"Or it was made to look like a gas leak," I answered him. Then stretching a little I added, "This is one helluva way to wake up."

"Tell me about it," Collin replied setting his empty cup on the coffee table. "I had to make up some bullshit excuse why a management consultant's phone is ringing at four in the morning. I mean, what the hell could be so important that I would have to get up and leave this early on a Saturday morning? An inventory crisis?"

"Excuse?" I knew the answer to my question before he answered me.

"I was at Maureen's house. The phone woke her up. I had to think of something."

"You slept with her." Again, it wasn't a question, but I still got a reply.

"Of course. She's hot and was all over me last night. It's actually a good thing I did. She lives over on Arapaho Road, not far from here. Nice house; makes me think that I should have devoted myself to the other side of the legal system. My apartment is a cracker box by comparison."

While I certainly hadn't expected Collin to realize the ramifications of what he'd done by getting involved with someone Jenna knew, I hadn't expected him to tell me how it was a good thing for the case because it was close by either. It complicated things dramatically. What we did when we were undercover was like a stage play. Too many actors on at once always confused the situation.

He must have read my face because he said, "I know you think this is a bad move on my part. I know you'll ream me for this, but I was not thinking about the job when I was with her. Maybe you're right, but I can't help wanting to get to know her better; she intrigues me."

It pissed me off that he was actually defending his actions to me, but I let him continue without interruption.

"I've had some time to think it through after I got the call. I think we can work this angle to our advantage. Trista works for Maureen, so it's only natural that she might find out something we can use."

"You're making a pretty big assumption," I countered.

"How so?"

"You're assuming that you were more than a one-night stand to her."

"I guess I'll find out at dinner tonight."

His cell phone interrupted our conversation.

"McShae. Yeah, he knows. What? Do we have an ID yet? I don't care what the security log says. Get a DNA analysis and call me back. That's not acceptable. Put a rush on it. Don't argue, just get it done and call me back."

I only heard his side of the conversation, but I gathered there had been fatalities. "How many?" I asked, the grim reality of what we faced daily in our job creeping into my voice unbidden.

"Two."

"Who?"

"A security guard named Paul Salerno and a chemist, Alex Fehr."

"Shit. There goes that link to Blackstone. Do we know what happened?"

"The security access logs show that Alex entered the building just after three this morning and went to the labs. Just before four, the guard left the building, but came back inside less than a minute later."

"That's odd," I muttered.

"They think he smelled the gas and went in after Alex."

Brave bastard, I thought as I let myself sink back into the couch, the ramifications of this event sinking in.

At ten o'clock Saturday morning, Jenna hit her snooze alarm for the third and final time. The temptation was strong to turn it off and sleep for a few more hours, but she thought better of it. She decided instead that a long, hot shower would be the perfect start to what promised to be a pleasant day.

Jenna replayed the details of her evening as she showered. All of the restaurants in Addison had been packed, being that it was a Friday night, so they decided to pick up sub sandwiches and go back to his condo. While channel-surfing, Jackson discovered a movie on cable they both wanted to see, so it was close to midnight before she came home. Of course, she stayed up writing until sometime after three so she could very easily go back to sleep for the next few hours and not feel guilty in the slightest.

Jenna wrung the excess water from her hair and wrapped it up in a towel while she did her makeup. Jackson had asked her if she knew where he could find a guide to the city so he could find his way around. There were several errands he needed to run, but he wasn't sure where to go. She volunteered to show him around.

It looked like Trista was finally rubbing off on her. She'd be so proud.

She smiled as she took her hair out of the towel and tousled it a bit with her fingers. After scrutinizing herself in the mirror for a moment she decided to wear her hair wavy and reached for the can of mousse on the counter. Jenna thought it would be a nice change for Jackson to see her when she'd actually bothered to do something to her hair.

Maybe that's what it will take for him to notice me, she thought to herself.

Jenna couldn't help feeling a bit put out as she flipped her head upside-down and began to dry it. Jackson made it clear that he was interested in her the first night they met, but he'd backed off significantly the following day. Since she assumed it was because of her odd behavior, she started to drop hints that she was also interested. Of course, she was probably a little rusty at sending signals.

Perhaps he was also rusty at receiving them. During the movie, she sat next to him on the sofa. Admittedly, it wasn't exactly the same as sitting on his lap, but the man did have two sofas and a recliner. About an hour into the movie she'd commented that it was chilly. Jackson left the room and returned with a small blanket for her. Jenna offered to share, which would force him to sit much closer to her, but he declined.

As Jenna reached for a butterfly clip it occurred to her that she was probably the only woman alive to complain that a man she just met was a perfect gentleman. She shook her head and gathered her hair into a loose ponytail at the back of her head before she twisted it upward. She fastened it with the clip and let the length of her hair spill over the top of the clip.

Jenna spent more time dressing than usual, deciding finally on a pair of well-fitted blue jeans and her favorite casual shirt she'd never worn. It was a stretchy red shirt with a squared neckline. She didn't usually make a habit of drawing attention to her chest, but decided to make an exception since she remembered how well it had hugged her curves in the fitting room. It didn't disappoint. If Jackson's eyes didn't stray at least once then she would have some serious doubts about his preferences.

After finding a pair of comfortable shoes that weren't ratty from playing in puddles with Lana, she gave herself a quick once-over in her full-length mirror. "Here goes nothing," she muttered to herself.

Chapter 8

Collin spent the better part of the morning at my place. The DNA results confirmed what we already knew from the security logs. Alex Fehr, our only link thus far to Blackstone, had died in the fire. To make matters worse, the car that was supposed to tail him on the drive from Houston to Dallas got a flat tire about an hour into the trip. I had a team stake out the address we knew his belongings were being sent to, but I still hadn't received confirmation that he'd arrived.

To say that Banks was not pleased when I called with my update would be to call Texas a tiny state.

"What the hell is going on down there, Caldwell?" she demanded.

"We'll find him."

"You better," she snapped. "We have a terrorist somewhere in Texas, which is a pretty damn big state, and you have no idea where he is. He could be fulfilling whatever his grand plan is as we speak and you're sitting at home scratching your balls."

Well, that *was* the best use of federal time on a Saturday morning. "Would you prefer I get in my car and drive back and forth to Houston until I find him? I'm sure that would only take me a few weeks, which I know I don't have to remind you we don't have."

"You're walking a fine line, Caldwell. Don't piss me off; just find him. Now."

She slammed the phone down loud enough for Collin to hear.

"So that went well."

"Yeah, she's a real kitten."

He shrugged. "He'll show up. He has no reason to suspect we're waiting for him. Do you want to go with me to scope out the area surrounding his apartment?"

I looked at my watch and was surprised by how much time had passed since his arrival. "I can't. Jenna should be here in about twenty minutes."

"Oh?"

"She offered to help me find my way around town so I can run all of my errands without killing the whole weekend."

"What errands?" Collin asked.

"Most of my dishes and cookware were damaged in the move."

"They were? Our people are normally more careful about that sort of thing."

"I guess I should say that they will be. Would you mind trashing all that stuff for me while I take a quick shower?"

Collin raised an eyebrow. "She's probably going to drag you to some mall, you know."

"I expect so."

"I can't believe you're willing to put yourself through that kind of torture just to get into her life."

"I'm not. I'm already in her life, but I need to be in closer so she feels she can confide in me if she should learn anything useful. She needs to consider me a friend."

"Or a lover?" he asked, a goofy grin plastered on his face.

"No, a friend," I insisted.

"You aren't even a little interested in her?"

"No. I'm more interested in your hundred bucks. Feelings cause complications that we don't have time for."

"So let me make sure I have this right. You plan to make this woman fall for you by being her friend?" He shook his head. "You may as well pay me now."

It may not have seemed like it to him, but I had things under control. Just because I hadn't used my moves in years didn't mean the skills weren't still there. "Take care of the dishes and let yourself out. Call my cell if you find out anything else."

I didn't wait for him to answer before leaving the room; I knew he'd do it.

Fifteen minutes later, Jenna knocked on my door as I was fastening my belt. I hated to admit it to myself, but she looked damn good. I grabbed my keys and wallet and followed her down the stairs. It was a nice view.

"So where are we headed?" I asked once we were in the car. Might as well find out I was being walked down the plank towards that special hell on earth known as the mall and get it over with.

"I don't know quite yet, but turn left on Preston and head north towards Frisco. There's a ton of stuff up by Stonebriar Mall that should be useful without actually having to go into the mall. I can't stand those crazed crowds."

Will wonders never cease? Too bad I was on the job or she might almost be worth the effort to get to know. Almost.

Jenna didn't really know what she'd been expecting, but she knew that she was disappointed. They had stopped for lunch before they attempted to shop for anything. She had come to realize over the past few days that Jackson was a wonderful conversationalist so none of the usual uncomfortable silences interrupted them. Most people considered that a good thing, but she couldn't help remembering a pearl of her mother's sage wisdom that had been imparted on her after a quiet first date. Though she couldn't remember the exact words, she knew it was something to the effect that a quiet date meant the guy was nervous and she'd get called to go out again.

As usual, her mother was right, but that didn't help her now. Jenna had to accept the fact that she might have scared him off the first night with her behavior. It was entirely possible he was only interested in her friendship.

She decided to let it play out as they left the restaurant. The parking lot to the store they decided to try was crowded, but Jackson was able to find a spot close enough to the door that they weren't forced to make an epic hike back to the car. Jenna pushed everything out of her mind except for maneuvering through the crowds to the section of the store that had all of the kitchen essentials.

They were looking at cookware when a voice from behind them startled her.

"Jenna Monroe, is that you?"

"Oh, my God. Chad, I haven't seen you in forever."

With a warm smile brightening her face, Jenna embraced her old friend.

I couldn't believe my eyes. The scoundrel half of the FBI was searching for, Chad Blackstone, stood right in front of me. He didn't appear like someone who would wreak havoc on an airport, but I'd learned to take a deeper look early on in my career.

I watched as Jenna pulled away from his embrace and turned to me.

"Chad, this is my neighbor, Jackson Caldwell. Jackson, this is Chad Blackstone. We went to high school together."

I extended my hand. "Pleased to meet you."

He took my hand. I was not surprised to find it was perhaps the weakest handshake I'd received. "And you."

"So, Chad, are you back in town for the reunion? The last time I heard from you was when you accepted the job in Houston. That must have been at least two years ago."

"It's been closer to three years, actually. I just got back into town today. I've been transferred up this way so I'll be based out of south Arlington."

Jenna frowned. "What are you doing in Frisco? Arlington is fifty or sixty miles from here. I hope they didn't stick you in corporate housing all the way up here."

I thought I saw a flash of anger pass through his grey eyes. Jenna didn't seem to notice, so I remained silent. The last thing I wanted to do was draw attention to myself, or alarm Jenna in any way.

"I heard the Dallas Stars had a new practice arena up here. I've always liked hockey, so I thought I would come check it out. I can't believe I ran into you on my first day back. I had every intention of looking you up once I got settled, but this is even better."

Somehow, I didn't believe that this was an accidental encounter. I had no reason to believe otherwise since he couldn't have known she would be up here with me today, but I had a strong feeling in my gut that there was something seriously not right with this guy. After he shook my hand, he hadn't even glanced at me. His eyes remained fixed on Jenna as though he was taking in her every detail. If I had not been positive this man was a danger before, I would believe he was a potential stalker, if nothing else.

"Well, let me give you my number so you can call me once you get settled. Maybe we can have lunch one day this week."

"I might just have to take you up on that. It was really great to see you again, Jenna. Nice meeting you, Jackson." With that, he turned and skulked off into the crowd.

Jenna turned to me after he left. "Sorry about that."

"What do you have to be sorry about?"

She made a face and said, "He was a little rude to you."

"I'm sure he was just excited to see you again. I don't mind."

"Even still..." Jenna stopped short and let out a deep breath. "Okay don't turn around, but I apologize for whatever is about to happen in advance." Turning slightly away from me she said, "Hi 'Laine."

I watched as a woman in her mid- to late thirties walked up and quickly embraced Jenna. It never occurred to me that I would meet so many people in Jenna's life during one simple shopping trip. It was immediately apparent to me that this woman must be a relative. Although she was a few inches taller than Jenna, she had the same delicate frame and deep brown hair.

The woman turned to me and gave me a quick once-over. With a slight smile playing at her lips she asked, "Who's your friend, Jen?"

I couldn't help the amusement I felt at the slightest shade of pink that was creeping over Jenna's face. She wouldn't be embarrassed if I wasn't getting to her. It had been a long time since I'd done the dating scene, but it would seem I still knew what I was doing. Nice to know.

"This is my new neighbor, Jackson Caldwell. Some of his things were broken in the move and I was trying to help him get everything replaced." She turned to me and said, "Jackson, this is my sister, Elaine Whitman."

"It's a pleasure to meet you, Jackson. Any friend of Jen's is a friend of mine," she purred as I shook her hand.

She didn't give me a chance to respond before turning back to Jenna and saying, "Oh, I am so glad that I ran into you here. There's been a slight change of plans about tomorrow night. Several of Lana's friends have caught some sort of cold, so we're doing her birthday party next weekend. Tomorrow will just be family...and friends," she said, eying me. "You'll be able to come, won't you Jackson?"

I was knocked off balance and said the first thing that came to mind. "Of course."

"Great! Come with Jen." She must have sensed the daggers Jenna's eyes were shooting at her, so she rushed on. "Gotta run. See you both tomorrow."

And she was gone.

"Please don't feel obligated to go tomorrow. 'Laine has a way of making people feel like they have to bend to her will."

"I don't mind going, unless you would rather I not."

"No, I don't mind," she said quickly. "It's just that I don't want to put you through that."

"Through what?"

"You will be grilled as though you're the new boyfriend," Jenna said as though it were a fact.

I gave her a sly smile. "Maybe it will be good practice."

"Practice for what?" I could tell she was intrigued.

"For when I am your boyfriend," I said with a wink.

Chapter 9

Jenna hadn't slept well at all on Saturday night. Jackson's comment had played through her mind on endless loop. It was frustrating to not know him well enough to read his face. She had no way to know whether or not he was serious or joking, though she did know she'd be disappointed if he wasn't interested.

As she got ready to head over to her sister's house for dinner, she reflected on the conversation and found herself hoping that Jackson hadn't been joking. Jenna was putting the last bow on the present for her niece when she heard a knock on her door. As expected, Jackson was on the other side, but with an especially frilly looking gift bag.

"What's with the bag?" she asked nodding toward his hand.

"I felt strange showing up to a birthday party empty-handed, so I picked up something that should go with what you got yesterday."

Jenna smiled warmly at him. "That was very thoughtful, but unnecessary. Her birthday isn't until later this week. Besides, Lana is one of the least materialistic children I've ever met, which is surprising given her parents." She saw the inquisitive look on Jackson's face and added, "You'll understand once we get there. I just need to sign the card and I'll be ready to go."

She could feel Jackson's eyes on her as she bent down to sign and seal the card. Excited waves of heat chased the shivers down her spine. If just his eyes could do that to her...

"Am I dressed okay?"

Jenna glanced up at him. Looked good to her. He was wearing dark beige khakis and a black golf shirt. In her periwinkle sundress and sandals, she must have appeared a little dressier to him.

"You're fine. I would be going over in a pair of cutoff shorts if it weren't for Lana. She thinks that, and I quote, 'girls should wear pretty things like dresses and skirts for as long as the weather doesn't make your legs cold.' I like to humor her. I think I'm the only one who takes her seriously."

"That's nice of you," Jackson commented. "Do we need to stop and get Trista on the way?"

"No. She and Blaine are meeting us there. Okay, I'm ready."

Twenty minutes later, they pulled into the driveway at the Whitman home. Once the car was off, Jenna stopped Jackson from opening the door by placing her hand on his shoulder.

"I want you to know how nice it is that you came here with me tonight."

"You don't have to thank me, Jenna. I enjoy spending time with you."

"You do?"

A lazy smile strolled across his mouth as equally unhurried fingers moved to caress her cheek. There they were again, the heat and shivers. She was either attracted to the man or she was coming down with an early case of the flu. But when he had that look in his eyes, he could be a carrier of ebola and she would happily fall victim to that entire host of ailments with a contented smile on her face.

His lips parted and she felt the tip of her tongue move to wet her lips on instinct, mesmerized by the twinkling in those crystal sky eyes and intoxicated by the tickle of lingering fingers. Her breath shivered through her throat and the single word escaped to cover or to inquire. "Jackson?" Though she knew on some vague plane of understanding she'd previously asked a question of him, the only answer she now sought was without words.

Before Jenna could get an answer to her question – either question – a squeal of excitement could be heard from the front door of the house.

"Aunt Jenna's here everybody!" They both abruptly turned from one another and watched as an almost-five-year-old Lana Whitman ran toward the car with her raven black ponytail bouncing behind her. Jenna got out of the car just in time to scoop her niece up with a hug. She was always amazed by Lana whenever she saw her. She was the image of her father, yet she had all of Elaine's grace and daintiness. Jenna sometimes even thought that she saw a little bit of herself at that age in her.

"Aunt Jenna, did you see the necklace that Miss Trista gave me?" the child asked, pulling a silver heart away from her throat for all to see.

"That's very pretty, Lana. Did you thank Miss Trista for it?"

"Yes, silly goose. I always do." Lana glanced over at Jackson and started to giggle. When she spoke her voice was an excited whisper. "Aunt Jenna, is he your boyfriend?"

Jenna laughed when Lana started to make kissing noises. "No, Lana, this is my friend, Jackson."

On cue, Jackson knelt down to her level. Jenna wasn't surprised by his response when Lana threw her arms around him in a big hug. He had been nothing but polite to everyone she introduced him to so far, but his hug went beyond politeness. She could tell he enjoyed being around children.

Here's hoping he didn't have any.

"What can I call you?"

Jackson looked up at Jenna, confusion in his eyes before he spoke. "You can call me Jackson."

Lana shook her head, causing her ponytail to whip around and hit her on either cheek. "No. My mom doesn't like it when I call grown-ups by their first names. She says it's misrespectful."

Jenna knew that the word her niece was trying to repeat was disrespectful, but she didn't correct her. She got enough of that from her parents. Luckily, Jackson took his cue from her and said, "We'll think of something for you to call me later. Should we go inside now, Lana?"

"Yes. Can I have a piggyback ride?"

"Hop on."

Jenna felt her heart melt into a slow pool of mush as she watched her niece throw her arms around his neck. She watched as the little girl whispered something into his ear and started to giggle. Jackson looked back and winked at Jenna before he answered, "Yes, I do." Something else was whispered in his ear and his response was the same, minus the wink.

Jenna's curiosity was piqued. "What are you two whispering about over there?"

"Nothing, Aunt Jenna."

Jackson grinned. "Yeah, nothing, Aunt Jenna."

Once they were in the house, Lana jumped down and ran into the kitchen to help her mother. Jenna was dying to know what had been said, but her brother-in-law walked into the room before she could speak. She closed the door behind them as the two men exchanged pleasantries.

It was well known in the family that Jenna was not Daniel Whitman's biggest fan, but she had to admit to herself each time she saw him that he was certainly handsome. As a teenager, Jenna remembered having the biggest crush on him, one she got over after coming to live with him and her sister. He had a nasty temper that turned those jovial green eyes into dark, sinister orbs. While he'd never so much as laid a finger on her, she had grown to fear him during her last year of school. He settled for nothing short of perfection out of every person who was to be associated with him.

Lana was no exception.

"Dinner's ready everybody!" Lana called from the dining room.

As she followed the others, Jenna wondered how much trouble Lana would get into for that faux pas.

Chad opened the door to Jenna's condo and switched on the light. Judging from the gifts Jenna and that other guy were carrying, he should have plenty of time to do what he needed to do. He set his lock picking tools on the entry table and instinctively walked down the hall to where the bedroom should be.

He took stock of the bedroom furniture in an attempt to decide the best place for his devices. Women were predictable and Jenna had much of the same furniture he'd expected her to have. Chad found he was well prepared. Moving swiftly from room to room, he was done in almost no time. The only setback he encountered was a pesky grey cat that wouldn't leave him alone. Chad hated animals. People gave those inferior creatures so much more credit for their capacity for intelligence than they deserved.

Especially cats.

He toyed with the notion of relieving Jenna of that particular burden, but he discarded the idea. She had always been the kind of sap who would cry at the sight of what had once been an animal on the side of the road. No, he would not do anything today, but he would be damned if that beast ever came to live with him.

He gave the apartment a final walkthrough to ensure he hadn't displaced anything she would be sure to notice. Once he was satisfied, he picked up the last of his equipment from the entry table and left as quietly as he had entered. Chad paused a moment in front of the condo across from hers. While he was tempted to plant the extra devices in his home as well, he knew that this guy wouldn't be around long enough to get in the way.

"You made a promise to me, Jenna," he muttered to himself as he walked down the stairs to his car. "You can have your fun with your new little boyfriend, for now, but you will be mine. You will keep your promise to me, my sweet, or it will be your last."

I was always the kind of guy girls loved taking home to their parents, so dinner was easy for me. The most difficult thing was that I had more knowledge about the situation than I should have. Daniel made a point to tell me Jenna lived with them after her parents' death. Though I wasn't sure why, I was immediately not fond of him.

Jenna had been right; I did understand what she meant once I was in the Whitman home. It was full of expensive furnishings and enough knick knacks to fill up my entire condo. Everything was so neatly in its place that it was hard to believe they had a child. How was a kid, even the best-behaved kid, supposed to be a kid in a place like this?

All through dinner, I was acutely aware of Jenna's presence next to me. Once or twice, she brushed her leg up against mine, but she apologized without hesitation. Still, I couldn't get rid of the thought that it had been no accident. I grew up with two sisters, so I was no stranger to what women did when they were trying to let you know they were interested.

A host of thoughts ran through my head as I interacted with Jenna's family, but mostly I felt distracted by my growing attraction to her. At times it was all I could do to keep from sliding my hand under the table and up that smooth porcelain leg of hers. In fact, the porno soundtrack was back with such intensity in my head that it became too difficult to focus on the polite conversation.

Actually, breathing was more than a little difficult when my mind was imagining in vivid detail all the things my hand could be doing to her without making anyone the wiser at the table.

No doubt she was a knockout, but it was more than physical. It was obvious she had a caring heart and she was easy to talk with. Truth be told, she was everything that I was looking for in a woman and that was why nothing could ever happen between us. I didn't want to like her; I wanted to wrap up my case, collect my hundred bucks, and get back to D.C.

Yeah. And I also wanted to move to the beach and make seashell jewelry from my cardboard box under the pier. See? I could fabricate ridiculous lies to tell myself all day long. I didn't want Jenna and I wanted to be the smelly guy selling crap under the pier.

Based on the twinkle in her eyes when she looked at me and didn't think I noticed, I could tell that she might make her own move if I didn't. It would be too easy – and oh so enjoyable – to let myself be seduced by her, but that wasn't my style. While many of my colleagues believed in "doing whatever it took" to catch the bad guy, I was not in the habit of using people. Even if I did let something real develop between us, it would never last.

At some point I would have to tell her the truth. I would have to tell her that everything she thought she knew about me was a lie.

Women always loved that.

Lana was an absolute doll. She thanked everyone for the gifts and insisted we all play charades after cake. It was obvious to me Jenna adored her. She asked if she could call me Uncle Jackson, but her mother was adamant that she call me Mister Jackson. Either would have been fine with me. I'd always been a sucker for kids and when it came to little girls...I was a goner.

Before we left, Lana made me promise I would go to the zoo with her and Jenna on Friday. I also was told by Elaine that I would be expected next Sunday for dinner. I didn't mind that either. It gave me a good excuse to be around Jenna; strictly business, of course.

Jenna was quiet during the drive home. I didn't know her well enough yet to know if that was a bad sign, so I didn't say anything to break the silence. I spent the drive wondering why I found myself flirting with her every time I opened my mouth, but the answer eluded me. Finally, when we were each at our respective doors, I turned to her and asked, "Are you ready for your rain check yet? Say tomorrow night? Around seven?"

"No fish?"

"Nothing from the water, as I recall."

"I'll be there."

"Good. I'll see you then."

I was about to close my door when she stopped me with a question. "Jackson...what was Lana whispering to you?"

"She asked me if I thought her Aunt Jenna was pretty. Then she asked me if I liked her Aunt Jenna."

"Oh. Goodnight, Jackson."

I liked the hesitant smile that crept across her face when I told her. It felt almost as good to see as that little shiver she'd made in the car when I'd touched her face. Would she shiver and say my name like that if I touched her anywhere else? Maybe I could take this just far enough to get my answer. Judging from her reaction to me, Jenna wouldn't mind that.

This was a line of thought that needed to be stopped, abandoned, left for dead. I knew this was dangerous, but she couldn't have a clue about that. Would she stop herself from falling for me if she knew? Could she?

If only she knew she was in for heartbreak.

Chapter 10

"I told you it wasn't just a one night thing."

I knew it was a bad idea to offer to take a shift tailing Blackstone. I had thought it would give me a chance to see how he operated firsthand. Instead, he hadn't left his apartment all day and I had to listen to Collin talk about Maureen nonstop for the last eight and a half hours.

"That's good, but be careful. We can't afford the complication."

"I know, I know, but it isn't like gorgeous, sexy women toss me into their beds every day."

"That's a shock." I loved to push his buttons.

"You can kiss my ass, man."

"Take it easy, Collin. I was just messing with you."

It occurred to me I stopped referring to my partner by his last name. I wasn't sure when that shift happened. Ever since my previous partner had stolen my wife, I preferred to keep things on a professional level. Seeing I had nothing left Collin could steal from me, I let it go. Besides, the little prick was starting to grow on me, though I would not hesitate to have him removed from the case if he screwed up again.

Changing the subject, Collin said, "We should probably head back."

"It's only three-thirty," I retorted.

"Traffic can be a nightmare around here."

"Again, it's only three-thirty."

"Rush hour starts before four. Anyway, I'm tired of sitting in a car with you."

I shook my head. "We can't just leave. What if he makes a move and no one's here to tail him?"

"Foster and Rodriguez got here about thirty minutes ago."

"They did?"

I was a little shocked. I prided myself in being able to make a Bureau man a mile away, but I hadn't seen anything out of the ordinary.

"Yeah. That bum over there is Foster and Rodriguez is the telephone company worker four cars ahead of us who's 'pretending' to be asleep. If Blackstone checks his mail, we'll know."

Collin hadn't been lying about the traffic. We were only ten miles from where I lived when traffic stopped moving. I was grateful I didn't have to commute to and from FBI Headquarters every day in this mess.

"Is there any news out of Houston?" I asked, hoping to make the time go by.

"Nothing left of the building. We have agents questioning all of Blackstone's former co-workers about him, but we haven't gotten anything useful from them yet. They all seem to think he was an exceptional worker, a little on the quiet side, but still a nice enough guy."

That was what they all said. A man could be butchering kittens in his dining room and his coworkers would all say what a nice, quiet guy he was. "Have we been able to get surveillance footage yet from the company?"

"The board of directors is hesitant to give it to us before they've had a chance to review it, but we've been assured we'll have it tomorrow morning."

"Do they have any theories about what might have caused their building to explode?"

"Cocaine residue was found in Alex's car. They believe he got high and tried to work."

"His sister was into drugs pretty heavily, wasn't she?"

"Yep. That was how we got to him. That stuff has probably been in his car for months and he was clueless about it."

"Have our guys developed a theory yet?"

"I asked this morning, but they don't want to venture a guess until they've seen the surveillance footage. What's your theory, Caldwell?"

"I think it was Blackstone. I can feel it in my gut that I'm right. I've come face to face with this guy and..."

"Whoa," Collin interrupted. "When did that happen?"

"Saturday, while I was with Jenna. I think Alex was acting strange and Blackstone got suspicious. He probably killed him and used the explosion to cover his tracks."

"We have no proof of that. Too bad we can't bring down a potential terrorist because of your gut."

"I've seen it in his eyes. I don't need proof, but I'll have more than enough on him by the time this is over. You can mark my words."

At just after seven that night, Jenna went across the hall to Jackson's place. She had heard him come home at half past five and thought he might need a little more time. However, once the aroma of whatever he was preparing wafted over to her, she knew he was ready for her.

Good thing, too, because she was ready for him.

"You're right on time," Jackson said at the door. "I just took dinner out of the oven."

"Is there anything I can do to help?"

"No. I have a few finishing touches. Make yourself at home."

Jenna did just that. Despite the fact that she had been in his home a few times already, she never looked around. A beautiful painting over the fireplace she hadn't noticed before caught her attention. She was looking for the name of the artist when Jackson walked up next to her.

"It's one of Monet's Water Lilies."

"It's beautiful," Jenna commented. "The use of color is spectacular. I've never been a fan of dark shades in artwork, or Impressionism for that matter, but this is rather well put together."

"I think so. Dinner's ready, if you're hungry, that is."

Jenna turned to face him. "I'm starved," she replied staring into those crystal eyes.

His eyes locked with hers and held it a moment too long. Her face was only a few short inches from his and she felt her breath snag in her throat. Rather than gapping the distance with a kiss, he turned away and led her into the dining room. She was slightly disappointed he didn't take advantage of the opportunity she had given him.

A moment later her disappointment turned to surprise. The dining room was lit only by two taper candles on the table. She watched as Jackson crossed the room to the kitchen and momentarily disappeared. When he returned, he had a single stem red rose in his hand.

"For you," he said as he handed the flower to her.

Jenna looked around the room in utter amazement. "What is all this?"

"I wanted you to have the true Jackson Caldwell dining experience," he replied as he pulled out a chair for Jenna.

A bit in awe, Jenna sat. In front of her was a plate full of salad greens and pecans. She took a bite and was surprised at how good the combination was.

"Where did you get this dressing, Jackson? It's wonderful."

"I made it."

"You did not."

"I most certainly did and if you aren't careful I'll never tell you how."

"I'll be good," Jenna promised as she continued eating the salad.

No sooner than Jenna set down her fork after taking her last bite, Jackson picked up their plates and whisked them into the kitchen. As quickly as he had left he returned with two more plates and a basket of crusty French bread. He gave her a quick smile as he set her plate before her.

"I hope there is no rule against chicken," he joked.

"Unless you've basted it with shrimp gravy, I think we're fine. This all looks wonderful, Jackson. I don't know how you ever had time to do all of this."

"That will have to be my little secret. Dig in. I'm anxious to find out what you think."

Jenna scrutinized her plate. Everything looked good; she didn't quite know what to try first. There was baked chicken with steamed vegetables, but she was certain after the salad it wouldn't be that simple. Her instincts had been correct, she realized once she took her first bite. The chicken was marinated and basted with some sort of a white wine sauce, but she couldn't place the other mixture of flavors. The vegetables must have been steamed with the same sauce, based on the flavor. To round out the meal were mushroom-garlic mashed potatoes, a flavor she knew well.

"Condensed soup?"

Jackson threw up his hands as he conceded, "You caught me. I spent so much time on the chicken and the salad dressing that I ran out of time for the potatoes. I hope you don't mind."

Jenna smiled at him from behind lowered lashes. "Not at all, but you should know I was just teasing you at the grocery store about your cooking ability. You didn't have to go all out to prove me wrong."

"I didn't," Jackson began as he refilled her glass of white wine. "I haven't treated myself in so long I thought it would be a nice excuse to make an old favorite of mine."

Jenna reached for her glass. "Thank you."

"Don't thank me. How do you know I'm not trying to get you drunk?" He winked.

"Easy. You wouldn't be giving me wine if you wanted me drunk. I have a high tolerance for it. Besides, why ever would you want me drunk, Mr. Caldwell?"

Jenna phrased her question as a joke, but wanted desperately to know the answer.

"Wouldn't you like to know?" he joked back.

She made a mental note to never ask a question she wanted answered as a joke again as she continued eating. A few times during the course of the meal, Jenna thought she felt Jackson's calf brush up against hers, but she dismissed it as nothing more than a lack of space under his cozy dining room table. With the exception of his few fleeting jokes, he'd given her no indication he was interested in romance. Unfortunately, romance had been on her mind since they met.

"So Jenna, how long have you known...what was his name...Chad?"

"I met him when we were in the ninth grade. He was so shy and awkward at that age that, well, I guess I felt sorry for him."

"Sorry for him?"

"In a way. I had been in the same district since I started school and he had just moved to town. It didn't seem like he was having an easy time making friends and the jocks were always picking on him."

"That was nice of you," he commented.

"I suppose. We stayed friends throughout high school." Jenna began to laugh as she had a sudden memory. "We even made this pact."

"Pact?"

"It was stupid."

"Tell me."

"He was sad after graduation - I guess because I was going off to Harvard in a few weeks. He wanted me to promise him that if we both weren't married, or otherwise involved, by the time our ten-year reunion rolled around that we would get married. I know how pathetic it must seem to you, but it seemed to perk him up a little bit. I can't believe I even thought about that. It hasn't crossed my mind in years. I bet he's forgotten all about it."

"I'm sure he has," Jackson responded as he began clearing the dishes. Jenna stood to help, but he wouldn't hear of it.

"I'll take care of this; I don't want you to see the mess I've made in my kitchen. It would ruin the illusion."

"Okay," Jenna conceded. "Do you mind if I turn on the stereo in the living room?"

"Not at all," he answered from the kitchen. "Coffee?"

"Sure. Oh, I haven't heard this song in ages. This used to be Trista's favorite love song."

Jackson entered the living room with a quizzical look on his face. He handed her a cup of amaretto coffee and sat on the sofa next to her before he spoke. "Def Leppard's *Love Bites* is her favorite love song?"

"You have to really know Trist to understand."

"Fill me in."

Jenna debated how much to tell Jackson as she sipped her coffee.

"I've known Trista since we were both five. She had a lousy childhood; parents always at each other's throats, but they refused to divorce. They wanted to stay together for her sake. When she got old enough to date, she played out her parents' relationship with every boyfriend she had. That's why this whole thing with Blaine is so terrible. He's the first guy she's gotten real with and started to trust."

"How's that going, by the way?"

"He swears he's innocent. I haven't seen the rest of the evidence, but so far it doesn't look great. Maureen is an excellent lawyer, though; one that you always hope is fighting on the right side. If anyone can find a way out of this for him, it'll be her." She paused and bit her lip. "I can't believe I'm telling you all this. It feels like I've known you longer than a few days. I guess that doesn't make a lot of sense."

"No. I get what you're saying."

Jenna set her coffee on the table and leaned back against the couch. She propped up her head with her hand and waited for Jackson to follow suit before she spoke. A sudden rush of bravery overtook her.

"Did you mean what you said to my niece?"

"I would never lie to a child."

"I suppose you also meant what you said about enjoying spending time with me then?"

"I don't want to lie to you either."

"If everything you say is true..."

"What?" His voice was soft, but coaxing.

"You've been giving me...mixed signals and, well, I don't really know how to interpret them," she began self-consciously. "At times, it seems like you're into me...but then you start winking and making jokes about it." She paused, beginning to realize how ridiculous she must sound. "I acted like a nut that first night and I just hope you can forget about that."

She let her lips quirk into a smile as she remembered something Jackson said to her a few days earlier. "Some people actually think that I'm a nice person. Of course, those people tend to be Trista and Elaine and I know you've realized by now that they're insane."

Jackson brushed his hand across her cheek and stared deeply into her eyes. "Don't say that, Jenna. There's nothing wrong with them and I don't think you're a nut. I wouldn't be hanging around all the time if I did."

"Oh."

"Of course I'm interested in you, Jenna. How could I not be? Any man with eyes would be interested."

Before Jenna knew what was happening, Jackson's lips were brushing against her own in a kiss. At first it was very soft and probing, but slowly it deepened and increased in intensity. He waited until her lips parted before he slid his tongue into her mouth. He tasted like the coffee; dark and sweet. She'd imagined this almost every night since she'd met him, but her fantasies had never come close to the reality of his kiss.

Her fingers played through his hair before Jenna finally wrapped her arms around his neck. Jackson's skin was hot; on fire, really, and Jenna wondered if he was feeling all right. Of course, she'd felt the excited chill run through her entire body when Jackson wound his fingers into her hair and pulled her head back enough to allow him better access to her neck so she was in no position to question.

And she didn't want to question anything...only feel.

When his lips came in contact with the sensitive spot behind her ear, Jenna heard the soft moan escape her lips as her whole body seemed to come alive with sensation. This was insane. Jenna always considered herself a reasonable woman, one who was perhaps a touch too conservative. What she was doing now…making out on the couch of a man she'd known for less than a week…aching for more…Well, that just wasn't Jenna, but she had a hard time convincing herself of it when she felt his hands slide down her body to her waist, his arms brushing against her breasts in the process.

Jenna realized she was leaning over backwards, pulling Jackson on top of her. Abandoning caution didn't seem like such a bad idea anymore.

As abruptly as the mood had hit, it ended and Jackson pulled away.

"I'm sorry, Jenna. I shouldn't have done that. I guess I got a little carried away." He cleared his throat. "I've got a meeting early in the morning and I didn't realize how late it was."

Chapter 11

"What the hell is wrong with me, Trista?" Jenna demanded of her friend as soon as she arrived the next morning.

"Besides the fact that you have no idea how to greet a friend at the door without sounding like a crazy person, I think you're great, sweetie. Why don't you take a step back and tell me what you're talking about." Trista set down a large stack of files on Jenna's desk.

Jenna relayed the events of the previous evening, leaving nothing out so she could appreciate how wronged she'd been. When she was done, she stared at her friend, waiting for some insight that would make her feel better; or at the very least, justified in her anger. Trista looked at her for a long moment before she spoke.

"Is it possible that he really did have an early morning meeting?"

"Probably; his car was gone when I got up this morning, but that doesn't mean anything."

"It means you're checking up on this guy's early morning habits, babe." She gave her a long look before continuing. "Okay. Have you considered he's one of the seven men on the planet that doesn't want to ruin a good thing by rushing into anything physical?"

Jenna scowled. "I guess that's possible, but..."

"But nothing," Trista interrupted. "You told me yourself he's a widower. Has it occurred to you that maybe he isn't ready yet? You, of all people, should understand that."

Jenna got the point. "You're probably right, Trist. I just...I just think I'm starting to like this guy and I'm scared he might not feel the same way about me. I don't know what to do."

"Starting to like the guy? I'd say you're passed that one already. Talk to him the next time you see him. Keeping things open is the way to go."

Jenna rolled her eyes and let out a sigh. "I think I miss the old cynical Trista. What did you do with her?"

"I told her exactly what I'm going to tell you now. I told her to grow up and go through that stack of files on the desk before I kick your butt."

Jenna let a smile play at the corner of her mouth. "You told her that, huh?"

"Tough love, baby. Get to work."

They both enjoyed a laugh before getting into the case. Jenna soon realized her condo had become their base of operations, which was even more evident when Maureen showed up around one o'clock with two more boxes of files. She hadn't understood how much help they needed when she agreed, but she couldn't quit now. Sable the Curious Kitty's next book would have to wait for a few more days; some things were just more important.

"So...what? I don't see what the big deal is."

Collin was starting to wear on my nerves.

"I kissed her, Collin. Don't you get how bad this situation is?"

"Because you had too much garlic in the meal and her breath was sour?" he asked me with a smirk.

"No! The kiss was amazing."

"I don't really see the problem with this. Consider it a fringe benefit of the job."

That did it.

"This is why I don't talk to you about anything. I refuse to use her and justify it by saying that it was for the good of the case. I'm not one of those guys."

"But you have no problem making a bet of her? You're a hypocrite, Caldwell."

"That's different."

"I don't see how."

"It just is. That was...before."

He appeared thoughtful for a moment. "Do you have any feelings for her?"

I hated admitting it aloud. "Yeah. I keep trying not to like her, but she's growing on me."

"If she had no involvement with the case, would you still pursue her?"

"The timing is awful."

"Fuck the timing, Jackson. Would you still want her?"

"I don't know. Probably. Yeah."

"Then you don't have to worry. If you were using her for the case, you wouldn't give a shit about her outside of it and we would certainly not be having this discussion."

"I'll just hurt her; we both know that."

Collin shook his head. "It doesn't have to go down that way."

I paused to think about that. It would be a perfect scenario. After last night's kiss, it was obvious she was open to more than friendship. Since I wasn't exactly ready for anything serious, it was perfect that I'd be going back to D.C. when the case was closed. Things could stay casual with us – or at least, for me because I had no intention of telling her about it.

I would have to think about it later. Collin was staring at me, waiting for a response. "It may not have to go down that way, but it will if I take things too far."

"Not necessarily. She doesn't have to find out the truth, you know."

"You're insane. My life is in D.C., not here. She would eventually find out I'm with the Bureau and that would be the end of that."

"You don't have to stay with the FBI. You could always get a job, hmm, as a management consultant. I'm sure you're well qualified for it after the number of times you've pretended to do it."

"I may have to if we don't stop talking about my love life and get to work."

"Point taken. The surveillance tapes should be queued up and ready to go in the viewing room."

Grateful for the change of subject, I followed Collin into a small conference room that was turned into our makeshift viewing room with the addition of a few chairs, a dust-covered table, a VCR and a monitor. I sat and waited for one of the audio-visual technicians to join us. He explained that the tape was of a pretty low quality, so he would be limited in enhancement options. Finally, he started the tape.

For the most part, it was as we had been told. Alex entered the building with his cap pulled down enough to cover his face. That gave credibility to the company's theory. If he was high, he wouldn't want his face to give him away on tape. He went into a room which I assumed to be the lab and stayed inside for several minutes.

Collin was getting impatient and was asking the technician to fast-forward when the door to the lab opened and Alex emerged. Less than ten feet down the corridor, he spoke to a guard who took off towards the lab. Alex continued walking the other way. The guard opened the door and within minutes, the narrow hallway was engulfed in flames.

Once the tape ended I turned to Collin and asked, "How did Alex die in the explosion if he wasn't there?" To the technician I asked, "Can you zoom in on the face of that guy right after the guard runs off?"

"As I explained, I'm limited in what I can do, but let me give it a shot."

He was able to zoom in, but the face was too fuzzy to make out.

"Can you clean that up any?" Collin asked.

The technician typed a few quick commands on his keyboard.

"Dammit! It isn't working. The quality of this tape is...so poor. I can try in black and white, if that would help."

"Do it."

A moment later I knew I was right as we looked at the somewhat fuzzy face of the man I had met seventy-two hours prior. Collin looked at me as if to ask if that was him and I nodded. I never forgot a face.

"Has the company already reviewed the tapes?" I asked Collin after the technician left to get pictures printed off for us.

"No. They had it sent directly from their central monitoring center. What do you want me to tell them?"

"We can't let them see this until our case is closed, that's for sure. Tell them that it was ruined. Get the audio-visual guys to make up a dummy tape that shows their hallway with lots of snow over it. Have them make sure to take out any evidence that Blackstone was there. We can't afford for them to jump the gun and try to prosecute him until we know he's no longer a threat."

"Consider it done," Collin said as he headed out of the room.

I knew I had seen murder in Blackstone's eyes when I'd met him. That thought sat heavily on my mind for the rest of the day. A murderer was in love with Jenna. If he was willing to murder two people in cold blood, one a close friend, and blow up a building; how would he react when Jenna told him she thought their pact was a joke?

I may not want to like her, but I would have to protect her.

The day went by quickly for Jenna. She abandoned her desk to spread out on the floor with the mounds of paper encircling her, made somewhat worse by the fact that her kitten wouldn't stop attacking imaginary bugs on them. By six o'clock, her mind was swimming with the details of the case.

The prosecution had a good case. Most of what they had was circumstantial, but, portrayed the right way in court, it could be very effective. His cell phone bill corroborated every date and time their witnesses mentioned and the witnesses wouldn't have been permitted to know that, so it wasn't faked. The bartender, who was cooperating with the prosecution to get a lighter sentence, was prepared to testify against Blaine as well. Mingled with the testimony of the girls who supposedly worked for him, as well as the knowledge that there was rarely a night Blaine wasn't personally overseeing the operation of the club, Jenna felt as though her work was cut out for her.

When they heard the familiar squeak of the building's access door, Trista jumped up.

"Finally. I thought Blaine would never get here with the pizza. I'm starving."

Once Trista opened the door, she gave Blaine a quick peck on the lips and frowned at something behind him.

"You two don't think you're going to sneak by without coming over to say hi, do you?"

"I figured you guys were busy. I didn't want to bother you."

Jenna jumped up off the floor as soon as she heard Jackson's voice. Her heart began to race and a swarm of butterflies gathered in her stomach. She wished she'd ignored the voice in her head that told her it would be too vain to put a mirror by the front door. She was dying to know if she looked as plain as she thought she did.

"We were about to quit for the night," Jenna said breathlessly.

Blaine must have sensed something and he joined in on the coaxing. "You guys have to join us. I've got a ton of pizza here and you know how women are; they eat half a piece and pretend to be full."

"Not me," Trista snapped grabbing the pizza out of his hand and heading into the living room. "I could eat all of this by myself, I'm so hungry."

To Jenna's delight, Jackson and Collin conceded and entered the condo. Jenna closed the door behind them and went into the kitchen to get paper plates and napkins for everyone. She was surprised when she realized Jackson had followed her.

"I wanted to apologize to you for last night," he began slowly. "I could have handled things differently, better. I'm sorry I didn't."

Jenna set the napkins on the counter and stood on her tiptoes to reach for the paper plates in the cabinet over the stove. "Don't worry about it. I got your point."

Jackson retrieved the plates for her and set them on the counter next to the napkins. "I don't think that you did."

"You made yourself clear, Jackson. I don't see what I could have missed?"

"This," he said, pulling her against him. "I haven't been able to think about anything else all day long."

Jenna locked her arms around his neck as he began to kiss her. "Really?"

Jackson's hands slid from her back to her butt, pulling her flush against him. It only took a second for Jenna to understand exactly how far his interest went. There was no question in her mind he wanted more from her than her friendship. He was hard as granite. That realization made her heartbeat thump out of control and there was no way that he wasn't aware of it.

Not with as close as their bodies were.

His lips left hers to explore her neck before making contact with that spot below her ear that turned her knees to mush. And her mind. After who-even-knew how long, Jackson whispered, "I've been trying to be good, to take it slow with you, but I've got to tell you that it's too damn hard. I have no idea what was said at the meeting this morning. All I could think about was what an idiot I was for pulling away last night. I won't make that mistake again."

Jenna was about to respond when he shifted his weight against her, causing the most erotic sensation that Jenna had ever felt. Instead of speaking, she arched against him. That was all the response Jackson needed because he captured her mouth again, crushing her lips with his.

He lifted her up onto the counter and Jenna wrapped her legs around his waist out of instinct, keeping him as close as was possible while they were both still clothed. A groan of satisfaction and frustration rumbled in his throat as he went to work again on her neck. What she wouldn't have given at that moment to get him naked and find out if her first impression of his body had been correct.

"Sorry to interrupt. I'm just going to grab this stuff for everyone. Sorry. Pretend I'm not here. I, uh, just see plates and napkins right now." Blaine's embarrassment was plain on his face.

After Blaine left Jenna's small kitchen, Jackson brushed a strand of hair out of her eyes and smiled. She buried her face against his shoulder, sure it turned a shade of crimson yet to be discovered. She shook her head as he helped her back down to her feet, and started to laugh.

"That was embarrassing," she told him.

"Not for me," he replied. "I was enjoying it."

"I was talking about Blaine walking in on us."

"And I was talking about this." Jackson placed his hand on the back of her neck and pulled her in for a rough kiss, erasing all thoughts of crimson from her mind.

With that, he turned and left the room. Jenna lagged behind in a futile attempt to regain her composure. There was no way that Trista would let the look on Blaine's face go until she found out what happened in the kitchen. At this very moment Jenna was certain Trista was discussing it with Maureen and Collin. The fact that there seemed to be a hushed silence coming from the living room, disturbed only by the sound of running water from the bathroom sink, wasn't helping to squelch her embarrassment.

Not even in her wildest dreams had she imagined Jackson would simply walk into her kitchen, announce that he wanted her, and go for it on her counter – with four nosy people in the next room. Just when she'd thought she had him figured out, he had thrown her for a loop.

As she joined the others, Jenna realized she liked that about him.

Chapter 12

I had to get a grip.

Before Blaine had walked in, I'd been about two seconds from carrying Jenna into her bedroom where I had every intention of having very wild sex with her for the better part of the night. Sure, it had occurred to me that there were four people in the other room, one of whom was my partner, but it didn't matter once I felt her against me. Even after Blaine left I was still holding on by only a thread. If Jenna hadn't looked so mortified then...

Well, I wouldn't be in the bathroom right now trying to think of anything to get rid of this raging hard-on.

Okay, this was bad. I'd been in here for long enough that everyone had to be wondering what the hell I was doing. I turned on the faucet and splashed some water on my face. My body was so hot right now that I was on the verge of combusting.

I tried to turn my thoughts to something, any-thing that would cool me down. Nothing. My mind was a total blank. It occurred to me when I made my move that Jenna might end up smacking me...but she didn't. In fact, she loved every second of it. She might not have minded if I'd carried her to the bedroom...

Wrong line of thought.

Blowing out a breath, I thought back to the last time that I'd gone from hot to cold in a split second. It was a day just like any other. I'd finished up some paperwork early and decided to surprise Melissa with take-out and flowers. She was sitting on the couch, talking, smiling. My partner was off that day and stopped by to see if I was home yet. They'd just been talking, but my wife had this look in her eyes...like she'd been caught in the act.

That was my first indication my marriage was over, despite the fact it took me months to realize it.

Yep, that did it. I opened the door and walked out to join the others. Luckily, it hadn't taken me as long as I thought to make myself presentable. Jenna looked like she'd entered the room just ahead of me. Maybe she also needed some time to compose herself.

"So," I asked, rubbing my hands together in expectation, "Is there anything left or did Trista eat it all?"

Trista shot me a look but didn't say anything. She didn't have to; her eyes said it all. I looked from Trista to Jenna, who blushed noticeably, and smiled. Once I had a few slices of pizza on my plate I sat next to Jenna on the floor and turned to Blaine.

"So, Blaine, what's your take on this?"

He looked startled. "This?"

I heard Jenna's breath catch so I put a casual arm around her shoulders, making sure she stayed very much aware of me. Collin gave me a stupid looking grin before clarifying, "Who do you think is framing you?"

"Oh." Blaine appeared thoughtful. "I can't figure it out. There are bound to be people out there who think I've wronged them in some way even though I always strive to be fair in my business dealings." He set his plate down in disgust. "How I didn't notice a prostitution ring was being run out of the back of my club for months doesn't help matters."

"It wasn't your fault," Trista snapped. "How could you be expected to know about that with me up there almost every night? I was too much of a distraction."

"Don't do that, darling. Even if you hadn't been there I doubt I would have thought twice about guys asking for an extra dirty olive in their martinis. Men hit on the bartender all the time." He turned to me. "She's about five-eight, blond hair, green eyes. She used to tell me she didn't mind getting hit on because it meant bigger tips. I guess the tips weren't enough anymore."

As I watched the exchange I let my hand move to the back of Jenna's neck and stroked it with my thumb. I could sense the exact moment her breath caught in her throat and her pulse quickened. It had been a long time since a woman had responded to me in that way and I had to admit that it felt good.

Damn good.

Jackson knew exactly what he was doing to her. He had to. Jenna realized Blaine and Trista were in a serious conversation at the moment even though she had no clue what anyone had said since Jackson began his maddening caress on the back of her neck.

It was wrong to think it, but Jenna wished everyone else would hurry up and go home. She'd say goodnight to her friends. Maybe think of some reason to keep Jackson there. Soft music. A few candles. They could finish that kiss that they'd started.

Of course, it was what would come next that sent a terrified shiver down her spine.

"What do you think about that?" Maureen asked.

Jenna realized that the question had been directed to her. "About what?"

Trista shot her a questioning look. "About the phone records, Jen. How do you explain those?"

"I don't know. There are too many calls to be co-incidence," Jenna replied.

Blaine nodded, a sad look in his eyes. "I know. It looks bad. If only there hadn't been a problem with the security system, I wouldn't have needed to keep calling to check on things."

"Whoa! Hold it right there." Maureen's tone let everyone know she was displeased. "What security prob-lems? Why is this the first time I'm hearing about it?"

He shrugged. "It didn't seem like a big deal. There were so many false alarms over the past several months I thought it most prudent to have the alarm company con-tact me instead of phoning the police right away." With a shake of his head he added, "The fines start to add up af-ter the first couple of times the police get dispatched for nothing."

Jenna realized this could be the break they'd been searching for. "Wait a minute, Blaine. I went over your cell phone bill with a fine-tooth comb. I didn't see a single incoming call on the night in question. How did the alarm company reach you?"

"Except for that night, they would always phone. For that one night I asked that they send text messages instead."

Jackson's hand went still on her neck. "Why?"

"It was our anniversary," Trista said. "I'm guess-ing he didn't want me to know about the problems at the club."

Collin was puzzled. "Why?"

Maureen flashed a cagey smile. "I believe it had something to do with Trista telling him that if he couldn't forget about the club for one night and pay attention to her that they were through."

Jenna's eyes widened. "Why didn't I know about that?"

Trista ignored her and turned on Maureen. "I can't believe you just announced my personal business to everyone like that."

"Trista..." Maureen began.

Trista jumped off the couch. "Don't Trista me. The only reason you even know about that is because you walked in while I was on the phone." She shook her head and Jenna realized her ears were the color of tomatoes. "I'm done for tonight."

Everyone watched in stunned silence as Trista stalked out of the room and slammed the door. For perhaps the first time since Jenna had known her, Maureen was speechless. Finally, Jackson broke the silence.

"So, uh, Blaine. Who all knew about the problems with the alarm?"

He shrugged. "Everybody who worked at the club knew."

"It's possible whoever is trying to frame you did something to set off the alarm so you'd have to call the club and give credibility to their story," Jenna mused.

"I don't know. The alarm has been giving us trouble for a long time."

"That could mean they planned this well in advance so that you wouldn't think anything of it when you got so many messages in one night. It's possible the alarm was purposely tampered with from the beginning," Collin offered.

"Uh, sure. Anything's possible." Blaine was distracted when he spoke. Rising to his feet he said, "I need to go check on Trista. This whole thing is taking its toll on her."

After a minute or two, Collin also rose from his place on the couch. "Was there anything else we needed to go over tonight, Jackson?"

He shook his head. "No. We can talk in the morning."

"All right. I guess I'll see you guys around. Unless…" Collin knelt down and whispered what must have been a very naughty suggestion in Maureen's ear, based on the look that passed through her eyes.

No sooner than Collin had righted himself, Maureen jumped up from the chair, announced she was exhausted and was going to call it a night. From the spring in her step as she followed Collin out of the condo, Jenna was certain that exhaustion wasn't the right word to describe Maureen's current condition.

Jackson turned to Jenna. "Well. They were about as subtle as a marching band."

"I know, right?"

Jenna hadn't been aware of it because of the attention she'd focused on the new information about the alarm, but Jackson's hand was still on the back of her neck. Now that no one else was in the condo to distract her, Jenna was very much aware of his nearness. He was about to kiss her again and, if he did, she would be a goner.

She jumped up from the floor with more force than she'd needed and began to collect pizza boxes and paper plates. "I need to get all of this cleaned up or it will drive me crazy all night."

"Well, we wouldn't want that," Jackson said, helping her carry everything into the kitchen.

Jenna hadn't been looking at him when he'd said it, but she was sure he'd have that damn sexy, mischievous grin on his face. It was just as well he couldn't see her face since his comment caused her cheeks to blush. Again. She tried to busy herself with things in the kitchen for as long as she could. Despite how much she was attracted to Jackson, now that they were alone again, things felt awkward to her.

Jackson was leaning against the door to the kitchen, blocking her in, when she turned to face him. One look into those intense blue eyes told Jenna what was on his mind. His grin did little to calm her nerves.

"So," he began, his tone casual, "What do you want to do now?"

Jenna was clueless as to how she was supposed to answer that question. She couldn't say she wanted to move this conversation into the bedroom. Then again, anything else she might say would sound contrived. Of course, she hadn't known him all that long so a part of her was screaming to slow down. Too bad, that was such a small part.

"I, uh…" Jenna stammered, looked away, saw the counter, remembered the way his body felt against her and blushed. She didn't think she could remember a time that she'd been this nervous.

"I get it," Jackson said. "I know what you want."

Because she didn't even know what she wanted, she was startled enough by his response to look up at him. Jackson advanced on her and backed her up against the wall, boxing her in by placing a hand against the wall at either side of her. Jenna fought to control her ragged breathing as she prepared herself for the raw passion of his kiss.

Instead of kissing her, Jackson moved his lips to her ear and whispered, "We don't have to rush this." He pulled back enough to look into her eyes. "Another night." He brushed a gentle kiss against her lips, then went home.

Wednesday, October 1

Something had been bothering me since last night. I was only vaguely aware of what it was at first. Collin was trying to get my attention about something in the file he was holding, but my concentration was shot.

"Are you even listening to me, Jackson?" Collin asked.

"No. I'm sorry, but I can't shake the feeling that something was familiar about last night."

Collin appeared thoughtful. "Now that you mention it, I've been thinking the same thing."

I kept replaying the conversation I'd been a part of the previous night at Jenna's. Everyone was discussing the facts of Blaine's case, which I already knew, but Blaine said something that hadn't been in the file I received on the matter. It seemed important, but I couldn't put my finger on it.

"Collin, is it my imagination, or has this exact same case been tried somewhere before?"

He shook his head. "No, I remember it too. What was that guy's name? It's on the tip of my tongue."

"Did it happen here?" I asked.

"No. I had to study the case as part of my entrance to the FBI. I would remember the details anywhere. A club owner wants a piece of the prostitution racket, so he gets his bartender to oversee it. When a customer asks for a martini with an extra naughty olive, he'd collect the money and have a girl sent over."

I nodded. Even though my recruitment had been unorthodox and my training was accelerated, I could remember someone standing at the front of a room droning on about a case like this. "I remember that case now. It was out of New York as I remember. It was a solid operation until an off-duty police officer overheard and thought it sounded like it might be a good drink. He got more than he bargained for with that one," I mused.

"Victor Ascenzi," Collin said, triumphant. "I know he did some time, but they were never able to find all the money he'd made at it. I wonder what happened to him."

I picked up the file on Blaine and rummaged through it until I found the picture I was looking for. I handed it to Collin and watched his eye's narrow.

"I'd remember those eyes anywhere. This is the guy. Where'd you get the picture?"

"His name is Victor Wellington now. He's Blaine's silent partner."

"Damn."

"That's not all," I began. "According to the partnership agreement, if either party is convicted of a crime involving the club, full ownership reverts to the remaining partner without a buyout occurring."

"I guess Blaine really was set up," Collin said.

"And Victor Wellington is about to become an even richer man."

"Unless we stop him. We can't let an innocent man go down for something like this when we know the truth."

"I know, Collin. I know."

Now I just had to figure out a way to leak the information to Jenna without her realizing what I was doing. Granted, I would have to find some way to be in a room alone with her, without tearing off her clothes, to make that work. It had taken every ounce of my willpower the night before to walk away from her. Knowing that she was as turned on as I was hadn't made it any easier. It would be a real test to accomplish this task.

Win or lose, I was willing to bet it would still be worth it.

Chapter 13

At six-thirty that night, Jenna walked across the hall and knocked on Jackson's door. She heard him come home about a half hour earlier, but she hadn't wanted to bombard him the minute he walked through the door. Spending time with him the previous night had been nice, even if she had lost her nerve and flaked out at the last second. Though she wasn't certain that she was any braver, she did know that she was ready to see him again, without the presence of four nosy chaperones.

"Hello, Jenna. This is a surprise. Do you want to come in?"

She shook her head. "No. I had a really nice time at dinner Monday and I wanted you to come over so I could return the favor."

"I was just there for dinner last night," he replied with a look on his face that made it clear he didn't think she was only talking about food.

"That was pizza, not dinner. Come on, it's just spaghetti with meatballs and a salad."

Jackson shrugged. "I can tell you aren't going to take no for an answer. Okay, I need to finish up something first. I'll be over in a minute."

Jenna accepted that answer and went to get the plates ready so they could eat once he got there. It was unnerving that he was acting so casual about last night, even though she would have been mortified if he'd commented on it. True to his word, Jackson walked in five minutes later. She was momentarily sorry she had used the dining room for her office instead of an actual dining room, but he didn't seem to mind eating in the living room.

"Where's the legal team?" Jackson asked after they'd eaten and made uncomfortable small talk about the weather, both of them avoiding the fact that they'd come very close to sleeping together the last time they'd been alone.

"Maureen thought we deserved a night off, or at least that's what she said. I think she had dinner plans with your friend."

"Probably, knowing Collin. How's the case going, anyway?" he asked.

Jenna shrugged. It goes before the grand jury on Friday. I can't imagine why it won't go to trial. There's a lot of evidence that points to the owner of the club."

"What do you think?" Jackson asked.

"I think he's being framed, but there's no evidence to support it."

"Well," Jackson began, "Is there anyone that would gain if Blaine went to prison? Maybe a relative or a business associate?"

Jenna shook her head, but stopped short. Blaine did have a partner, but she didn't know if he had anything to gain. She remembered the partnership agreement in the stack of paperwork. Maybe there would be something in there.

"Jackson, I don't mean to cut the evening short, but you gave me an idea. There's something I think I should look into."

Jackson stood. "Don't apologize. Dinner was wonderful, but I need to be getting back to work myself."

He hesitated at the door; Jenna wasn't sure why until he walked back over to her. Jackson put his arm around her to hug her, but Jenna pulled away enough to give him a soft kiss. A look of uncertainty passed through his eyes before he pulled away.

"Goodnight, Jenna," he said softly before leaving.

Jenna wanted to run after him, but she kept her feet planted where they were. That look in his eyes made her wonder if maybe he hadn't wanted to say goodnight so soon and Jenna knew she hadn't wanted the night to end with a quick kiss. She almost managed to talk herself into showing up at his door and throwing herself at him when she caught sight of her office from the corner of her eye. It was going to take her quite a while to find anything in that mess, especially given that her kitten had chosen to spread the contents of one of the files across the room while playing.

"I'd better get started," Jenna said with a sigh. "It's just as well."

Or at least, that's what she told herself.

Thursday, October 2

"That's pretty weak, Jenna, but I'll see if I can use it," Maureen said after Jenna explained the reason she was at her office.

Jenna sighed. "I know, but it could be something. It could, at least, be reasonable doubt."

Maureen nodded. "I'll have one of my investigators check Victor out. I'll let you know if it turns into anything."

Jenna stood. "Okay. I just hope it helps."

"Not so fast, Jenna. While I have you in my office I want to talk to you."

Jenna sank back down into the chair. "What about?"

"When are you going to stop messing around and take the Bar? You have a knack for this, you know."

They'd been having this same discussion from the first day they'd met and Jenna was sick of it. Why couldn't people understand she was doing what she wanted to be doing with her life? She was grateful when her cell phone rang.

"Jenna, its Chad. I'm up on your side of the world and I was hoping you might be available for lunch."

Jenna wasn't in the mood to catch up with old friends, but anything had to be better than getting interrogated by Maureen for the thousandth time.

"Sounds good. Where are you?"

"Keller Springs and the Tollway...I think," he answered uncertainly.

"Okay. There's a Mexican restaurant there. I can meet you in about fifteen minutes," Jenna offered.

"Yeah, I see it. I'll see you then," Chad said before ending the call.

Jenna turned to Maureen and shrugged. "I'm sorry, but I couldn't get out of that. We'll have to finish this conversation another time."

After circling the small trailer park for the third time, Collin was convinced we'd found the right place. I thought it was obvious from the empty driveway that the trailer's occupant was not at home, but I humored him by leaning against the truck while he knocked on the door. He gave up after the third knock and returned to the truck.

"Where could she be? Our records don't indicate that she has a job," Collin muttered, thumbing through the file.

Of course, had he actually *read* the file on Henrietta Grace instead of just glancing at the bullet points, he might have realized Blackstone's maternal grandmother, and only living relative, was heavily involved with her church. I suspected she was there, though I kept that tidbit to myself for the moment. Something told me it would be more fun to see how long it took Collin to arrive at the same conclusion.

It was insane for us to be here. The chances that Blackstone's grandmother would tell us anything we wanted to know were slim to none. More likely, she would tip him off we'd been here and he'd get real careful, real fast. Unless he got careless. Either way, she was the only lead we had to work at the moment.

Except for Jenna.

Things were steadily heating up between us since I'd met her and it was becoming more unlikely that I'd be able to focus on my case while I was with her. It was rough to feed her the information I had last night when I had no desire to chat about the weather and Blaine's case. I knew it was my job to stay close to her, but the line was blurring, making it difficult to determine how close was close enough.

And how close was too close.

"You have the attention span of an ant, Caldwell," Collin growled. "How have you managed to last in this line of work for this long?"

I glared at him. "What's that supposed to mean?"

"It means you haven't heard one word I've said since we got here." He rolled his eyes. "Actually, you haven't heard anything I've said since the chick you're watching got you all hot and bothered."

"She has a name, you know."

"Right. Jenna. She has you so twisted in knots that you're driving me nuts. You need to hurry up and get laid so we can put this case to bed."

"I am not discussing this with you, McShae."

He shrugged. "If you can't take the heat then get out of the kitchen."

"We aren't in the kitchen," I muttered, knowing full well to what he was referring.

"Stop trying to change the subject. I'm not the one who was nailing her on the kitchen counter."

"I was not..." I paused to regain control of my voice. "It wasn't like that. Things just got out of hand."

"Can I help you boys with something?" a maternal voice asked from behind.

I turned and sized up the woman in front of me. Blackstone's grandmother looked far older than her seventy years of life should have aged her. At one time, she had been five foot five, if the file was accurate, but age caused her shoulders to slope at the expense of several inches of height. Her grey eyes were still bright even from behind her thick glasses. Her thin hair had turned the same color as her eyes and was swept back into a tidy bun at the base of her neck.

She could have been on a package of cookies.

"Mrs. Grace," I began, extending my hand. "I'm Special Agent Caldwell and this is Special Agent McShae. We'd like to ask you a few questions."

Rather than accept my hand, Henrietta pulled her glasses further down on her nose and regarded me with unabashed skepticism. "Agents, huh? Do you boys have anything to prove that?"

We handed our identification over for inspection.

When she had scrutinized to her satisfaction she said, "Thank you for humoring me. A woman can't be too careful about letting strange boys into her home nowadays. Can't be too careful at all."

We nodded and followed her inside the tiny trailer.

"Can I get you boys something to drink?"

"No, ma'am," Collin replied. "We'd like to ask you a few questions and we'll be on our way."

"I see." She lowered herself onto the worn sofa. "Have I done something wrong? I know I shouldn't have parked in the fire lane at the market, but there were no spaces and I had to pick up my pills. It was only supposed to take a quick second, but then I ran into Olivia Marcicolo and she was in a sour mood. Now, it seems that Olivia's husband was at Peter Kawakanski's drug store and...Let me back up. You have to know Peter Kawakanski to understand what happened. You see..."

"Actually, Mrs. Grace," Collin interrupted. "We're here about your grandson."

"Chad?" She squinted at us. "Why that boy is an angel...a living angel."

I knew this was going to be tough so I got right to the point. "Have you noticed any strange behavior in him since he came back to town?"

"Good heavens, no. It's been a blessing...a gift from God to have him back." She glared at me over the top of her glasses again. "What exactly do you want to know about my little Chad?"

I exchanged looks with Collin. He must have guessed at my thoughts because he gave an almost imperceptible shake of his head.

I cleared my throat. "We're investigating his employer. Has he mentioned anything to you about that?"

"No, I can't say he has, but then he has been a touch busy with that woman friend of his." She hoisted herself up to her feet. "If you boys will excuse me, it's time for me to take my pills. I'm overly tired from my work at the church and I need to rest a spell."

Chapter 14

As Jenna sipped at her tea, she realized she had never been this uncomfortable at lunch in her life. They had been close in school, such good friends that it was difficult for her to understand how they could have so little in common, even after ten years. Actually, she had to wonder how she had become such a bad friend. For the last ten minutes, she'd been thinking about Jackson while Chad talked about a clinical trial. Even if she had given her undivided attention she doubted that she'd have understood most of what he said.

Chad had changed little since high school. He'd grown a couple of inches, filled out some, but that only bumped him from scrawny to lanky. His eyes were a flat shade of grey that brightened when he spoke of his work. Jenna had to smile every time her eyes strayed to his hair. It was the same as it always used to be: an unruly mop of forgotten hair atop his head. Perhaps it was the absent-minded scientist in him that always forgot most people owned combs.

Jenna wondered if her illustrator would be able to capture that careless style for the book. She had halfway spun the plot in her head of an eight-year-old boy, with forgotten blonde hair, conducting science experiments in his mother's attic when she realized Chad was asking her a question. "I'm sorry, Chad. What was that?"

"I was asking how you like being back in Dallas after all the time you spent in Boston."

Jenna remembered she'd last spoken to him while she was still in law school, long before she'd been forced to move home. Long before Tony...It wasn't something she wanted to get into with him so she searched for something plausible to say. "You know, Boston was never home. I missed my family and my friends."

"But you gave up on being a lawyer? That was all you ever talked about wanting to be when we were in school. You had your life planned out. How could you walk away from all that?"

Jenna slunk back against her chair. "Life happens. Things change." She looked away and caught sight of the waitress staring at them from the corner. Apparently, she wasn't thrilled about having a table stay for almost an hour after paying the check. Turning back to Chad she said, "We should get going. I have a lot of writing to do tonight."

Chad nodded and followed her outside to her car. "It was great getting to catch up with you after all this time." He touched her face. "Jenna, I've missed you so much."

She was still trying to figure out what his hand was doing on her face when she felt his other hand grasp the other side of her face. He pulled her to him and forced his lips against hers, a sloppy tongue licking at her lips.

You've got to be kidding me with this, she thought.

Pushing him away and wiping off her mouth she demanded, "What are you doing?"

Chad looked startled. "I was kissing you."

Jenna let out her breath slowly and tried to make her voice calm. The last thing she wanted to do was hurt him. "I'm flattered, really I am, and in another time then maybe..." It was such an obvious lie to her own ears that she paused. "I'm seeing someone, Chad. I value you as a friend, but I'm involved with someone else."

"Well that went about as expected," I muttered once we got back to headquarters.

"Better," Collin countered, "She could have made us listen to the rest of that story."

I knew there was no point to questioning Blackstone's grandmother. Or, at least, trying to question her about him. It was clear after only a moment that she was in deep denial about him. More likely, she didn't know what he'd become since moving away. She'd raised him from the age of thirteen and was his only living relative. After re-evaluating the background information we had on him, I could see why she was protective of him.

His parents were total losers. His father ran a heroine lab out of the family's home, but was caught when Blackstone was eight. He was sent to prison where he died after a prison yard squabble.

The guy's mother was even worse. She'd claimed no knowledge of her husband's activities and was given immunity when she helped put him away. She'd never worked a day in her life and couldn't maintain the lifestyle she was used to by working nine to five, so she'd turned to the streets. She turned tricks for a few years before her throat was slit and she bled out in some seedy alley.

If I didn't know anything else about this guy I would have felt sorry for him. He'd had a rotten life by anyone's standards. It was more than a little surprising he had excelled in school.

"Are we sure the government seized all of his father's drug money?"

"They took every cent they knew about at the time. I suppose it's possible he had a secret safe-deposit box stuffed with cash somewhere for his son. Why? Do you think that might be how he's financing this little fiasco?" Collin replied.

I shrugged. "I don't know. I'm reaching at straws, I guess. Has anything new turned up yet?"

"If you mean a bar napkin with his master plan on it, the answer is no. The only angle we have right now is Jenna. Is she still distracted with the case?"

"It goes before the grand jury tomorrow. I think she figured out the Victor thing, so let's hope they can put it all together in time. I think I'm going to head out."

"I'll see you tomorrow morning," Collin said.

"No," I reminded him. "I have to go to the zoo tomorrow, remember?"

Collin smiled. "Oh, yeah. Lions and tigers and all that. Have fun."

I knew he was being sarcastic, but something told me I would.

Jenna climbed into her bathtub and tried to let the bubbles wash her day away. Lunch with Chad was okay, boring, but okay until they were leaving. She couldn't believe he'd kissed her.

It was no secret he had a crush on her when they were in school, but she was certain that would have vanished by now. At least Chad had understood she was seeing someone else and they'd parted on good terms.

Jenna wished she could figure out if she really was seeing someone else, or if it was all in her head. She'd overcome the urge to go and see Jackson that night; instead convincing herself to get into the tub. She should be able to go a night without seeing the man. After all, she was spending the day with him and her niece tomorrow. It wasn't the most ideal date, but it was a start.

Once Jenna got out of the tub, she played her messages and was pleased to have received a call from Maureen about the case. She played the message a second time, just to make sure she hadn't misunderstood, then smiled.

"Hey, lady, it's Maureen. I wanted to let you know that Victor's last name isn't Wellington, it's Ascenzi. Apparently, Mr. Ascenzi has a rap sheet longer than most of my skirts. He used to do the exact same thing in New York. I can't wait to see the look on his face in court tomorrow. Thanks Jen, I owe you one."

Jenna took her hair out of the towel on her head and tried to shake out some of the water as she walked down the hall. No sooner had she flipped on the bathroom light, a knock sounded at the door. She glanced at herself in the mirror and decided her robe covered enough for her to answer the door. Still trying to towel of the excess water from her hair, she answered the door.

Jackson blew out a breath when he saw her. "Damn."

Jenna frowned at him. "That's a different greeting. Do I look that bad?"

"No. Can I..." His voice trailed off and he just stared at her.

"Come in?" she finished for him. Stepping aside she added, "I swear you get stranger every time I see you."

Jenna closed the door and felt him come up behind her. His arms circled her waist and pulled her back against him, making her drop the towel in her hand when she realized how aroused he was. At least that explained his inability to form words.

Trying to make her voice light, she asked, "What's up?" She realized the moment she said it that her words were poorly chosen.

He nibbled on her earlobe. "I think that's obvious."

As one hand pulled back her hair to allow his lips free reign over the back of her neck, the other hand slipped inside her simple terrycloth robe to cup her breast. It had been a long time since any man had touched Jenna in such an intimate manner, so long that she gasped when his thumb rasped across her nipple. Her heartbeat throbbed in her ears and her mind shut down.

Jackson pulled back the hand and stepped away from her. She turned to face him in shocked silence, not understanding why he'd stopped. He looked at his hand as though it were an alien before turning away.

"I swear I didn't come over here for that. I wanted to find out what time we needed to leave in the morning, but..." He looked back at Jenna. "The sexy, wet hair and robe were more than I could handle, I guess."

Jenna looked down at herself, confused. This robe was the least sexy thing she owned. Maybe if she'd been wearing the short silk one Elaine had given her for her birthday one year she could understand his reaction. Come to think of it, she should probably figure out where she'd put it before too much longer...

When Jenna didn't respond, Jackson continued, "I didn't realize that I, uh...the hand, uh..." He started to move towards the door. "I should go. You look like you were getting ready for bed." He paused, his eyes raking over her. "Hell."

Jenna reached out and placed her index finger over his lips to silence him. "If you would stop babbling for a second then you might be interested in hearing you read this all wrong."

Jackson's eyes grew dark with interest, but he remained quiet.

"First off, I never get to sleep early so you aren't keeping me up or anything. We should leave at ten, but I don't care what your reason for coming over here is because I've been trying to talk myself out of going over to your place for most of the night and..." She flicked her tongue over her now dry lips. "You don't have to apologize about the hand because I liked it."

"Wait. Which hand?" Jackson asked, eyes dark, intense. He moved around her and pulled her back against him, pulling her hair back as he had moments earlier. Grazing the back of her neck with his lips, he asked, "This hand or," He paused long enough to slide his other hand into Jenna's robe. "This hand?"

Jenna shuddered and arched back against him. "Both."

Time ceased to move. His lips moved from the back of her neck to her ear, then to her jaw as she twisted around in his arms. Their lips met in a ferocious kiss, shoving all thoughts of the mishap with Chad or the case from her mind. He was all that mattered; his taste and his touch were all that existed.

More than anything else, she wanted him. It didn't matter how long they had or hadn't known one another. It didn't make sense and it didn't have to. Jenna wanted all of him; couldn't stand the layers of fabric standing between them. Blind, useless fingers tugged at his shirt until he broke the kiss to yank it over his head.

Their eyes met as the forgotten shirt fell to the floor. Something as timeless as it was dangerous flashed through his eyes. He held her gaze while moving towards her in a wordless seduction. She didn't realize she moved until her back met the wall. Why she would ever move to put space between them, she didn't know.

His body crushed against hers, melding to all her curves. "Jackson..."

Hurried lips moved over her neck and face before teeth met earlobe. "Tell me to stop right now."

She nearly choked. "What?" If this was some kind of sex game, she wasn't getting it.

His breath came out in heated, ragged gasps, tickling her ear and igniting her desire. "If you don't want this, Jenna...If you don't want this to go any further then tell me to stop right now." His knee pressed between her thighs. "Unless you tell me to stop…I won't."

Jenna writhed against him until her arms were between them with her palms flat on his muscled chest. "Don't…" The word was no sooner passed her lips then he started to pull away. Why had she even bothered to test it? She hooked her foot around his leg to stop him. "I don't want you to stop. I want this. Now. Tonight."

"Oh, thank God. I think it would kill me to wait any longer."

She wanted to tell him she felt the same way, but his lips were already moving over hers, surprisingly un-hurried after the fervor of his words. But his hands were a different story. They fought with the robe's sash until the knot gave way and it fell open, giving her the first de-licious high of feeling their bodies skin against skin.

His hands moved away from her body and the lock clicked at her side. Before she understood he'd locked the door, Jackson's hands were back on her, mov-ing under the robe to grasp her bare hips, lifting her up until the hard ridge of his denim-clad erection was exact-ly where it would do the most good. She wrapped her legs around him and arched into him, using her body to beg for more.

He didn't disappoint.

Jackson grasped her wrist and lifted it high over her head, forcing her back to arch even more. Jenna gasped to catch her breath when he tore his lips from hers to take in her body with hungry eyes. His hand re-leased her wrist to trail down her arm, her shoulder, be-tween her breasts. He managed to drag his eyes from her trembling body long enough to take in the wanton need in her eyes.

Her chest heaved in anticipation. She couldn't handle waiting for his next move. It already felt as though a lifetime had passed since his last touch. Desperate for more, she reached for him, tangling her fingers into his hair, pulling his lips back to her.

But he didn't kiss her. Instead, he matched her by tugging back on her damp locks and exposing her throat for lips and teeth and tongue. Her pulse throbbed beneath his mouth, then raced out of control when it moved lower, taking his time with each breast in turn. Teeth teasing against her nipple were nearly more than she could stand and she cried out in pleasure, tightening her legs around him even more than she thought possible.

"Jenna..." He growled out her name and tightened his grip on her hips. "I can't wait another second. I need you right now."

"Now. Jackson...now."

With her legs still wrapped around his waist, he moved in the direction of the living room, careful with his steps in the darkened condo. The thought of the mood being spoiled by the screeching of one of her cats being stepped on flitted through her mind. It didn't stay. It couldn't. His nearness, the friction of their bodies, the desperate need evident in the pattern of both their breathing...It all crowded out any thought from her head that didn't involve getting him naked and satisfying her desire.

As he was attempting to kick off his shoes, Jenna unwound her legs from him and lowered them until she felt carpet beneath her feet. "Need some help getting out of those?"

"My shoes?"

She trailed her hand down his muscled chest and abs. "You seem to have those under control. I meant your pants."

He gestured to them. "If you insist."

Swift fingers made short work of his belt; attacked the zipper with a gusto reserved for the most decadent of desserts. He may as well be a sugary treat. She craved him more than she ever had a chocolate bar.

His erection beckoned to her once freed from the confining pants as though inviting her to indulge her sweet tooth. Taking a taste wasn't a half bad idea. Torturing him the way he always did her was a better idea. Turnabout, after all, was fair play.

The devil was in her eyes when she looked at him and she knew he knew it by his grin of expectant mischief. Her hands teased against what beckoned her with feather light fingers. Her lips explored his muscles on the way down. He treated her ears to a gasp of anticipation each time her mouth moved lower, and his groans of pleasure grew more frantic as she kept up her light stroking. Just as she reached that spot where her breath was warm against his excited flesh and a deep growl rumbled in his throat, Jenna righted herself and shoved against his chest, toppling him back over the arm of the couch.

"What the..."

She wasted no time in joining him on the couch, straddling him. A shiver raced up her spine. All that stood between them now were very thin boxers – boxers that did little as a barrier.

Jackson stared up at her, reaching for her. "Come here."

How could two syllables sound so damn sexy? "I am here."

"Kiss me."

Her hair fell against his face when she kissed him and her open robe covered them both. His hands were warm as they slipped underneath the robe, pressing against the small of her back to hold her body as near to his as it could be. He broke the kiss to move to her neck and Jenna whimpered, wanting so much more, but not wanting him to stop anything. A hand stole away from her back to trace her hip until stroking fingers found their way between her thighs.

"Oh...God!"

Was he really moving in slow motion or did it only feel that way because all the patience she'd ever managed to muster snapped at his touch.

His fingers were probing deeper when they heard a knock at the door. He gave Jenna a questioning look, but she shook her head and angled her hips to give him more access. "Ignore it. Whoever it is will go away," she whispered.

Despite her hopes, the knocking persisted and was followed by, "Come on, Jen. I know you're still up. Turn off the damn computer and let me in. The door's locked and you never lock the door," Trista whined from outside.

Jenna fought to block out her friend's voice. This wasn't happening. It couldn't be happening, not when she was only a few inches from getting several inches of pure pleasure. Building anticipation was more than she could take.

The knocking started again, softer this time. "Jen, if you're not asleep then please open the door. I'm really worried about the trial tomorrow. I can't handle losing Blaine over something he didn't do."

Jackson sighed in frustration. "She's not going anywhere, is she?"

"No."

His head dropped back against the couch. Through gritted teeth he said, "She needs you right now. We can pick this up later."

Jenna pulled her robe closed and forced herself to move off him. "Hold on a second, Trist. I'll be right there," she called out. Once Jackson's pants were back on and he was heading for his shirt by the door, she whispered, "I'm so sorry about this."

He crushed her against the wall and kissed her hard. "It's not your fault. We'll have other nights." With obvious effort, he pushed himself away from her trembling body. "If I didn't think this visitor could be here all night, I'd say we'd have later tonight and the early part of the morning." Opening the door, he said, "I'll see you tomorrow at around ten." To Trista, "I'm sure everything is going to be fine."

Trista walked into the condo and took in the dimmed lights and the towel carelessly left on the carpet. "Was his shirt on inside-out?"

Jenna shrugged it off. "Probably. So what's going on?"

Chapter 15

The call came around three o'clock Friday afternoon while Jenna and Jackson were at the zoo with Lana. She was skipping ahead of them on the path when Jenna's cell phone rang. She glanced at Jackson, who must have understood that Lana was getting too far away from them and quickened his pace to catch up to the energetic little girl while she took the call.

"What happened, Trist?"

Trista's voice was excited when she spoke. "The judge threw the entire case out. They took Victor into custody right there in the courtroom. Blaine will have to testify against him at his trial, but other than that, this whole nightmare is over. You have no idea how relieved I am, Jen."

"That's great. I'm happy for you. And for Blaine."

"My cell is cutting-. Blaine wants to celebrate tomorrow night at the club; private room. Bring Jack-"

Jenna put the phone back in her purse and hurried to catch the others. She couldn't wait to tell Jackson the good news, but she stopped short when she saw them. They were both standing on one leg with the other foot resting on their knee.

"Look, Aunt Jenna. We're flamingos. Can I have an ice cream from the man in the cart?"

"Okay," Jenna said as she handed Lana a few dollars.

They watched as she skipped to the ice cream cart six feet away before either of them spoke.

"Was that Trista?"

"They dropped the charges. It looks like our hunch about Victor was right. I don't know how I can ever thank you for thinking of that."

"You came up with it. I was just there when you did. However," Jackson's tone became playful, "I can probably think of a few ways for you to thank me."

"Oh, really?" Jenna turned her attention from Lana who was selecting a flavor to Jackson. "What might that be?"

"Hmm." She could tell that Jackson was pretending to appear thoughtful. "I'll have to think of something. Unless you have any ideas."

"I have a few of my own," Jenna replied. After last night, that was an understatement. If his prediction about Trista staying into the early hours of the morning hadn't proven correct then she would have found herself at his door to finish what they'd started. When Jackson knocked on her door that morning, he'd declined coming inside, clearly not trusting himself with her any more than she could trust herself alone with him.

So, yeah, she had more than a few ideas about what she wanted to do to him.

His hands stroked up her bare arms. "I can't wait to hear more about these ideas of yours. Care to share?"

"Nope. You'll just have to wait."

"Wait?" He pulled her close to nip at her neck. "What if I can't wait?" Teeth tugged at her earlobe. "What if I have to have you right now?"

Jenna didn't have a problem with that, not once she was sandwiched between his body and the railing to the flamingo area. No hint of reluctance to be affectionate in public tainted his kiss once their lips met. It took every ounce of her self-control to keep from whimpering and moaning in response to him. The whole day of platonically walking and occasionally holding hands was maddening, but this...his kiss...It was the cruelest and most delicious form of torture.

"Now can I call you Uncle Jackson?" a tiny voice interrupted.

Jenna pulled away and shook her head as she laughed.

"I think it's time to get you home, Lana."

"Okay, Aunt Jenna, but can we get a picture first?" Lana pointed to one of the instant photo booths.

Jenna looked at Jackson, who shrugged in response, eyes still the color of molten sky from their kiss, then smiled at her niece. "Why not?"

I was glad Jenna suggested we leave the zoo when she did. The traffic from Dallas to Frisco was moderate, but I could imagine what it would have been like if we had let another half hour pass. Lana was a cute kid, no doubt, but I sure didn't want to be stuck in a car with her for hours waiting for traffic to move five feet.

All I wanted was to be alone with Jenna. Every time she kissed me, I forgot about why I was here. What I was supposed to be doing would fall away from my mind and she would fill it. That already proved to be a dangerous behavior, so I knew I would have to be more careful. I'd almost made love to her the night before without protection; something I never did. I mean, *never*. It wouldn't be a bad idea for us to make a pit stop after we dropped off Lana. I'd already decided I would stop under the guise of refueling. No way I could be alone with Jenna again until I'd taken the necessary precautions. At this stage in the game, a non-sexual evening stretching in front of us wouldn't be an option...for either of us.

Of course, after the way I remembered Black-stone looking at her, not having any condoms was the least of my worries.

Almost as soon as we entered the Whitman house, Elaine pulled Jenna away into another room and Lana skipped off. I decided against standing in the entry to wait. Even though I wanted nothing more than to skip the small talk and get Jenna out of her clothes, I knew how that would appear. Instead, I headed to the den where I found Daniel and Lana watching television. It struck me as odd that she could be so wholly engrossed in what she was watching when she'd only been home a mere matter of minutes.

"Was that really me, Daddy? I look so small," Lana asked.

Lana's eyes were filled with wonderment as she spoke to her father. I realized they were watching a home movie of a past birthday party. I sat quietly next to them on the sectional.

"Yes, honey, it's you there. You look smaller be-cause you were only three."

I didn't know most of the people I was watching, but I recognized Jenna when I saw her. She had changed little in appearance, but there was definitely a change in her. When a man walked up behind her and wrapped his arms around her waist, she looked happy. It was the kind of joy people rarely found and managed to hold onto in a lifetime.

Conflicting emotions rose from a place inside me I didn't know existed. In jealousy, I wanted to know who the hell this guy was and why his hands were all over *my*

Jenna. From a deeply protective place, I wanted to know why he'd screwed up that happiness for Jenna. I couldn't imagine she'd done anything to end that. Why would any man dream of leaving a woman like her?

Once Jenna and Elaine entered the room things began to happen in such rapid succession that I could scarcely keep the order of events straight.

"Who's that with Aunt Jenna, Daddy?"

"That was your Uncle Tony."

"Daniel, please shut that off," Elaine snapped.

"I remember Uncle Tony. He used to play horsy with me."

"Daniel, shut it off," Elaine's voice was pleading.

"I don't think I remember him after the party," Lana said.

Jenna was still.

"Daniel, please..." Elaine was begging now.

"What happened to Uncle Tony, Daddy?"

I saw Jenna's face go pale out of the corner of my eye.

"He went away, Lana," Daniel said, quiet.

"When is he coming back, Daddy?"

Jenna fled the room, tears flowing. Elaine chased behind her.

"He can't come back, sweetie. We talked about this."

"But I miss him. Where did he go?"

"He went away to Heaven, Lana."

It was suddenly clear to me why Jenna left Boston so abruptly two years ago.

Jenna didn't remember the ride home. It seemed like they just left the zoo, but now she was sitting on her couch at home. She always planned to tell Jackson about what happened at some point; just not at this early stage in their relationship. As awful as the whole thing was, there was a sense of relief, too. She'd been living with Tony's ghost for so long that once she'd been able to move on she hadn't wanted to think about it for fear of ruining everything.

But it was all out in the open now. Whatever was going to happen, would now happen. It was out of her hands.

Maybe it was never in her hands at all.

Jackson returned from the kitchen after what felt like forever with a cup of hot tea. Jenna accepted it, but didn't drink. She set it on the coffee table and stared into space for what she imagined to be hours, but knew was probably only a minute or so.

Jackson hovered for a moment before breaking the silence.

"Do you need anything, Jenna?" His voice was soft.

"No."

"Do you want me to go?"

"No."

Jackson sat next to her on the couch as though he didn't know what else to do. He put his arm around her shoulders to comfort her, but remained silent. Jenna let herself slump against him and rested her head against his chest. The fact he was even still there was a comfort in itself.

"I was engaged once," Jenna began, unsure how she was supposed to begin this kind of conversation.

"You don't have to talk about this."

"I know," Jenna said as she pulled away to face him. "I want...I need to."

Jackson remained quiet.

"I met Tony when I was interning at a Boston law firm. He was a Homicide Lieutenant with the Boston PD and my firm was defending the guy he was trying to put away. Getting involved was clearly a bad idea, yet...it was like it was inevitable that we would.

"We kept our relationship a secret, for the most part. It would have caused problems for him at work and I would have been fired. We weren't doing anything wrong, but we both realized a need to be discreet. Cops and defense attorneys, at least from my firm, they didn't mix well."

He nodded. "I can see how that would be an issue."

"We came down here for Lana's birthday party after I graduated. I didn't know it at the time, but he came with me to ask for Daniel and Elaine's blessing to marry me.. Anyway, he asked me just before the party that you saw on video earlier."

Jenna paused to wipe a rogue tear away from her cheek and continued.

"We agreed not to tell our friends in Boston or set a date until I passed the Bar, which I was scheduled to take that December. He didn't want anything to distract me from it. He didn't like the fact that I would be defending the people he was trying to put behind bars, but he was still supportive. We could find a way to make it work.

"Everything fell apart at the beginning of November. His partner was the only person who knew about us there, so he had to deliver the bad news to me. Tony was in a convenience store when some guy high on meth tried to rob it. He was off-duty, but tried to stop the guy. There was a struggle. He was shot. He was gone before the ambulance arrived."

"I'm so sorry."

"I was given time off from the firm to study for the exam, so I didn't have to tell anyone why I needed time off for the funeral. That was when I found out my firm was defending the guy who killed Tony. They won and I never went back."

"I guess that's why you gave up the law," Jackson said.

"That's a part of it."

She hadn't talked with anyone about Boston in years, not even Trista. She always avoided the subject to avoid dealing with her feelings. The sense of closure washing over her now was unexpected. It felt as though a weight was lifted from her shoulders. And her heart. It felt as though she could face her pain and move on.

She finally felt peace.

"My father was a lawyer, a very good one actually, and it was always his dream for his children to follow in his footsteps. He learned Elaine had no intention of fulfilling that wish for him when we were still young. It all fell on me. I went to law school out of a sense of duty, not because I wanted to. I didn't even pick Harvard Law. He was an alumnus. Being a legacy and the daughter of Michael Monroe held a lot weight. It was a done deal before my senior year ever began."

"How did you end up writing?" Jackson asked.

"The mechanics of it are a long, boring story, but it was a dream of mine to write since I was a child. After Tony died, I needed to do something that was for me. Only me. I moved here and shut myself off from the world. Until I met you, that is."

Jackson was quiet for a long moment. It looked to Jenna as though he was about to say something when his cell phone rang. He looked at the display for a moment and frowned.

"I'm sorry, Jenna, but I have to take this. It's my sister Sherry. She's had a rough time with her husband lately."

"I understand," Jenna lied. "I need to change anyway."

Even though Jenna left the room to change, I knew that she might return at any moment. I didn't think she would try to eavesdrop on me, but I couldn't risk her hearing anything that might blow my cover. I slipped into the guest bedroom and closed the door before answering the call.

"Hello, Sherry."

"Well, that's a nice change from your usual gruff greeting. I suppose you aren't alone from your tone."

My tone was rushed, hoping she would get the hint and also be brief.

"I'm at Jenna's, but I can talk for a minute. What's going on?"

"I called to find out if there were any new developments since we last spoke. I'm getting a lot of heat up here for the lack of results thus far."

"I've got a team covering Blackstone and Collin is..."

"I don't care about that. I want to know what you're doing. You're the agent I sent to deal with this and nothing's happened yet. I knew I would regret sending you instead of Franklin from the moment I called you into my office, but we both know his current assignment had to take priority so I was stuck with you."

I could feel the muscle in my jaw contracting at her words. It took every ounce of my being to stop myself from letting her know what I thought of her opinion about me and Franklin. Her and her golden boy could burn in hell for all I cared. If they took Melissa with them on the way down then all the better.

If she was expecting a smartass comment from me, her disappointment didn't show in her voice when she resumed speaking. "You've been spending a great deal of time with Miss Monroe and I'm not getting a benefit from it yet," she said matter-of-factly.

"She doesn't know anything, Sherry."

"Or she doesn't trust you enough to tell you what she knows."

I fought to make my voice calm before I spoke.

"She trusts me enough to tell me why she left Boston."

"I'm going to need a little more than your fluffed up pillow talk, Caldwell."

"Don't excite yourself over there. You'll never hear or hear about my pillow talk."

There was silence for a long moment before she replied.

"Have you considered the possibility she's in on it and playing you? Or can your fragile male ego not handle being used again?"

"She isn't," I sputtered.

"Perhaps. Perhaps not. Step it up, Caldwell. I want you to get her phone tapped."

"I'll take care of that," I said even though I had no intention of doing it.

"I want you to do whatever it takes to make certain you are not wrong, and I do mean *whatever* it takes. Keep in mind, this country may not officially condone torture, but I sure as shit do when it comes to an agent gone soft. Get it done," she ordered before ending the call.

I tossed the cell phone onto the bed and sighed. I wasn't surprised by her attitude and I couldn't blame her for wanting results. I would feel the same way if I were in her position, but that realization didn't make things any easier for me.

Jenna had been hurt in the past; I knew that. She would be hurt again if I stayed involved with her. I should walk out her front door and not look back. I knew Blackstone was up to something and I was reasonably certain I could prove it if I personally kept tabs on him until something went down. The best thing for everyone involved would be for me to walk away, but I couldn't do it.

Not now.

Jenna poured her soul out to me not fifteen minutes before. If I had known, I never would have told her my wife died. I assumed she felt some sort of natural connection to my 'loss' when, in reality, I had no idea what she'd gone through. Even though my wife, ex-wife, was dead to me; she wasn't dead. It was a definite she would be furious with me once she found out the truth. I knew she would think I had said that only to get closer to her. She may have started out as a case and a bet for me, but it had turned into more than that. Would I have done that, used that personal pain of hers to further my investigation?

Maybe. I didn't know.

All I knew for sure was if I wasn't careful then I was going to fall in love...

My thoughts were interrupted by a soft rap at the door. The door opened and Jenna hesitantly stepped inside. Despite all my reservations, I couldn't help thinking she looked great, even though she was wearing plaid, flannel pants and a t-shirt at least two sizes too large for her. Actually, it was the same frumpy thing Melissa would wear when she wanted to make sure I knew I wasn't getting laid that night. On Jenna, the effect was much different.

"Is everything okay, Jackson?" Jenna asked quietly as she sat next to me on the bed.

"Yeah," I lied. "My sister is a tough cookie; she'll be fine."

"That's good."

"How about you? Are you okay?"

"Sure. I feel much better now that I'm out of those clothes. Lana managed to get chocolate on my back, though I'm not sure how."

I could tell she was being evasive with me on purpose.

"I think you know that isn't what I meant, Jenna."

"I do, but I'm ignoring it. I've been living in the past for two years." She leaned back on her elbows. "I'm ready to move on and I think you should move on with me, Jackson. I think I'm ready to pick up where we left things last night."

Jenna tugged on the back of my shirt until she succeeded in pulling me back onto the bed with her.

"What are you doing?"

"You know exactly what I'm doing. Don't pretend you don't, Jackson." Her voice was whisper soft against my neck.

She trailed kisses across my jaw before her lips met mine. I wasn't sure how I'd let it happen, but she managed to pull me on top of her. Her intentions were evident to me by the liquid way her body moved against me, by the desperate sounds in her throat. No doubt I was tempted.

Damn, was I tempted.

It took every ounce of willpower I could muster to pull away from her. I rolled onto my side and propped myself up on an elbow. I looked into her eyes before I spoke.

"You're right, Jenna, I do know what you're doing. I don't think you do."

Her eyes narrowed. "I'm fully aware of what I'm doing. What I don't know is why you're stopping me."

"I'm stopping you from doing something you'll regret tomorrow, Jenna."

"You believe that," she said evenly.

"Yes, I do." I took a deep breath before continuing. "Look. Things have progressed quickly between us and I'm fine with that. I'm not afraid to tell you that I care about you a great deal, Jenna, and I don't want to do anything that would hurt you. I can't take advantage of you like this."

"But you didn't seem to have a problem taking advantage of me last night."

I sighed. "That was different, more of a lust-fueled reaction to you. Your emotions are too raw right now. I still have every intention of making love to you, but doing it like this isn't right. When it happens, I need to know it's me you want and not just an escape from your past."

Jenna exhaled sharply, but said nothing. Even though it was only seven o'clock I could tell she was worn out by the events of the afternoon. I repositioned myself to lean back against the pillows.

"Come here."

Jenna hesitated then curled up next to me, allowing me to envelop her with my arms.

"You know I hate it when you're right, don't you?" she asked wearily.

"I know." I also knew I needed to lighten the atmosphere and added, "What's the deal with the canopy bed? I didn't figure you as the ruffles and frill type."

Jenna was half asleep now, but she answered, "Lana is the only person who ever stays over. I keep it cute for her."

"That's nice of you."

"I really love her," she said, even sleepier.

"I think I'm falling in love with you, Jenna."

She didn't respond. At first I started to panic, but I realized she was asleep. It was just as well she hadn't heard me; things were complicated enough.

Chapter 16

Jenna opened her eyes and looked around the dark room. She knew she was in bed, but it wasn't her bed. She sat up and rubbed her eyes in an attempt to wake herself up. Then it all came back.

She was alone and she was sure Jackson wasn't in another room. Jenna was always able to sense the presence of other people in her home. Though it wasn't abnormal for her to wake up by herself, she hadn't wanted to this time. That simple fact told her all she needed to know.

Probably more.

"I scared him off." That thought haunted her in the time it took to wash her face and brush her teeth for bed. A part of her knew while she was talking to Jackson earlier that it was too much information to dump on him at once. Or maybe it was that some of it was the kind of information she was never supposed to share. She couldn't blame him for running at the first opportunity. It's what any guy would do.

Why did he have to be any guy? He was supposed to be special – or at least, she wanted him to be special. She wanted more than anything for him to be that one percent of men out there who could handle – really handle – when things got tough and real and honest.

If only wanting something made it real.

But deep down, Jenna knew how unfair that was. Once in a lifetime was all anyone could hope for something like that. Her once upon a time had already come and gone long ago. Everything she ever wanted in a man, she'd already had in Tony. To try to project all his qualities onto Jackson wasn't just unrealistic, it was insanity.

It was also cruel.

To Jackson.

How could he think anything about the way she'd thrown herself at him that night other than what he thought? Why would he believe her desire for him was separate from the rush of emotional release she'd experienced just before? She couldn't blame him now if he was wondering now about each time things had grown heated between them. Would he be able to realize her need to touch him, kiss him, feel every inch of him had nothing to do with filling the void left by Tony?

Could he understand it?

She didn't.

In so many ways, Jackson did remind her of Tony and that terrified her. Tall, dark hair, wicked sense of humor. Then there was the powerful authority that exuded from his very being in even the most casual of situations. It made sense for Tony to have that being that he was a seasoned member of law enforcement, but Jackson...She'd never in her life met an accountant who could pull that off. While some might fire off a few shots at the firing range, there were few accountants who would ever have that same sense of confidence that came from wielding a weapon to save lives, knowing that they could beat anyone to the draw.

Except Tony hadn't the one time it counted.

"Damn frustrating misplaced male ego." Two glowing yellow orbs met her gaze from the bedroom as she made her way to the lonely comfort of her own bed. "No, Buddy, I don't mean yours. You're allowed to have an inflated ego."

It was eleven o'clock. Four hours passed since she drifted off yet she didn't feel rested. Something danced on the fringe of her memory; something she sensed she should remember. What was it? It was as if she gained some insight from an already forgotten dream. Maybe it didn't matter. She wanted this frustrating day to be at an end. Once tomorrow came she would be able to sort things out.

Things were always better in the light of day.

Jenna had no sooner turned off the lamp on her nightstand when she heard the soft click of her front door being closed. Her heart leapt into her throat, causing her mouth to go dry. Someone was in the condo, but she was too terrified to move. Instead, she strained her ears to hear the footsteps, desperate to know where they were, where they were going, but they were too quiet. This wasn't some junkie looking for cash for a quick score.

Whoever was there had done this before. What did they want? Her mind raced through the possibilities. She didn't have priceless antiques and Elaine had the bulk of the family jewelry worth anything. Her purse contained maybe twenty dollars in loose cash and change. She herself would be worth little in terms of ransom.

Reason took over before panic fully took hold. Jenna nearly convinced herself her mind was playing tricks on her. Her condo wasn't all that big so an intruder would already have made their way back to her. The years of living alone while reading crime and murder mystery novels were finally catching up with her. Maybe if she were a dog person then she'd be less jumpy. How could anyone not be paranoid when they lived with two cats that chased imaginary monsters down the hall and stared at random spots on the wall as though they were concealing leering slime monsters?

What was that? The familiar squeak of the loose floorboard in her hallway made her heart skip two beats. It was just outside her bedroom door. Unless her imagination had taken corporeal form, this was not a drill.

A shadowy figure filled her doorway and she prayed it was someone after money or electronics. Should she use the element of surprise to knock them off balance and get away? Would playing possum work? Why didn't she know what to do? She did her level best to appear as though she were asleep as the figure approached her bed.

Oh, God!

Jenna's heart stopped as the intruder knelt beside her. This wasn't a jewel thief. This wasn't a jewel thief. This wasn't...

Something was somehow familiar. There was the hint of an aftershave she had come to know well in the air that hadn't been there before. She realized who it was just before he spoke.

Jackson brushed a strand of hair off of her forehead and kissed it lightly. "Jenna, are you awake?" His voice was a whisper.

Relief flooded her veins. "Yes," she said sitting up and smacking him on the shoulder. "And don't do that to me again. You scared me half to death. I thought you were here to kill me or..."

"Hey...everything's all right." Strong arms circled her waist in an attempt to calm her. "I'm sorry. I didn't want to wake you up if you were still asleep, so I didn't turn on any of the lights. I would never do that to you on purpose.

"Where did you go? I didn't think you were coming back."

"What gave you that idea?"

"I don't know," Jenna lied.

"I thought you might be hungry when you woke up. I only meant to run out for a few minutes, but I didn't realize everything decent around here closed at ten. I had to settle for fast food. It's in the kitchen if you're hungry."

Jenna hadn't realized almost twelve hours had passed since she'd eaten until he mentioned food. She became aware of the vague rumbling in her stomach, but something else was bothering her. There was something that she had to straighten out first.

"I need to say something to you, Jackson, and I need you to try not to rationalize what I'm saying until I'm done. I need you to hear me – really hear me. Okay?"

Jackson pulled away to look at her. She could make out his face in the small amount of moonlight streaming through the window. "Okay," he replied.

"I heard everything you said to me earlier," Jenna began. Her lips were suddenly dry and she flicked her tongue over them before continuing. "I appreciate everything you said and I have a lot of respect for you for not wanting to take advantage of the situation, Jackson, but I...I want you to know what happened earlier hasn't changed anything for me."

He started to respond, but Jenna shook her head to let him know she wasn't done yet. "I want you now as much as I wanted you last night and you should know...It's you I want, not some meaningless distraction or escape. I want you, Jackson. You."

Jenna waited for what felt like an eternity for him to respond. Her mind searched for every argument he might be formulating to be ready for his response, but he remained silent. The air between them grew thick and she found it difficult to think about anything except his nearness. After a lifetime, Jackson spoke.

"Are you done?"

Not really the response she'd hoped for or expected. "I am."

"Okay. I didn't want to be accused of not hearing you out."

Silence.

"Um...I thought you might have more to say about it."

"I'm done talking tonight."

While she was still trying to make heads or tails of what that might mean, his lips moved over her own.

Huh?

Oh.

Ohhhh...

Jackson rose slowly, pulling Jenna up onto her knees on the bed, never once breaking the kiss. Something, and she didn't know what it was, in that slow intensity told her this was happening. Now. Tonight. Since the wait was over, all need to rush through anything was no more. She could spend all eternity in that moment, basking in the unhurried unraveling of passion through the kiss. More would happen when more happened. What mattered was that it was happening.

Except...The scratchy fabric of shirts between them was incongruous. That anything could exist to stand between them was impossible. And wrong.

So wrong.

Her fingers found the evil shirt's hem, tugging in seamless motions until she was forced to tear herself from the kiss to discard it onto the floor. She felt Jackson's strong hands slip under her shirt and lift it over her head. Then his arms were around her again, pulling her so close their bodies were one continuous, provocative line.

Jenna could feel Jackson's hot, ragged breath setting her skin on fire as he kissed her neck and a strange mixture of emotions filled her. She'd wanted men before, but none as desperately as she wanted him at this moment. Tony had been the only other man in her life to awaken such strong desire in her.

Jackson pulled back, almost as though he guessed the turn of her thoughts. "It isn't too late to stop if you're not sure about this."

In the past, she might have taken the out he offered and shut herself away again, but there was no going back for Jenna. Not now. Not anymore. Her mind was now ruled by her body's longing for him and the time for being rational was a distant memory. Her need for Jackson was an all-consuming flame inside her.

"Jackson, you are the only thing I'm sure about right now," Jenna replied, unfastening the button of his slacks.

"Good," Jackson said, husky. He caressed her cheek with his thumb and gazed into her wanting eyes. "You have no idea how badly I want you, Jenna, how much I've wanted you since the first moment we met."

She allowed herself to take in the tension in his well-muscled torso with her eyes and knew what was stirring inside her would sweep her away if she let it, if she let him, but she realized with a sudden clarity that she didn't care. "You're wrong. I do know because I feel it too."

Quickly, Jackson stepped out of his pants and laid her back onto the bed. He brushed a rough kiss on her lips and began to explore her body, first with hands, then with lips. Jenna could tell he was enjoying taking his time in removing the few articles of clothing remaining between them. She let him prolong it for as long as she could stand, but her skin was alive with sensation and that unhurried unraveling sensation from before was kicked away by the unruly waves of want rolling over her. Every inch of her body ached for him as he placed fiery kisses all over her, dying from the building anticipation.

"Jack...son..."

Their mouths found each other again and she kissed him with a ferocity she didn't know existed, much less that she possessed. Jenna let her hands play through his hair and heard a soft moan, but it took her a second to realize it came from her. Jackson lifted his head slightly so they were looking into one another's eyes. It frightened and excited her all at the same time to see the raw desire she felt mirrored in his sexy blue eyes.

"Wait."

Chad glared at the monitor, enraged. The tape from a few hours ago he'd finished reviewing was enlightening. This guy was an agent. A fed. A motherfucking fed. Yeah, yeah...he hadn't said exactly that, but Chad was able to put it together from the phone call. He'd underestimated this guy and now he too would have to die.

And it would be a pleasure to snuff out the spark of life in his body.

Especially now.

Of course all that was nothing compared to what he was watching now. Jenna's bedroom was dark, dark enough to interfere with the quality of the images, but enough light came through the window for Chad to see everything going on. Her rejection of him earlier in the week was nothing compared to this new betrayal.

She was actually letting him touch her, defile her. The perfection of her half-nude body was marred by the image of him all over, diminishing her pristine beauty. He was...tainting her.

"I will punish you, my darling," he whispered to her image on the monitor.

Chad's eyes became tiny black orbs as he fixed his stare on her face. As he reached down into his pants, he imagined he was the one who was with her. He should be the one with her. She knew it, too. She would need a reminder of how she felt about him, about the passion meant only for the two of them. He would make that happen soon.

Very soon.

As he was nearing his climax, the image vanished and the monitor filled with snow.

"No!"

This would be the last time Jenna would leave him unsatisfied in the cool darkness. One way or the other, she would give him everything he wanted. She would fulfill his every desire.

And, with a smile on his face, Chad would gut anyone who stood in their way, starting with the agent bedding his girlfriend...

There was confusion in Jenna's eyes as she looked at me. Things were happening too fast, but I knew she didn't understand. Hell, I doubted I would be able to explain it to her no matter how hard I tried.

"What's wrong, Jackson?"

A lot was wrong, actually. I was an FBI agent who'd been sent to watch her, not fall in love with her. It might be possible for me to pretend I didn't love her if we stopped now, but I knew I wouldn't be able to deny it to myself if we made love. She would never understand; probably never forgive me if I didn't stop this now. I couldn't give her what she wanted. I couldn't give her forever. We had maybe a month at most before my case would be closed, one way or the other, and I would have to move back out of her life.

I wouldn't hurt the woman I loved in that way. I couldn't. Truly, it would be better if I walked away now and continued to tell myself I didn't like spending time with her.

"I didn't come here prepared for this tonight, Jenna. I shouldn't have started it." I averted my eyes. "I should go."

"Like hell," she snapped.

Her words caught me off guard. I think this was the first time I'd heard Jenna swear. My eyes met hers again in surprise.

"I'm not going to let you keep doing this to me, Jackson. You can't come over here night after night to turn me on and leave me unsatisfied."

"That's not what I'm trying to do."

She rolled her eyes. "Hmm. You sure could have fooled me. You've got a twisted idea of how to do the right thing."

I opened my mouth, but there were no words.

"Look, Jackson. I want you. You want me. I'm ready. You're ready. We're in bed. What else do you want? A gilded invitation to sex?"

I swallowed hard. "Protection, Jenna. I hadn't planned on making love tonight. I didn't come prepared."

Her lips curved into a smile. "Oh." She laughed.

"I'm sorry, but I fail to see the humor in this situation."

She pulled me down onto her and kissed me lightly. "Nightstand."

"Huh?"

"Condoms, Jackson. They're in the nightstand."

"You planned this?" I was amazed. Then again, I'd been planning on the same thing before seeing the video at her sister's house.

She arched her body to reach into the nightstand drawer. It was perhaps the sexiest thing I'd seen. Tossing the box at me she said, "After almost not being interrupted by Trista, I thought it would be a good idea to hit the store early this morning before you picked me up."

As a fresh wave of lust washed over me, I started to pull off her underwear, but stopped short. If this affair was sure to end with her hating me then the least I could do was make sure I left her with the memory of at least a single amazing night. I nipped at her skin just above the fabric, grinning at her response.

Her breath drew in sharply. "What the hell are you waiting for?"

"For you to want me more than you've ever wanted anyone else."

"Men and their egos," she muttered.

"It's not ego when the skills back it up, babe."

Before she could respond, I trailed my mouth down her thigh, using teeth again at the sensitive flesh at the inside of her knee. Her gasped response spurred me back up her thigh, pausing just left of the promised land until her anticipation became palatable tension in the air. Then I repeated the exact same thing on the other leg, again stopping just to the right of where I knew she wanted me. When I did get around to removing that slip of fabric, it took all my willpower to work my way back up her body to devour her mouth with mine while sliding a hand up the inside of her thigh. She tore away from the kiss and cried out when I slid a finger inside of her.

"Jackson...now."

"Not yet." I did something clever with my hand and she screamed.

"Now..."

I stilled my hand, wanting her to be sure about this. "Are you sure you want to do this?"

Her breathing was ragged. "Yes." She arched against me and I felt her hands against my boxers, stroking me. I fought to remain in control.

"Do you want me?" I asked as I quickly discarded the last of my clothes to the floor.

"Yes."

I tore open one of the packets and unrolled it over myself. "You're sure?"

"Dammit, Jackson! Just do it already!"

Well, she was going to hate me when it was all said and done, but I couldn't make myself care in that moment. It took every bit of my control to go slow, inching my way into her slick heat without hurting her. Fuck, I wanted to ravage and destroy her after the past few days of stopping and starting. Once I settled in as far as I could, I realized she wasn't breathing. "Are you okay?"

Jenna didn't answer. Instead, she wrapped her legs around my waist and kissed me with a force I didn't think I'd ever expected from her. Her arms found their way around my neck as I began to move against her. I took it as slow and easy as I could stand, enjoying her kiss, the feel of her body, the building storm that I could barely control raging within me.

When her breathing quickened, I realized she was close from some part of my brain still capable of thought. She buried her face against my shoulder as I thrust harder, driving her over the edge. Her climax was intense, pulling me over the edge with her. It was the damnedest thing, though. Even though I had just had the most mind-splintering orgasm of my life, I was still hard as a rock.

I withdrew, discarded the condom in the wastebasket by the nightstand and sheathed myself again before Jenna even realized what was happening. I drove myself back into her with one hard thrust as that final thread of my self-control shattered violently. I took her mouth with mine one last time before I began to move hard and fast, thinking of nothing; only feeling.

The feel of her body was amazing. I might have whispered something into Jenna's ear, but I'd be damned if I had any idea what I'd said. My mind was telling me to slow down, to not be this rough with her, but my body ignored the message. Her nails bit into my shoulders as we rocked, her breath became more ragged and her cries more insistent. When I couldn't hold back a second longer I emptied myself into her and collapsed against her as she shuddered from the intensity of her own climax.

We stayed like that for a long time before I was able to find the strength to move myself off her. I stared at the ceiling and fought to catch my breath. Without a word, Jenna got out of bed and left the room. The soft click of the bathroom door being closed had the effect of a door being slammed in my brain. It didn't take a genius to know it was never a good sign when a woman jumped out of bed and hid in the bathroom after sex.

"Fuck."

Chapter 17

Jenna splashed cool water on her face in an attempt to regain her composure. She'd lost her mind this time, of that she was certain. Jackson had thoroughly made love to her and she'd fled the room like a complete psycho.

"Idiot," she said to her reflection in the mirror.

It was never like that before for Jenna. Nothing could have prepared her to get so lost in the moment, to so completely lose herself to Jackson. She couldn't think, much less know how to react to that. The longer their bodies stayed entwined in silence, the more time she had to realize how nervous she felt.

Perhaps waiting out the silence wouldn't have been such a bad idea. The weight of his body on top of her felt...right. Was it supposed to feel that way? Had it ever felt so meant-to-be with Tony?

In the ever-building wall of silent tension that ensued, Jenna realized one of them had to say something at some point. A few moments before, it wouldn't have been such a big deal, but now...Once her mind started going to the destined to be together place, well, that was it for her. Her mind was spinning out of control, jumping to conclusions that existed only in her head. Now, either she'd have to break the silence or Jackson would. And if he was the first to speak then she'd have no choice other than to respond.

But how were you supposed to respond to the man who just took you to places you never knew existed? Escaping to the solitude of the bathroom was the only option that made any sense.

From the way he knew just how to touch her, how to kiss her, to get the response he wanted, Jenna could tell he was far more experienced than she. In a separate league, really. Maybe she would get lucky and he'd slip out if she stayed in the bathroom long enough. That way, she wouldn't have to face him until she'd figured out what to say.

There was a soft tap at the door. "Are you all right, Jenna?"

No such luck. She cleared her throat. "I'm fine."

"Can I come in?"

"No."

Jenna heard him sigh through the door before asking, "Did I hurt you?"

The concern in his voice touched her. She was about to open the door when she realized she was stark naked. The conversation about to take place required she have some level of confidence, confidence she wouldn't get without putting something on first. Jenna wrapped her robe around her and opened the door. "You didn't hurt me."

He reached out and touched her face. "What did I do?"

Jenna gazed at him, trying to figure out what to say. He was so handsome that her mind went blank. Though his boxers were back on he was still naked otherwise. It took Jenna a moment to drag her eyes back to his. "You didn't do anything wrong."

"Then what is it?"

The look of concern in his eyes broke her heart so Jenna turned away. "I just felt...awkward."

She felt his hands on her shoulders applying a gentle pressure. "What do you have to feel awkward about?"

Jenna turned to face him. "We slept together."

A grin played at the corner of his lips. "Actually, we hadn't got around to the sleeping part yet."

Her cheeks flushed. "I was a virgin when I went away to college," she blurted out.

Jackson looked confused. "I don't understand what that has to do with anything."

She took a deep breath to steady herself. "Yeah, I guess you wouldn't. Never mind."

Jenna tried to turn away again, but he stopped her. "Just because I don't understand doesn't mean I don't want to."

"Okay." She blew out a breath. "I knew the moment I was accepted to Harvard that I was going to law school so I didn't make a lot of time for guys when I got there. I didn't make any time, actually. You know, other things were always more important than dating. Law school is intense anywhere, but it's especially bad at Harvard because they consider themselves to be the best." Jenna realized she was babbling, but she couldn't seem to stop herself and get to the point. "Between case studies and term papers there was never any time."

"Jenna, what are you trying to tell me?"

"I'm trying to tell you that until tonight I'd only been with one man," she whispered, her voice weak.

Jackson pulled her into his arms and hugged her close. "Is that why you think things are awkward now?"

Jenna nodded.

He lifted her chin until she was looking into his eyes. "I don't care how much experience you have or don't have. I just want to be with you. There's no reason for you to be uncomfortable with me."

"I've only known you for a week."

"And?"

"And nothing." Jenna pulled away. "I've known you for a week and you've already seen me naked. It's embarrassing."

Jackson appeared thoughtful. "You know, it was dark in there and you're wearing your robe now so I can't tell if you have anything to be embarrassed about."

Jenna didn't know how to respond to that so she remained quiet.

He reached out and untied her robe. Jenna didn't resist when he pushed it from her shoulders. Jackson sucked in a breath as he looked at her. "I'm not seeing anything here to be embarrassed about. Your body is perfect."

"You don't understand."

He grinned. "Oh, I get it." He reached out again and stroked her cheek. "I see the problem now."

Jenna looked on in confusion as Jackson turned on the faucet in the shower. "What do you mean you see the problem now?" she demanded. She turned her attention from him to her naked body. Was there something wrong with it? What problem did he see with her?

"You still want me and you think you haven't known me long enough yet to know how to tell me you want another go. Well, that's just fine because I don't mind one bit."

He disappeared from the room for a moment. When he returned, he set a few condoms on the edge of the bathtub and removed his boxers. After testing the water temperature with his hand he turned to Jenna and asked, "What are you waiting for?"

"For you to tell me what you think you're doing."

Jackson moved close to her. "Well, first I thought we might take a quick shower, then I plan to go down on you." Something in his eyes danced in the most mischievous and delicious manner. "After that I'm going to make love to you...I haven't thought much further ahead than that, but I know it's going to be over and over until you're smiling again."

Jenna was stunned. This was a side of Jackson she'd never seen. He was being cocky and arrogant and...damned if it wasn't turning her on.

"Don't you think that you might be presuming too much?"

He cocked his head to the side. "How's that?"

"You're assuming I want to have sex with you again."

"Are you saying that you don't?"

"Maybe."

Jackson raised an eyebrow. "Maybe isn't going to cut it here, honey." His lips ravaged hers until it felt like her bones were liquefied. When her body trembled, she felt him grin against her lips. "That's what I thought. If you don't want this then tell me now."

Jenna gave up on playing it cool. She allowed herself to be led into the steamy shower, careful to avoid getting her hair too close to the spray. He angled the nozzle to help avoid her hair and pulled her under the water with him, kissing her with tender care. Understanding swirled with the desire hazing her mind. It wasn't that he was being arrogant; he was taking her mind off her shyness. Once out of the way, he reverted back to the same man who had made her fall in love.

"Are you still mad at me, Jenna?"

"I never said I was."

"You didn't have to. I could tell I pissed you off."

It was her turn to smile. "Looks like you'll have to make it up to me."

"With pleasure," he replied, reaching for her body wash and sponge.

Jackson proceeded to make it up to her with his soapy fingers, teasing her until she couldn't remember how to think. He followed that up by putting his smart mouth to better use, licking and nibbling at all her sensitive areas until she forgot what he was trying to make up to her. Jenna was grateful for the tiled wall at her back when her orgasm ripped through her like a runaway train. Without it, she might have ended up in the emergency room with a concussion. She opened her eyes when she heard the sound of foil ripping. "What are you doing?"

He grinned. "I told you I was going to make love to you again. Trouble is, I'm not going to make it to the bedroom – just like I knew I wouldn't."

She watched him with drowsy fascination as he sheathed himself in one expert stroke before his hands came to grip her by the hips, lifting her up, pressing her back against the wall. He entered her with one deep thrust that almost had her screaming in ecstasy. She clung to him as he moved inside her. His kiss was liquid fire and Jenna couldn't seem to get enough.

Of any of it.

Undiscovered sensations ripped through her body as his lazy thrusts increased in urgency. When Jenna thought she might shatter from the intensity of it all, Jackson tore away from the kiss to brush his lips against her ear. "Don't close your eyes, Jenna. Look at me and let go."

Jenna opened her eyes and gazed into his crystal blue depths. She remembered what he'd confessed to her before she'd fallen asleep. She wanted to say something to him, to let him know, but it was too late. As soon as she'd looked into those sexy eyes, his rhythm changed and the wave of tension in her body built and crested, sweeping her away with it.

A moment later, Jackson followed her over the edge. They both collapsed into a heap in the tub. At first, neither of them moved, but Jenna found his lips and poured all of her love for him into her kiss, unready to confess her feelings for him. She felt his surprise at her raw emotion and let herself be rolled to her back...well, as much on her back as she could be in the bathtub. He was reaching for another condom when the shower began to rain pellets of ice down on them. The hot water heater, it would seem, was no match for their passion.

Jackson managed to shut off the water then stroked her cheek with his thumb. "How much did that kill the mood?"

She couldn't suppress the shiver. "I'm freezing," she admitted. She gazed at him from beneath lowered lashes. "I think you'd better take me to bed and warm me up.

"I can do that." He reached for the towel. "I can definitely do that."

Saturday, October 4

I opened my eyes and squinted because of the light streaming into Jenna's bedroom. A glance at the clock revealed that it was well past noon, but I wasn't surprised. Dawn's first light broke before we finally slept. Ah...just the thought of the previous night brought a slight smile to my face.

As Jenna started to stir next to me, I became aware of the weight on the pillow above my head. When a fluffy grey tail began to flick me in the face I realized her cat was just about sitting on my head, glaring at me. I resisted the urge to shove the cat over and turned my attention to Jenna.

She was more enjoyable to focus on anyway.

She was sleeping on her side with her back to me. I put my arm around her waist and gave her a kiss on her shoulder. Her skin was like ice against my lips so I pulled the covers up over us and said, "Good afternoon."

"Huh," she answered me, voice heavy with sleep. "What time is it?"

"Almost one."

"Hmm...I haven't slept this late in ages."

"It is a Saturday if that makes you feel any better."

"I don't know that anything could make me feel any better than I do right now," she said, snuggling back against me.

"You sure about that?" I kissed the nape of her neck and pulled her closer.

"Well...the obvious is excluded from that."

"How about we pretend that you didn't exclude that and let's put it to the test?"

I could detect the exact instant her pulse quickened and she gave in. After everything we had done the night before, I doubted she'd ever be able to hide herself from me again. Of course, after everything, I knew better than not taking full advantage of her mood.

Jenna reached back and ran her fingers through my hair. I traced my lips across the back of her neck, enjoying the provocative way she wriggled against me in response. My hands slid up her stomach until they reached her breasts and I wondered if it was possible to retrieve the contents of the nightstand without taking my hands off her. I didn't think there was anything I loved more than her body.

Somewhere close, a door slammed.

"Jen! It's time to get up, sleepyhead. Your phone must be off the hook and I've been calling you for...hello." Trista stopped short at the bedroom door. I could tell she was more than a little shocked to see me feeling up her best friend under the covers.

Shit. Were we even still covered?

"Hi, Trista," I said in an attempt to diffuse the tension, not that I thought it would be a success.

"I, uh...Jen, uh...I'll talk to you later," Trista stammered as she fled the condo.

Jenna sat up, brushing my hands off her in the process. "Crap! I'm sorry, but I have to go after her. Do you, uh...do you have plans?"

"I have to get a new cell phone."

She sighed. "I've already apologized for that. Do you have plans beside that? I'd...well..." She retrieved her robe from the floor. "I'd sort of like to see you again..."

"No other plans," I said, enjoying the sight of her slipping into her robe. I liked that she didn't want me to slip off while she was gone. "I'll be here when you get back."

The cat leapt over to the edge of the bed nearest Jenna as soon as she rose and was looking up at her, head cocked to the side.

Jenna scratched the cat under his chin. "I know you're hungry, Buddy. I'll feed you as soon as I get back."

"I can feed him if you want me to."

"That's sweet of you, Jackson. I won't be long," she said, exiting.

I allowed myself to linger in bed after she left, something I never did. Of course, falling in love was also something rare for me. I meant what I told her the evening before while she was sleeping.

With great reluctance I got out of bed. After I put on my pants I followed the cat down the hallway towards the kitchen. I decided to get a pot of coffee brewing before I retrieved the can of cat food from the pantry where he was rubbing his face. I threw away the wrappers from the food I picked up while I waited, glad I made the call to pick up something. It had come in handy at three that morning when we finally took a break from each other, starving for something else.

Last night had been perfect, I thought to myself as I set the plate of food on the floor for the bossy grey cat. The little one was nowhere to be found. Well, okay, perfect might have been a bit of a stretch. It would have been except for one minor incident. I hadn't counted on Jenna flipping out on me afterwards. Good thing I had a way of calming women.

"Damn hot water heater," I muttered.

After my first cup of coffee, I turned my thoughts to the case. I knew I didn't have much time left to figure out what Blackstone was up to and even though it was my job to stay close to Jenna I also knew it wasn't yielding the results I needed. I would have to find a way to split my time to meet both of those objectives.

At some point I would have to face facts. Jenna was part of my job. As much as I wanted to pretend I had any future with her, I didn't. Regardless of the outcome of the case; it would be over soon. I would go back to D.C. and Jenna would be here, hating me.

Once I heard Jenna open the door to the condo, I decided to set my thoughts aside. It was too late for me to walk away now; we passed the point of no return. Until the case was over, I couldn't let Jenna sense I was conflicted. For the time being, she was all mine.

"That was long," I commented as I handed her a cup of coffee.

"Sorry. It couldn't be helped. Apparently, once you shock the hell out of your best friend, she doesn't just drop it."

I followed Jenna into the living room. She plopped down into the chair and placed her feet on the ottoman. I took that as a sign she wanted to talk, so I sat on the loveseat nearest her.

"Has she forgiven you?"

"Of course; I'm very lovable. Besides, she needs a maid of honor."

"Really?" I realized how that sounded. "The maid of honor part, not the lovable thing."

"They got engaged last night, which is why she's been calling all morning from his house," Jenna said, a faraway look passing through her eyes.

"Are you okay?"

"Yeah, it...brought back memories, that's all."

"Okay." Time to change the subject. "I don't think your cat likes me much."

Jenna smiled and shook her head. "I wouldn't take it personally. He was Tony's cat. I imagine he wouldn't like any man in my life," she replied, absent, her gaze again far away.

I got the impression something else was on her mind, something she wasn't telling me.

"Okay, what's going on here?"

"Nothing."

I could tell she was lying. I was trained to read people and she was an awful liar. I rose and walked over to where she was sitting. As if she were reading my thoughts, she moved her feet off the ottoman so I could sit down.

"Come on, Jenna. I can tell something else is on your mind. You aren't having second thoughts about last night, are you?"

"No, of course not. It's just..."

"You can tell me anything."

"I know, Jackson. I guess I feel, uh, awkward."

"I thought we already talked about this and you felt better about it?" If not, I had zero problem hopping back in the shower with her.

"No, we did, but...I'm not usually as forward as I was last night. I'm not the kind of woman who keeps a supply of condoms by her bed and..."

"I'm glad you did," I interrupted her.

"Me too," Jenna replied, averting her eyes.

"While we're on the subject," I began, taking her hand in mine, "you should know I don't make a habit out of this sort of thing, either. As far as you being too for-ward; I don't think that's possible. Anything short of what you said wouldn't have gotten the point across to me. I can be dense about this stuff."

"I noticed."

"Finally, I get a smile out of you."

Jenna set her coffee on the table next to her chair. The knot on her robe was not tight – at all – and I could see a provocative triangle of creamy skin peeking through. I found it difficult to tear my eyes away and focus on her face when she turned back to me.

"Jackson, you haven't done much dating since your wife died, have you?"

Slippery slope. Not good.

"Only the obligatory fix-ups my friends tricked me into. I can't remember the last real date I've been on."

"Me neither, but I think I made up for lost time last night."

I wasn't keen on the idea of talking about my fake dead wife. I knew I needed to change the subject, but I also knew it had to be subtle. Mmm, I had the perfect solution.

"You did?"

"Yes. Why?"

"Because I don't think I did." Come on, Jenna…take the hint and run with it.

"You're kidding, right?" Jenna looked shocked. "I can't even remember how many times we had sex last night. How could you not…" She got the hint and changed her tone. "Huh. Well we should do something about that."

I scooped her into my arms. On the way to the bedroom I stopped at the door to make sure it was locked. I didn't want any visitors walking in. At least, not for a few hours.

Chad looked at the clock on his dashboard for what must have been the tenth time that hour. He'd been waiting for his chance to get back into Jenna's condo to replace the malfunctioning camera. When he saw the fed Jenna was screwing leave her condo a few hours ago he assumed they would be going somewhere soon. After slouching down in his car for more than three hours, he learned he was mistaken.

Finally, he observed them leaving the building with Trista. After waiting a respectable period of time to ensure they weren't coming back, Chad grabbed his bag and crossed the parking lot to her building. As before, the lock was easily picked.

Once they were together, he'd make sure there were better locks. No one would be getting in to get her. No one.

No sooner than the camera was replaced and he was heading for the front door, it opened. Chad froze, chiding himself for not locking the door behind him. He would have to think fast to get out of this one.

"Hey, lady, I think I left my tablet...Who are you? Wait. I know you. You're a friend of Jenna and Trista. Chad, right?"

Damn the luck, Chad thought to himself. It would have to be Maureen. He disliked her when he'd stopped by her office to say hello to Trista. Granted, few lawyers existed he liked; they had too good an eye for details.

And they never forgot a name.

"Yeah. You're Trista's boss, right?"

"Uh-huh. Is Jenna here?"

"No," Chad responded as his escape plan began to come together in his mind.

"Should you be here? Jenna's a private person. She doesn't like strangers in her home unattended."

Chad was enraged and took a step towards her.

"I'm not a stranger. Jenna and I are to be married," he replied without emotion.

Panic flashed through Maureen's eyes and Chad took great pleasure in her knowledge she was in danger. Things escalated so quickly with Alex that he hadn't had the opportunity to revel in his fear. But it was different now. He was in complete control of this situation.

"It was good to see you again, Chad, but I have to be going if I'm going to get to the club in time to meet everyone."

Chad allowed her to turn and open the door. He wanted her to breathe in the fresh air of freedom before she died. It was sweeter that way. Knowing she must think she would live long enough to warn Jenna was intoxicating to him.

He reached into his bag and pulled out a wrench. Locking the door behind him, Chad followed Maureen down the stairs. Once she reached the first floor, Maureen sprinted to the door, but he was too quick for her, too smart for her. He slammed the door closed with his hand just as she was able to open it. Before she could move, he smashed the wrench against the back of her skull with a satisfying crunch.

Problem solved.

Chapter 18

Even for a Saturday night, Blaine's Rain was packed. I was grateful we met in a private room at the back of the club. As a rule, I wasn't a fan of large crowds. The situation was nearly impossible to control. Anything could happen and I wouldn't be able to do anything to stop it.

Jenna looked amazing. Until now I only saw her conservative side in public. The black leather pants and barely there shirt were a nice change, though I was certain she borrowed both from Trista. On the other hand, I didn't like that every guy in the club was eyeing her when we arrived.

Collin was driving me insane by eleven o'clock. He kept looking for Maureen, who was strangely absent. Trista assured him Maureen did this kind of thing all the time, but he just wouldn't drop it.

"But she told me to meet her at nine sharp, Trista," he complained.

"Collin, if you're going to be involved with Maureen then you're going to have to get used to this," Trista explained. "She once vanished for a week before she bothered to call and tell me she was on vacation in

Bermuda. Don't get me wrong, I like her, but she's possibly the least considerate person I've ever known. Blow it off. There are plenty of women here right now," Trista said.

I could tell Collin wasn't going to accept that at all. It was obvious that the FBI agent in him was working every possible angle of this in his mind. It was too bad that he didn't put the level of energy into his job that he did in figuring out a woman.

As if that was possible.

I tapped Collin on the shoulder. "Come on. I know you won't shut up unless we go stand outside and wait for her." I turned to Jenna. "I'll be back in a while."

She grabbed the collar of my shirt and playfully pulled me towards her.

"Okay, but don't stay gone too long."

"I won't," I said, giving her a quick kiss.

Once Collin and I were outside I demanded, "What the hell was all of that in there? They're trying to celebrate."

"And you weren't?" Collin retorted.

"What's that supposed to mean?"

"You didn't answer your cell phone," Collin answered, matter-of-fact.

I couldn't figure out where he was going with this and it was starting to piss me off.

"And?"

"And you always answer your cell phone."

"You could have misdialed."

"Not twenty-seven times, I couldn't."

"What the fuck happened that you called me that many times? And why am I just now hearing about it?" I could hear the blood pounding in my ears. "Was he on the move?"

"No," Collin said. "Blackstone hasn't left his apartment."

"Well...what then?"

Collin smirked. "After the first couple of times I figured you were having some fun of your own. I thought it would be fun to piss you off. Did it work?"

"You're a real dick, Collin. You know that?"

"I guess it did," Collin said, a hint of satisfaction in his voice.

"Actually, Jenna threw it at the wall when she couldn't get it to stop ringing. I had to get it replaced this afternoon."

Collin started laughing. "She threw your phone at the wall?"

When Collin said it, it sounded ridiculous. I gave in and laughed with him.

"Hey, she was trying to sleep."

"Somehow, I doubt that."

He was right, but I kept my mouth shut. None of his business.

"Yeah, I know what silence means. Interesting."

"What?"

"I thought you didn't want to complicate the case?"

"It couldn't be helped." I was getting uneasy with the turn of the conversation. "Have we got anything new out of Houston?"

"I'm going to be a nice guy and let you change the subject. Actually, yeah, I think we did."

"You think we did?"

I was annoyed. This was his job. Lives were at stake. He should know, not think.

"Any hard evidence was destroyed by the fire, but the woman who took over his files thought she saw something out of place on one of them. A date was scrawled on a scrap of paper. She said she thought it was the date of a clinical trial at first, but she couldn't find anything to substantiate it. She tossed it."

"Why did she mention it then?"

Collin shrugged. "I guess the agent asked her if there was anything unusual. I don't know why, but I'm glad she told him."

"Are we sure it wasn't a date that went with a different file?"

"Yeah, it's a week from tomorrow and I was able to confirm that they don't do any trials on Sundays."

I exhaled sharply. I underestimated Collin's dedication to the case after all.

"So, we have a date. Have you met with the local TSA guys yet?"

"No. I figured you'd want to handle it yourself since you're such a control freak and all. I've got a meeting set up for Monday morning at ten o'clock."

"Good thinking. Do you think they'll be a problem?"

"No. Once they find out why we're there, I think they'll bend over backwards to help. DFW Airport is one of the busiest in the country. They can't afford not to help us and end up with any sort of national security nightmare."

"That's good to know. Dulles is a real pain in the ass."

Collin yawned. "I'm going to head out. I don't think Maureen's going to show up. Congratulate Trista and Blaine again for me. I'll meet you at your place Monday morning to head to the airport."

"Okay, Collin. Enjoy what's left of your weekend." It was too bad we wouldn't get to work together after the case was over; I was starting to think of that guy as a friend. I turned around to go back into the club and came face to face with Blackstone.

"I need to make the rounds to see if everything is running smoothly. Will you two be okay by yourselves?" Blaine asked.

"Hmm. Private room, fully stocked bar, I think we'll manage," Trista replied with a wink.

Jenna snuck a glance at her watch. Jackson had been gone for a while. She wondered if she should go after him, but discarded the idea. It would seem too needy.

"Is it time for you to turn back into a pumpkin, Jen?" Trista asked.

"Huh? Oh, the watch. No, I was wondering how long Jackson had been gone," Jenna said as she poured herself another daiquiri.

"Okay, spill it, Jen."

"Spill what, Trist?" Jenna took a sip of her drink.

"Don't play innocent with me, girlfriend. I invented that game. I'll spell it out for you. First, I have to practically force the guy on you. Now, you're his shadow. What gives?"

"Nothing," Jenna lied.

"Look, you don't have to get defensive with me. It doesn't seem like you to sleep with a guy and get all clingy. Actually, it's not like you to sleep with a guy you've known for all of five minutes like this."

Jenna slammed down her drink on the table. "I am not all clingy."

"Jen..."

"Okay, so what if I'm clingy. I haven't been in love in years and..."

"You love him?"

Oh, great, Jenna thought to herself. She hadn't meant to say that. Aloud, she said, "No...maybe...hell, I don't know. He knows about Tony."

"You told him?"

Jenna sighed. "I hadn't planned to tell him yet, but Daniel was playing the video of that birthday party for Lana. Lana didn't know not to say anything about him."

"Well, that was ideal."

"Talk about it. Jackson was great, though. It felt good to talk to someone about it after all this time."

"See? That's what I've been telling you for the last two years. You never listen to me."

"That isn't all of it, Trist." Jenna leaned forward, her tone confidential. "I think I heard him say he was falling in love with me."

Trista shrugged. "And? I don't see what the big deal is about that."

"Huh?"

"Don't give me that look, Jen. I'm trying to keep you grounded in reality before you start planning your wedding."

"I don't understand what you mean."

Trista shook her head. "I hate to be the one to tell you this, sweetie, but you had sex with him last night."

"Trista..."

"Men will say a lot of things to get a woman into bed."

"It wasn't like that Trista. He didn't say it to get me into bed..."

Trista's turquoise eyes were ablaze. "Don't tell me he said it once you were already in bed? How predictable. Did he say it before or after he c—"

"Trista, will you please stop and listen to me for a damn minute?"

"I guess I hit a nerve, but I'll listen if it will make you feel better."

"After I told him everything, he got a phone call and I went to change. I found him in the guest room and I basically threw myself at him, but he shut me down..."

"He shut you down?" Trista looked amazed.

"Yeah. He didn't want to take advantage of me when I was upset. Anyway..."

"That's so sweet."

"Trist, stop it. This isn't the important part. After he shut me down, he was holding me and I started to fall asleep. I can't be a hundred percent sure of what I heard because I was half gone, but I think he said he was falling in love with me."

Trista frowned and bit her lip in thought. "Did he know you were asleep?"

"I'm not sure. He didn't say anything else and I fell asleep, so I don't know. I'd forgotten about it when I woke up and I didn't remember until we were in the shower, but I didn't get the opportunity to mention it."

"The shower, huh?" The look on Trista's face was worth a million bucks. "So, uh, Jen…what was going on in the shower that kept you from telling him?"

Jenna felt her face grow hot. Trista laughed. "That good, huh? I'm going to want details, you know."

Jenna had no intention of sharing the intimate details of last night with her right now. Changing the subject, she said, "Do you think I should say something to him about it?"

"Definitely not."

"What happened to being open and honest?"

"Nothing. It's still important, but this is way heavier than why he won't make out with you."

"Trista!"

"I'm serious. If he meant it, he'll tell you when he knows you're awake. If he didn't, he's glad you were asleep and you should leave it at that. He'll mean it soon enough. Look, Jen, quit wasting your time in here with me and go find him. We'll talk more tomorrow."

"Thanks, Trista," Jenna said, giving her friend a hug before hurrying off.

"Hello, Jackson. Fancy meeting you here."

The sound of his voice made my blood run cold. His tone was cordial enough, but something insidious lurked in his eyes. I pulled my thoughts together as rapidly as I could. He couldn't know I was onto him.

Not until I was ready to slap the cuffs on him.

"Hey. You're Chad, right."

"Good memory. We only met the one time. Briefly."

Was that suspicion in his voice? "I meet a lot of people in my line of work and it helps if I remember names."

"And what is it you do?"

He was too interested. "I'm a management consultant."

"Oh, really?"

I could have sworn he was mocking me with his tone. "So, what brings you here?"

"Jenna mentioned this place when we had lunch last week. I thought I would check it out."

Or you thought you'd run into her here, you sonofabitch. Aloud, I said, "It's not bad, if you like the club scene. It's one of the more tolerable ones."

"Here you are, Jackson. I've been looking everywhere for... Chad? What are you doing here?"

"You spoke highly of the club, so I thought I'd check it out for myself. Good to see you again, Jenna."

With that, Chad entered the club and left us standing outside. His voice seemed strained when he spoke to Jenna. Maybe I was throwing my own spin onto it because I knew what he was capable of, but maybe not. I had a hunch more was going on than I knew. If nothing else, I knew I was right about the way his eyes popped out of his head at the sight of Jenna.

Jenna shook her head. "That was weird. What happened to Collin?"

"He got tired of waiting on Maureen and went home. Should we go back in, or are you ready to go?"

Jenna faked a yawn. "I'm beat. Let's get out of here."

The drive home was a fast one, but it was much too long for my taste. Not because I couldn't wait to be alone with Jenna again – which was a given – but something Collin said gnawed at my mind. How did Blackstone get to the club if he hadn't left his apartment all day? Clearly, I couldn't call Collin to find out with Jenna beside me.

If I didn't need the alone time to make a call, I'd be pouncing on Jenna when she followed me into my condo. Fucking job was in the way. Again. I had a sexy woman ready to attack me and I wanted to call my partner.

"What's wrong, Jackson? You've been quiet since we left the club."

"I don't like that guy," I answered on instinct, regretting the lack of thought I'd put into it.

"How come?"

"No reason in particular. I get a strange vibe from him. That's all."

That was true, at least. Well, the first part.

"I think that's my fault."

"How's that?"

"He came onto me when we had lunch, but I shot him down. He must figure you're the reason why." Jenna cocked her head and raised an eyebrow at me. "Do you want to be talking about Chad right now?"

"No."

"Good. I haven't seen your bedroom yet. Let's fix that."

"Collin was upset when he left and I think he might have had a few too many. Let me call to make sure he made it home." I grinned at her. "Then I'll be happy to give you the tour of my bedroom all night long."

"I'll be waiting."

Once I knew she was out of earshot, I dialed Collin's number.

"McShae."

"I'm not alone, so I can't talk. Blackstone was at the club. How was he there without us knowing first?"

"I'm on it. Have fun, tiger." He hung up.

"Jackson," Jenna called from the bedroom, "I didn't know you had mirrors on your headboard. Kinky." After a beat, "I like it."

A smile crept across my face. I forgot about those. Maybe the FBI knew what they were doing after all.

Chapter 19

Jenna struggled to get out of Trista's leather pants for a moment before remembering she hadn't taken off her shoes yet. She reached for her shoes and tumbled back onto the bed. The shoes hit the floor with a thud and she winced. Good thing Trista was staying at Blaine's that night. Even if she weren't too drunk to avoid making noise with her shoes, the walls in the condo weren't as thick as she'd like. Especially not when the nosy best friend's bedroom was directly below.

She'd just discarded the pants to the floor when she noticed Jackson walk in and lean against the door. "You like the mirrors, huh?"

Jenna crossed the room to him. "Would you really like to know what I'd like?"

"After last night, I already know what you like."

"Take off your clothes, Jackson."

He regarded her for a moment. "Yours are still on."

"Not for long. Now take off your pants."

Jackson looked intrigued and worked the buttons on his shirt while he kicked off his shoes. Every other time his clothes came off it was dark or things happened too fast for Jenna to enjoy the sight of him. Now, she watched for the first time as he finished the last of his buttons and shrugged out of the shirt. He looked at her with eyes full of lust. "Come here."

Jenna closed the last step's gap to him and ran her hands over his muscular chest. She gazed into his crystal eyes while her hands slid down fit abs and rested on his belt. His breath caught in his throat when she dropped to her knees, trailing her lips down his stomach as her hands tugged off the pants and boxers.

His erection strained in front of him, beckoning to her. With cautious fingers, Jenna stroked him and, emboldened by his groan of desire, used her mouth to drive him wild. She felt his fingers tangle into her hair, further fueling her desire to drive him over the edge. Just when she was getting into things, she felt Jackson's hands grasp her by the shoulders and pull her up.

She blinked in surprise. "What? What did I do?"

Jackson slid his hands underneath the strings on the back of her halter top and began untying them. "You did one hell of a job turning me on, that's what you did."

"But you stopped me. I wasn't done yet."

"I'm buying Trista a new shirt," he muttered, ripping it in his hurry.

"Someone's impatient," she commented. "Wait a minute...was it that obvious it wasn't mine?"

"Later," he growled, pushing her onto the bed.

Jenna was about to respond when Jackson covered her mouth with his and kissed her with unbridled passion. His hands ran down the length of her body until they found the edge of her panties. He pulled away long enough to pull them off and went to work on her neck. "What the hell have you done to me, Jenna? I can't control myself anymore around you."

The thought that it might be more about the amount he'd had to drink and less to do with her briefly floated through her mind.

Without warning, Jackson jumped up and fled the room. That was a strange reaction. Jenna pushed herself up onto her elbows and tried to see what he was doing in the other room. It sounded like he was trashing the living room, but she realized what he was doing as soon as he came back into the room. He seemed pleased with himself to have found the contents of the bag he'd carried back from his trip to the convenience store.

Jenna grinned. "Did you get a big enough box? What is that, a six month supply?"

"Naw. We'll be lucky if this lasts the night." He tore the box open with his teeth. "I'm about to rock your world."

Sunday, October 5

As I'd expected, this week's Sunday dinner turned out to be a birthday party for Lana, complete with fifteen five year olds. I could tell Elaine put a great deal of effort into the 50s sock hop for her daughter, though I couldn't figure out why. They were far too young to be familiar with any of the music. More than one little girl asked me during the 'pin the kiss on Elvis' game who he was.

Elaine expressed her gratitude to me for my help numerous times during the party. Conveniently, Daniel Whitman had to work. Of course, I knew there was more behind his absence. On a hunch, I placed a tail on him to see if we could uncover what he was hiding. Chances were, it wasn't relevant to the case, but I didn't usually dislike people for no reason and I couldn't take a chance that he was somehow involved with more than he let on.

By five o'clock, the last parent had come to collect their child and Lana was sitting in her room reading a picture book a friend gave her as a gift. I wondered what in Lana's short life happened to make her so obedient.

Most children her age were wild and energetic, not poised and demure.

It occurred to me that I hadn't seen Jenna or Elaine in a while and I went in search of them. Part of me hated admitting it, but when I heard hushed voices speaking in the laundry room, I stopped short of entering. The agent in me wanted to know the reason for the secrecy.

The man in me wanted to know what kind of review I was getting.

"I don't like the guy, Jen. There's something not right about him," Elaine said.

I strained to hear who they were talking about because I knew it wasn't me.

"'Laine, I'm sorry. I had no idea he would come over here to talk to you. He's an old friend. Nothing more." Jenna's voice was an aggravated whisper.

Had to be Blackstone. The terrorist was busy doing more than evading my surveillance team.

"Even when you were in high school, you know I didn't approve of that friendship."

"You mean Daniel didn't approve."

"Don't put this off on him like that. I didn't like Chad back then and I don't like Chad now. After what he did to those animals, I don't know how…"

"Stop it, 'Laine. You and I both know he wasn't the one who vandalized the shelter and slaughtered those animals."

"Jen, I know another student took the rap for it and got expelled. But I don't buy the story. When guys get kicked off the football team for hazing, they don't slaughter animals. They go after whoever got them kicked off the team."

"Look, I've had lunch with him once since he came back to town and I can count on one hand the number of times I've run into him outside of that. He's an old friend, not my boyfriend. Can we drop it now?"

Why didn't I know about her having lunch with him? Wait, I guess I did know, but telling me last night after a few too many drinks didn't count.

"Okay, I'll drop it. There is something else I've been dying to talk to you about."

I heard Jenna groan. "And what might that be?"

"You had sex," Elaine said, triumphant.

"Elaine! You talked to Trista?"

"No. I didn't have to. You've got that happy-goofy-tired glow about you. Besides, your bottom lip is swollen, like you've been kissed for hours."

Oh yeah, it had been hours...and hours. I couldn't control the smile creeping over my face. The only thing to rein it in was the knowledge of how little Elaine would like me if she knew the truth about me.

"Don't give me that look, Jen. I'm not coming down on you; I think it's great. I'm just wondering what changed. I thought you swore off men after Tony."

That was news to me.

"You never listen to a word I say. I said I had sworn off men with dangerous jobs."

Uh-oh. So much for entertaining the thought of keeping Jenna in my life once I told her what I really did for a living.

"You know he wasn't on duty."

"No, he wasn't, but he *was* the job. If he hadn't been a cop, he never would have tried that heroic stunt. We both know I'm right." Jenna paused. "Besides, none of that matters now. I'm with Jackson and he has the most boring career I could imagine. I think I could have a real future with him."

That was enough. I crept away without a sound. Once I closed the back patio door behind me, I ran my hands through my hair and sighed in aggravation. Why couldn't I be who I said I was?

My cell phone interrupted my thoughts before I could grow more depressed about the situation.

"Caldwell."

"I know how Blackstone slipped past us," Collin said.

"Great. How?"

"He has a second car. There's a ledge underneath his back balcony that makes it easy to climb down to the first floor."

I was puzzled. "Why would he sneak out of his own home? That doesn't make any...sonofabitch! He's onto us. Dammit, someone must have tipped him off that we were asking questions about him."

Collin was quiet for a moment before he spoke. "Probably the grandmother. I could tell she didn't appreciate our questions. Should I pull Foster and Rodriguez?"

"No, I'm not going to make it easy on him just because he knows about us. Tell them to be on guard. We'll have to get someone to cover the back now, too," I added.

"Taken care of."

"Good. Oh, I almost forgot. I overheard Jenna and Elaine talking about him. Do we have anything on a possible animal mutilation involving him when he was in high school?"

"No. I'd remember something like that. Why?"

"See what you can dig up on it. Another student took the rap for it. This might be nothing, but..."

"It fits the profile. I'll see what I can find out. See you tomorrow."

I was beginning to like the way he thought.

"Damn it all straight to hell!" Jenna shouted, tossing her cell phone to the floorboard of the car.

Jackson gave her a sidelong glance. "Everything okay?"

"No. Chet left a message."

"Chet?" Jackson raised an eyebrow. "Is that your other boyfriend?"

"No. He's my agent and...My other boyfriend? I didn't realize I had a boyfriend in the first place."

He placed his hand on her bare thigh and gave it a light squeeze. "Yeah, I guess we skipped that conversation."

"So...you want the job, I suppose?"

Jackson's hand drifted higher. "It seems like a natural progression, you know, since we're sleeping together and all."

"Then you should know that Chet is my agent. He calls all the time and this time he called to say the release date for my new book has been moved up. They want it out in time for Thanksgiving."

He seemed unconcerned. "That's like a month away."

Jenna sighed. "Yeah, but with the illustrations and the press kits...I have a week until I have to have it to him. I've never missed a deadline before and I don't want to start now."

"Why would you miss the deadline? I thought that you were working on it all the time."

"Well, I have been working, but not on this book." She could feel her cheeks flush. "I thought I'd try my hand at some, uh, adult fiction."

Jackson grinned and changed lanes. "Am I in it?"

"Your ego continues to astound me."

"It's not ego if it's true, babe."

He had a point. "Do you really think I'd let you know if you were?"

"Sure, why not?" he asked, his fingers grazing the edge of her panties. "You should let me read it. I might get some new ideas."

Jenna's breath snagged in her chest. "I doubt I'd be the one to give you any ideas. Besides, I have to switch gears long enough to write a children's book."

"How much do you have left?"

"All of it," she admitted.

"How long will it take you to write?"

"I can get it done in a week if I chain myself to the computer and ignore everything else."

"Chains...hmm." He glanced at her. "See? You're giving me new ideas already."

Jenna groaned. "You don't understand, Jackson. If I'm going to pull this off, I'll have to spend every free minute working and..."

"Don't worry about it, Jenna. This is going to be a crazy week for me at work anyway. You don't know how much you'll be helping me out."

What an odd thing to say. Jenna turned to face him as he parked the car. "How does this help?"

He cut the engine. "If I knew that you were sitting at home with nothing to do, I would skip out of work early to get back to you and get myself fired."

"I guess it's a good thing I'm under a deadline."

Jackson leaned towards her. "Yeah. I'd hate to disappoint millions of children."

"You're mocking me, Caldwell. Keep it up and I'll find another boyfriend."

"No, you won't," he said, brushing his lips against hers. "I'm a great boyfriend."

Jenna grinned. "I'm going to need some proof of that."

"Proof?" Jackson feigned shock. "You don't need proof. Don't you remember last night?"

Jenna blushed. "No, not after we left the club."

Jackson pretended to be mad. "How can you not remember? It was magic..." He grinned. "Okay, it's just as well you don't remember because I was too drunk to deal with the condom and we both passed out."

"I might have had a bit too much to drink last night." Her blush deepened.

"I love it when you blush, Jenna. You have no idea how much it turns me on."

No, she didn't have any idea how much it turned him on, but she started to get the picture when they could barely make it up the stairs and into her condo before they started pulling off each other's clothes. Jenna had to wonder if they'd even make it down the hallway to the bedroom.

They didn't. They were already on the carpet.

For all of the passion of the moment, the fierceness of his kiss, the way his hands possessively claimed every inch of her body, Jenna was surprised by the tenderness of his lovemaking. He moved with such an agonizing slowness that she could hardly stand the sweet torture of it. She found herself trying to move her hips against him, to move in any way to speed him up, but he changed his position and her best efforts became useless. She was helpless and was forced to let her body go where Jackson was taking her. Out of frustration, she bit his shoulder.

"Hey! What the hell was that for?" he asked, stopping to look at her.

"I don't think a good boyfriend would be torturing his girlfriend this way."

His eyes were full of mischief. "He would if he knew it was going to make it better."

"You don't know that."

"I do so." He strained to look at his shoulder. "That really hurt."

"Whatever. I hardly used teeth."

"That's definitely going to leave a mark."

"Poor baby." Jenna kissed his shoulder in apology. "Is that better?"

In lieu of a response, Jackson claimed her mouth. He slid his tongue passed her lips and explored every inch of her mouth as he began his maddening rhythm again. Jenna wound her fingers into his hair and felt a contented sigh somewhere in her throat. She was utterly, hopelessly in love with him; even if he was an expert at pissing her off. Despite her complaints, she could easily let him continue what he was doing for the rest of the night.

Maybe even for the rest of her life.

Jackson thrust deep. No warning, just feeling. Jenna broke the kiss and screamed from the sensations that tore through her body. "There. That's better," he said, taking her hard and fast.

Jenna clung to his shoulders as the vibrations of ecstasy rolled over her, each more intense than the one before. She thought she'd shatter from the building pressure. She almost couldn't keep her feelings in check. She bit back the words just before she told him she loved him. It was too soon. It wasn't the right time. It was the quickest way to destroy the mood when he ran for the hills as a result. Instead, she gasped, "Don't stop."

"Not a chance," he replied, his voice breathless.

As Jenna began to tremble from her climax, Jackson fastened his lips over hers, never slowing for an instant. She realized it was a good thing because she couldn't be held responsible for anything she said at that moment. She let the calm wash over her, only to feel the tension build again and break violently.

Long after she'd screamed out his name, he held her, kissed her softly. She looked into his eyes and saw something in them, a look that went beyond what people who were mere lovers shared.

"So? How about it?"

Jenna couldn't remember the question. "How about what?"

He smoothed her hair back. "Do I get the job or what?"

She grinned. "Why do you want it so much? What's the catch?"

"No catch. I love...I just love being with you and I'm a possessive guy. I don't want to give you the chance to figure out you can do better."

Jenna gazed into his eyes and knew he loved her. He might not be able to say the words, but by the look in his eyes, his kiss, the way his body moved with hers, she realized she knew everything about this man she needed to know. "Yeah, okay. You've got the job. Happy now?"

"Yeah, but now I'm supposed to leave you alone for a week. Not fair."

"Well, not right away. I don't have to start working tonight. Do you have an early morning?"

Jackson raised himself up onto his elbows. "Not too early. What do you have in mind?"

Jenna pretended to look thoughtful. "I haven't had time to think it far ahead, but I'd like for my new boyfriend to help me up off the floor before I end up with the mother of all carpet burns. After that, I could probably be talked into a quick shower."

He grinned and helped her up. "I'll just bet you could. What else can I talk you into?"

"I don't know," Jenna answered with a shrug. Leading him down the hall, she added, "I don't see a whole lot of sleep in your future."

Jackson pretended to be annoyed. "The things I put up with to have you as a girlfriend..."

Jenna pushed him into the bathroom. "You'll live."

Chapter 20

"Blackstone is on the move," Collin told me as I got in his car around nine o'clock on Monday morning.

"Yeah?"

"He left through the front door this time. I should know if he's heading anywhere important soon. Oh," Collin reached for a file on the backseat before continuing, "I got something from the tail you put on Daniel Whitman."

I opened the file and realized why I didn't like the guy. The first page was a computer printout from a surveillance camera showing him cozying up to a blonde. The guy missed his daughter's birthday party to meet up with another woman. That was low, but not surprising. He seemed like the kind who would keep a girlfriend in every town he flew to. Did Elaine know about it and keep quiet to maintain her current standard of living?

The rest of the file contained copies of restaurant and hotel receipts, none of which shocked me either. The last page confirmed he visited a casino in Atlantic City on his way home. I let out a long, low whistle when I saw the bottom line.

"That was my reaction," Collin said.

"How do you lose fifty grand in a few hours?"

"I don't know about that, but I checked his financials."

"And?"

Collin shook his head. "It's not pretty. It looks like he's a compulsive gambler. Most of his 401k has been wiped out as a result. The sad thing is that I don't think his wife has a clue."

I closed the file and faced him. "How's that possible, Collin? I thought that Texas was a community property state. Shouldn't she have to sign off on any substantial withdrawals from a retirement account?"

"The blonde you saw on the first page is a notary public. Elaine's signature appears to be a notarized forgery," Collin answered as he parked in one of DFW's numerous parking garages. "Ready to meet the wizard, Jackson?"

"As long as you don't forget where you parked again."

"Keep it up and I'll leave your ass here, Caldwell."

"Chad, what are you doing here?"

"Do I need a reason to come by and see how the best Nana in the world is doing."

"Oh, you're an angel, but then again, you always were." Chad's elderly grandmother wrapped him in a frail embrace. "I wish you called first. I've got to get to the church. I'm helping to organize our annual rummage sale for the homeless this year."

You should organize a fundraiser for yourself, Chad thought bitterly as he looked at the dilapidated hovel in which she lived.

"Don't worry, Nana. I was in the area running an errand anyway."

"You're such a sweet boy," she said, disappearing into her house, presumably to collect her keys and handbag. Chad wandered over to the corner of her tiny yard while he waited.

"Boy, what have I told you about getting too close to that Oleander bush; it'll stop your heart dead," she scolded.

Chad turned toward her with a smile on his face. "Don't worry, Nana, I wasn't chewing on the leaves. I was noticing how it's still blooming this late in the year."

"I've been meaning to dig that thing up for years and get rid of it, but, ah, my back. Maybe you'll bring that sweet little fiancé of yours over here one weekend and help an old woman out. Hmm."

Chad stuffed his hands in his pockets. "I'll bring Jenna by soon, Nana. I promise. She's been busy lately with all of the wedding plans."

"I always liked that Jenna. I knew God would send an angel to watch over you for me. I won't always be here, you know," she mused as she got in her car.

"No more talk of that, Nana. You'll outlive us all yet."

"I don't know about that, but, the good Lord willing, I'll be here long enough to see you married."

"I love you, Nana, and I promise to bring Jenna over next week to see you," Chad said as he closed her door for her.

He watched as her car vanished down the street. Every time he visited, he was reminded of his painful teenage years in that house, not that any of it was her fault. Soon enough, he would have his revenge and the woman he loved. Life would be perfect for him at last. He would see to that.

Chad had what he'd come for.

"Well Agent Caldwell, if everything you say is true, please rest assured that you'll have complete cooperation from this facility. I apologize, but I have a pressing meeting. Please make yourself comfortable and Mr. McNamara will be in momentarily to facilitate things."

After he left, I turned to Collin. "If he had another meeting, why did he bother talking to us for five minutes?"

"That was my doing. I kept getting the runaround from his assistant, so I threatened to inform Homeland Security of their lack of cooperation in the matter." Collin smiled. "I got a call ten minutes later."

"Have you worked with these guys since you've been with the Bureau?"

"No, but I dealt with them plenty when I was with the Dallas PD."

"How was it?"

"Not horrible, but it can be if you don't let them retain some sense of ..." Collin stopped short as the conference room door opened.

"Good morning gentlemen. I'm Eric McNamara, Assistant Director of Airport Security, and I'll be assisting you."

He had a firm handshake, but I could tell I shouldn't trust him with any more information than was necessary. From his manicured hands and expensive shoes, I knew this guy was a suit, nothing more, who would use the situation for his own advancement purposes.

After McNamara poured himself a cup of coffee and took his seat across from us at the expansive table he said, "I've taken the liberty of having my assistant start putting some things together for you. I'll have a complete set of location maps for you by the time this meeting is over. Of course, you and your agents will have total access to all areas, with the exception of upper level management offices, that is."

"I'll need a master key," I said flatly.

"Under normal circumstance that would not be possible. However, Agent Caldwell, I anticipated that request and I will be able to provide you with one key which is to remain on you, and only you, at all times. I understand that much of what you do is classified, but certain details would aid me in making security preparations."

"Such as?"

"What are we dealing with, Agent Caldwell? A terrorist threat is rather vague."

I could tell he was fishing. I mulled over what to tell him as I took a sip of my coffee. Finally, I decided to show my hand.

"We have a freelancer on our hands, Mr. McNamara."

"A what?" he questioned.

"A psychopath with enough knowledge to do serious damage. We have reason to believe he will stage an attack on this airport on Sunday, but the rest of our details are sketchy at the moment. We know who the individual is and will provide you with his picture, but we don't have enough to hold him with yet."

McNamara's expression hardened. "What kind of threats are we looking at?"

"Biological or chemical. Nothing that would show up during a normal passenger or luggage screening," Collin answered.

"What do you propose we do?" McNamara asked, his face now void of color.

I cleared my throat. "I hope to be able to narrow it down to a single terminal to keep under watch, but I'm prepared to have over a hundred plain clothes agents here to cover each terminal. I'll need a complete list of everyone with any level of clearance to be here."

"If you take into account airport personnel, airline personnel, and private contractors; that could be several thousand people. That will take me some time to put my hands on," McNamara said.

"I'm aware of that, but we don't have time on our side right now. Please do what you can."

McNamara rose. "I'll get started on it right away, unless there's anything else."

I was thoughtful as I stood. Remembering what I learned on the way over I asked, "Do you have the authority to change the security clearance of an airline employee?"

"No, that would have to go through the airline itself. I can have the employee flagged, if that would help."

"Would that enable us to keep tabs on him?"

"It would as long as he was in an employee restricted zone."

"I need you to flag a pilot for me. This has to be kept confidential because there's an excellent chance he has no involvement."

"I understand, Agent Caldwell. Just give me a name and, with the exception of the technician who flags him, it will stay in this room," he assured me.

"Daniel Whitman."

"I have your cell phone number, Agent Caldwell. I'll see to it that you're contacted directly with his whereabouts."

Once we were in the car, Collin turned to me and asked, "Daniel Whitman? What are you thinking?"

I shook my head. "I may be wasting his time, but something occurred to me earlier. Whitman has complete access to the aircraft and the hangers. He's also in financial distress."

Collin started the engine. "I think I see where you're going, but put it together for me anyway."

"What if Blackstone needed someone on the inside to help him? This guy is obsessed with Jenna, so we have to assume he's done his homework on her family.

"What if Blackstone offered Daniel Whitman a substantial amount of money to get him in, or plant a device for him? I think a man in Whitman's position might take him up on it."

"Problem," Collin stated, "Blackstone doesn't have anywhere near the amount of money that would justify a, for the most part, law-abiding citizen to break the law."

"We know that because we've done a thorough background check on him, but Whitman wouldn't know it until it was too late." I paused and blew out a breath. "I'm in love with Jenna."

Collin gave me an odd look. "I know. Is that a good thing or a bad thing?"

I shook my head. "I don't know anymore." I looked out the window as he merged in with traffic. "I'm going to come clean with her...tell her everything and hope to hell she doesn't start throwing things at me."

"Am I supposed to be in support of this hair-brained idea of yours?"

I shrugged. "I know it's a bad idea, but I don't have anything else. If you've got an alternative, let's hear it. I can't live with myself anymore. Every time I'm with her, I have to lie to her about who I am. It's ripping me to pieces."

Collin sighed. "Love sucks, Caldwell, but this is your job. If you blow your cover in the middle of an operation...I'm certain your boss will have you tossed into jail for the next five years."

"Longer, knowing Banks." I thought about the way Jenna looked at me last night and again before I'd left this morning. "If there's even a slim chance she'd be waiting for me when I got out...it would be time well spent."

Collin chuckled. "Dead man walking."

Chapter 21

Jenna was going stir crazy. It was a long day for her. She hadn't imagined missing Jackson the way she did.

"I'm getting pathetic," Jenna said to herself. "I saw him this morning."

Even though they were lovers, neither of them thought to exchange numbers. When the phone rang at seven-thirty, Jenna jumped up to answer it. She noticed Jackson hadn't come home yet and a part of her hoped that he might be calling her from somewhere she could meet him, even though her home number was unlisted. A break from her writing might do her some good; seeing him definitely would.

"Hello."

"Listen carefully, Miss Monroe," a throaty voice ordered.

"Who is this?"

"The person who is going to kill you if you don't listen and do as I say. Do I have your attention?"

Jenna felt her heart skip a beat. Her voice was barely a whisper. "Yes."

"Go into your spare bedroom and remove the drawer to the nightstand. There's a present for you taped to the bottom."

Jenna walked down the hallway and removed the drawer. This was surreal. It couldn't be real. As promised, there was a letter-sized manila envelope taped to the bottom. She opened it and dumped the contents onto the bed.

What she saw almost killed her.

A picture of Lana sitting on the swing in her backyard. Another picture showed her taking a drink from a water fountain at her school. The last picture was the most disturbing. In the background, Lana was skipping rope with one of her friends. In the foreground was a gloved hand holding a hunting knife.

"By your silence, I'll assume you understand how far I'm willing to go," the voice said, icy calm.

Jenna couldn't rip her eyes away from the image of the knife so close to her niece. This wasn't happening. It wasn't.

"What do you want?"

"One tiny favor is all I ask. Your brother-in-law is a pilot, yes?"

"Yes," Jenna whispered.

"Get me his security badge."

"How will I get that to you?"

"I've enclosed information on when and where to make the drop. I suggest you memorize it and burn everything. A word of caution to you: tell no one about this. The police will not find a trace of evidence on what I've left you. If you tell anyone, including your boyfriend, I will gut that precious child and leave her head on your doorstep."

"Why are you doing this to me?"

"So self-centered, Miss Monroe, always thinking of yourself. This is a means to an end for me. The decision is yours. You can choose to do the simple task I've requested of you, or you may choose to kill your niece. I'll leave you to it. Have a pleasant evening."

Jenna held the phone long after the line went dead. She stared at the pictures for an eternity, the reality of what was going on seeping into her brain. When the full implications hit her, first came tears, then bile.

If someone wanted airline security clearance bad enough to murder a little girl, what would they be willing to do when they had it?

Her legs didn't get the message to move before her stomach emptied its contents.

Tuesday, October 7

"Caldwell, please tell me I didn't hear you correctly," Banks said, fighting to remain calm.

"I can't do that."

"Okay, we're going to play a little game. Let's pretend I'm your boss for a second. Oh, wait; no...I am your boss. New game: explain to me why in the fuck there isn't a wiretap on her phone!"

"I've been with her non-stop this entire weekend and I'm telling you she doesn't know anything. Blackstone is fixated on her, but that's as far as it goes."

"Look, Caldwell, you need to start thinking from above your waist. I am not happy to hear that Blackstone already knows we're watching him. If he can figure it out, why couldn't she? How do you know they haven't been in cahoots the entire time?"

"Because I know her."

"You know what she wants you to know and nothing more. This would not be the first time a woman hopped into bed with an agent to throw him off the scent." Her voice was as cold as ice when she spoke.

I remained silent. Nothing I could say would matter, even if I had words for this.

"Good, I see I have your attention now, Caldwell. Let me make this crystal clear for you. I've tolerated your insubordination thus far because I like you; you were one of my best agents before your home life turned to shit. If those wiretaps are not on her phones by the end of today, I will have you removed from the case. I will have you locked up. I will have you charged with aiding a terrorist and obstructing an investigation."

"You can't do that and..."

"Don't underestimate me, Caldwell. Trust me when I tell you that you don't want to call this bluff. I'm well-connected and I can have you locked up for the rest of your life with one phone call. Get it done!"

After I hung up the phone, I relayed the conversation to Collin.

"I've never worked for the woman, Jackson, but everyone in my office knows of her. She isn't bluffing."

"I know," I said. "Do you think she's right? Am I being played?"

He shrugged. "Only Jenna can answer that for you."

"You know I can't ask her."

"No, you can't. Not without blowing you cover, anyway. Do you want me to have her followed?"

I couldn't believe I was considering this. Collin was suggesting I have the woman I loved followed like a common criminal. Then again, her wounded dove demeanor could all be a carefully constructed ruse. Fuck me. At least I didn't have the opportunity to come clean with her yet. Maybe having her followed would give me the peace of mind I needed to fess up.

"Jackson?"

I nodded. "Phone it in."

*****

"What are you doing here, Jen? I wasn't expecting to see you until the weekend," Elaine said in surprise, hugging her sister.

"I'm sorry to pop over like this, but Jackson and I have dinner plans. I was hoping you'd let me raid your closet," Jenna lied.

"Of course, sweetie. I was about to make a few phone calls for the Cancer Society fundraiser, so you go ahead and help yourself to whatever you need."

Jenna watched Elaine disappear into the study and shut the door behind her. Lying to her sister wasn't something she was in the habit of doing. It left a hollow feeling in her stomach as she opened the closet door.

Jenna went through the pockets of all of Daniel's uniforms hanging in the closet to no avail. She began to panic. She had to have it for tonight. For Lana's sake.

Thinking of Lana was the only thing that kept her sane during this insanity. Something bad would happen regardless of what she did, but in one scenario that something didn't happen to her niece. She couldn't think about what happened after she delivered the security badge. It would only prompt a breakdown. That couldn't happen. Not yet. Not until after.

In sheer desperation, Jenna crossed the room to the dresser and began searching through the drawers. Nothing. Then it occurred to her that he might keep it in his car since he needed it when he flew.

Jenna crept up to the study and pressed her ear to the door. From what she heard, she knew Elaine would be on the phone for quite a while. She tiptoed through the kitchen into the laundry room and opened the door to the garage.

Luck was on Jenna's side. The car was unlocked, but a quick search didn't yield any results. His badge wasn't in the glove box, the center console, or behind either of the visors. As a last resort, Jenna felt under the seats.

Bingo! She found it under the passenger seat and slipped it into her purse.

"What the hell are you doing, Jenna?" a booming voice questioned from behind her.

Chapter 22

"What do you mean she isn't there? I thought you told me she would be at home all day, Jackson," Collin said in shock.

"That's what she told me. I've got to get in there to tap her phone, but I can't risk her walking in on me."

"Give 'em here. I'll do it," Collin said, gesturing for me to hand him the two wire taps.

"You can't get caught either," I replied.

"I'm not going to, because you're going to cover me. Stand outside her door while I'm in there. If she shows up, tell her that you were about to knock and do anything to get her out of here."

Without waiting for my agreement, Collin snatched the wire taps from my hand. With reluctance, I followed him across the hall to her door, where he picked the lock. He emerged two minutes later.

"That was quick."

"I'm that good. Any sign of her?" he asked me.

"No."

Collin sensed my disappointment and said, "At least you didn't get the brush off."

Closing my front door behind us, "I guess that means you still haven't heard from Maureen."

Collin flopped down on the couch. "Nope. I even went over to her house to see if she was there, but it was all dark. I guess her one night stands last for a week before she discards them."

Ouch. "You don't know that for sure. She did ask you to meet her at the club Saturday," I offered, though it didn't sound convincing even to my own ears.

"An invitation doesn't amount to much when she never shows up. You don't have to try to cheer me up, Jackson. I've been wrong about women before and I'll be wrong again. Plenty of times."

A knock on my door stopped me from responding. I wanted it to be Jenna, but instead it was an obviously distraught Trista. She didn't give me an opportunity to say anything before she spoke.

"Is Jenna over here? I need to talk to her and she isn't answering her phone."

"I haven't talked to her since yesterday. Only saw her briefly this morning."

It was apparent to me by the way Trista paced back and forth that something was wrong. It was out of character for her to be home this early. Something was wrong.

I exchanged glances with Collin before adding, "What's going on?"

"It's Maureen, I think," Trista said before bursting into tears.

I guided her to the couch and let her sit down before asking, "What happened?"

"She didn't show up for work today."

"I thought you said she did this sort of thing all the time."

Trista shook her head. "She does, but she always thinks to cancel appointments first. She missed a client's deposition this morning. I've tried to get a hold of her every way I know, but it's like she's dropped off the face of the earth or something."

Collin was concerned, but I was relieved he was able to contain it when he spoke. "Is it possible she forgot about the deposition?"

Trista sighed. "I guess, but she's normally so good about that kind of thing."

She was holding out something vital and I decided to push harder.

"There's more than you're saying, isn't there?"

"Yes. Victor has friends and I don't mean the kind you invite to golf at the country club; real low lives. I'm worried that he holds Maureen responsible for being in jail. What if he retaliated?"

When she broke down again I sat next to her, putting an arm around her shoulders in comfort. I thought fast and decided on the best course of action.

"Don't worry, Trista. We'll find out what happened to her."

Collin's eyes grew wide, but I shook my head and winked.

Trista looked up at me and asked, "How can you do that?"

"One of Collin's poker buddies is a cop. I'm sure he wouldn't mind looking into this." To Collin I said, "Why don't you use my office to call him and see what he can do?"

Jenna's heart leapt into her throat at the sound of her brother-in-law's voice. Daniel was the last person she wanted to see on a good day and this wasn't a good day. He'd had a way of seeing right through her since they first met and she didn't have enough time to make him understand the severity of what was going on. She turned to face him and was met with a fierce glare.

"Hmm?"

"What the hell are you doing in my car, Jenna?"

She realized with a sudden rush of relief that from where he was standing in the garage he hadn't been able to see what she'd done. She searched her brain for something, anything that would sound believable. When she spoke, she didn't know exactly what she was going to say until she heard the words come out of her mouth.

"I needed to borrow something from Elaine," Jenna answered, surprised at how calm her voice sounded.

"In my car?"

Jenna got out of the car and closed the door. "I couldn't find an outfit that would work, but I remembered she's got this great pair of earrings that could really dress up something I already have."

"Why aren't you looking in her jewelry box for that?" Daniel asked. It was clear from his tone that he didn't believe her.

Jenna walked past him to the door that led outside and placed her hand on the knob, ready to escape.

"They weren't there. She's been on the phone, so I didn't want to bother her over it. I thought she might have worn them to a gala or something recently."

"What are you up to?"

"Nothing," Jenna replied, praying her tone sounded as light as she intended. "You know how 'Laine is. She always buys the most painful earrings and takes them off on the way home. I thought they might have fallen under the seat, but I didn't find them."

Daniel shrugged. "Next time ask. I don't like people snooping around in my car."

"I'm sorry, Daniel," Jenna said as she opened the door. "I've got to run now. Tell her I decided not to borrow anything after all."

Before he could respond, she exited the garage and crossed the circular driveway to where her car was parked. She felt for keys in her purse, but dropped it in her haste. The contents, including Daniel's badge, spilled onto the ground. She reached for it.

"Jenna?"

She palmed the badge and looked up. "Yes?"

He walked over and knelt beside her. "You seem jittery. Is everything okay?"

"I'm in a hurry to meet Jackson," she lied, praying he wouldn't look at what she held in her hand.

He nodded. Handing her purse to her, he said, "You don't have to be so nervous. I can tell the guy is nuts about you."

She accepted the purse and pressed the badge up against it in her hand, hoping to keep it concealed while he helped her retrieve the rest of its fallen contents.

"Thank you, Daniel."

"It's good to see you happy again. It's a nice change."

Jenna stood and watched him walk into the house. She fumbled with her keys again, unable to unlock the door because of her shaking hands. That was far too close. If Daniel realized she had his pilot's badge...Well, it wouldn't have been good. Only after she was safely on the highway did she allow herself to breathe.

After assuring Trista we would find Maureen, she left to go back to work in case she called. Collin left right after that to get a team briefed about the disappearance. I tried to spend the rest of the afternoon looking over the maps I had of the airport to determine the best placement of agents, but I couldn't concentrate.

At eight o'clock that night, Jenna still hadn't returned home.

The one consolation I had was the phone call I received a few hours earlier. Jenna's car was spotted outside of her sister's house. I was informed they would call me if she went anywhere or did anything I should know.

At least there was some comfort in knowing I could pick up the phone at any moment and know her exact whereabouts.

My relief was short-lived once the machine in my office monitoring Jenna's phone line started to beep. I made certain my door was locked and walked down the hall to my office. What I wanted was a mundane call to reassure me when I slipped on my headset and pushed the button, allowing me to hear what was being recorded at headquarters.

Please, let this confirm what I know.

"Hi Jen, it's Elaine. I'm sorry I didn't have anything you were looking for. I talked to Daniel after you left and he mentioned you seemed nervous. It sounds like this date with Jackson you're on is a big deal. Call me when you get this. I want details. Bye."

I shut off the machine and tossed my headset onto the desk. My forehead joined it a moment later. I didn't want to believe what I heard. Maybe Elaine misunderstood Jenna, but I didn't see how. The only plans we made for this week were for Saturday night, but going to Jenna's high school reunion couldn't be confused with a dinner date.

Something didn't add up. Put together the pieces, Caldwell.

I let out a sigh and realized how stupid this was. Banks was one of those special bosses who enjoyed toying with people. She would be having one hell of a laugh if she knew I was sitting at my desk doubting my relationship with Jenna.

No, there had to be a logical explanation to where Jenna was all day. I knew she was under a deadline, but I couldn't pretend to know her process. Maybe she couldn't concentrate knowing I was across the hall. It was a conceited notion that at least made me feel a little better. For all I knew, she was out right now putting the finishing touches on her book.

Maybe she made dinner plans for us to celebrate and was on her way over here right now to tell me...

My head shot up when the phone rang. It would be a relief if it were Jenna on the other line, even though I never actually gave her the number. Imagining it was her kept me from thinking about what I'd feel if it weren't her.

"Caldwell, it's me," Collin said, hurried even for him.

My heart sank. "What do you have?"

"It isn't good news, but I thought you should hear it from me first."

My mouth went dry.

"About ten minutes ago Jenna went to a park and tossed a brown paper bag into a trash can." He paused. "I just confirmed Blackstone picked it up. Jackson...I'm sorry."

Collin might have had more to say, but I hung up anyway. Automatically, I walked into the kitchen and poured myself a glass of water – not that I could swallow over my building rage. The implication of what I learned washed over me and I didn't realize I'd thrown my glass until I heard it shatter against the wall.

Banks was right after all. I was being played by the woman I loved. She wouldn't get away with this.

At ten o'clock, Jenna knocked on my door. I debated whether or not to let her in, and scolded myself for even having the thought. Over the past hour it finally occurred to me how much easier this made things. I spent too much time being concerned with how she would react once she found out I was with the FBI, but none of that mattered anymore. Now that I knew the truth about her, her feelings were off the table. I couldn't toy with Blackstone, but she was fair game.

Besides, I needed to tap her cell phone.

"I thought you were writing," I said once I opened the door.

She gave me a quick kiss and walked past me to the living room where she sat.

"That's not much of greeting. What's wrong with you," she asked.

I hadn't meant that to come out as harsh as it did.

"Sorry. Work stuff." At least that was the truth.

"I know the feeling. This book is driving me insane. I had the worst case of writer's block all day."

"I'm sorry to hear that. Can I help?"

"No. I spent the day at the library reading some of the books that inspired me when I was a kid."

Lying bitch!

"Did that help?"

"I think so. I feel ready to write, but I wanted to see you first."

"Why?"

She looked surprised. "I missed you. I hoped that maybe you wanted to get something to eat."

"I already ate."

"Oh." She snuggled up close and whispered in my ear, "Can I interest you in some dessert then."

I knew what she was getting at, but it was out of the question, for tonight, at the very least. My emotions were too raw right now. I would have to get them in check first.

"No."

She pulled away and looked at me. "Are you sure I can't tempt you?"

She had a hint of pain in her voice. I felt a twinge of guilt over hurting her, but I squashed it. She was good at this little game.

I was better.

"I've got a lot to finish before tomorrow and I have an early morning. I'm sorry."

Jenna jumped up. "That's okay. I understand. You warned me you had a busy week. I should probably write anyway. I guess I'll see you." She didn't take a single breath when she spoke.

In her haste to leave, she grabbed her keys and purse, but left her cell phone.

Score.

Chapter 23

Wednesday, October 8

"You have to pull it together," Collin said to me after I told him about what happened with Jenna.

"I know; it's just harder than I thought it would be to be around her."

Collin walked over to the coffee machine and poured two more cups of coffee. We were in one of the larger rooms at FBI headquarters. I'd been here since five o'clock this morning looking over flight manifests for every flight out of DFW that Sunday. By the time Collin joined me at ten, I'd scarcely made a dent. The process was made more difficult by having no idea what I was looking for.

I accepted the cup that Collin handed me and said, "She's even got her sister fooled, you know."

He slammed his fists down on the table. "Stop it! Sooner or later everyone gets played. I know this is my fault for pushing you to get involved with her, but you've got to look at this in a more positive light."

"Positive? How?"

"You're in a rare position. She doesn't know you're onto her. If you stay as close to her as you've been, it'll be difficult for her to make a move without you knowing about it. I know it sucks, but you've got to continue things with her exactly as you did before you found her out. That's the edge we've got right now."

I knew he was right. Too bad that knowledge didn't stop the twisting in my gut. It was a pain I hadn't felt since Melissa left.

"Mr. McShae," a timid voice said from the door.

Collin glanced up. "Yeah, Petey."

"He's in room A, sir," he said before exiting.

"New intern?"

Collin shook his head. "First day. What are you gonna do?" He stood and tapped me on the shoulder with a file. "Come on. I've got something in room A that will cheer you up."

"What's that?" I grabbed my coffee.

"I had the guy Blackstone got expelled brought in. He's got quite a story."

"When did you have time to talk to him?"

Collin paused at the door to room A. "What did you think I was doing this morning? Sleeping in?"

"Oh, come on! I've got to talk to another one of you guys?" the man seated at the table yelled once we walked into the room.

To be in school with Jenna and Blackstone, he had to be in his late twenties, but the years had not been kind to our witness. His light brown hair was thinning in all the usual places and his face had enough lines to fill a road map. Though he was reclining in his chair with his feet perched up on the table, it was obvious he had a beer gut. I was hard-pressed to ever picture this guy as an athlete.

Of course, if someone asked me twenty-four hours earlier I would have been hard-pressed to picture Jenna as anything other than what she appeared to be.

"Cool it, Eddie, or you aren't leaving here any time soon," Collin said, knocking his feet off the table. "This is Special Agent Caldwell. He's running this investigation and I suggest you play nice."

I was impressed. I'd never seen Collin interact with a witness. His years with the Dallas PD must have taught him something after all. It was also nice to have my authority recognized.

Not that I cared about much at this point.

"Fine, I'll tell you what you want to know, but only because I want to see y'all throw the book at that piece of shit. Where do you want me to start?"

"The beginning would be nice," I said dryly.

"Fine. I first met him during my junior year. I could tell right away he was a total loser. I got stuck with him as a lab partner, but he was a real science geek and it was all good. We gave him hell all year, you know, stuffing him in trash cans and shit. There was this one time we locked him in his locker and left him there during football practice. It rocked."

"Get to the point," I ordered.

"Yeah, I'm getting there." He cleared his throat. "Anyway, after the locker thing, his grandma complained and the coach got onto us. He made it clear that we had to consider him untouchable, so we dropped it for the rest of the year. Okay, senior year comes." Eddie put his fingers out like he was framing a scene. "Picture it. Varsity, babes, glory, you know. That insect of a sophomore wasn't even on the radar as far as I was concerned. Then it happened.

"Coach said I had to bring my history grades up and I got this tasty treat of a tutor, Jenna something. Damn, she was fine! She was a couple grades behind, but I thought she'd make for a nice roll in the hay."

The muscle in my jaw tensed. Despite what I knew, I wanted to deck the guy. Collin must have picked up on it because he said, "Speed it up."

"Whatever. She didn't go for the Edster; stupid bitch. Then, next thing I know, I've got Chad in my face about it. Dude tried to punch me over it, so I knocked his ass up against the wall. Then, the day before I'm supposed to start in the big homecoming game, coach calls me into his office. His grandma called again, 'cept I didn't do what she said I did. He comes back to school with two black eyes, a busted lip, and a broken arm. He was fine when I left him."

"Can you tell us about the animals?" I asked. I was getting a little bored with his rambling.

"Okay, but you need to know something first. Some of the younger guys on the team were pissed at him after that. We lost 'cause of it. They got the lame idea to bust out all the windows to his house. They didn't know anyone was home when they did it. The old lady had a heart attack 'cause of it. She was fine, but Chad blamed me."

"How do you know?" I asked.

"He walked up to me in the parking lot and told me I'd suffer for it. Two weeks later, someone breaks into this animal shelter that the coach's wife ran. Ten cats and dogs got butchered. I got expelled for it and spent some time in juvie. They thought I was pissed at the coach for kicking me off the team."

"And you didn't do it," I confirmed.

"Hell no, I love dogs. Cats are all right, I guess. Look, a whole bunch of my stuff was planted there to make it look like I did it. I may be a lot of things, but I ain't a killer, not even of animals. I lost everything, scholarships, babes; you name it. Just because I made a pass at some girl he was stuck on. He came to visit me in juvie and he told me exactly how he did it, not that anyone ever believed me. He fed them some load of crap about how he came to be a good Christian and forgive me."

I turned to Collin and nodded towards the door. Without a word we stood and left the room. Once the door was shut, I turned to him and shook my head.

"Is this guy reliable?" I asked.

"No, but I believe him. I did some checking around before I had him picked up and he's been singing that same song since he got out. His life is shit compared to what it could have been, but he's reformed."

I nodded. "Okay. Get this information to a profiler and see what they think."

"I just don't get it," Jenna complained after they ordered lunch.

"Get what?" Trista asked.

"Jackson. This whole weekend was perfect, but he was completely cold to me last night. I don't understand what I did to piss him off."

"He's a man…They can't handle it."

Jenna was confused. "What are you talking about?"

"You are so naïve sometimes, Jen. Men all want a woman who will sleep with them, but as soon as they get the goods they can't handle the fact they found a woman who actually would sleep with them. It's pathetic, really."

"I don't think that's the problem." Jenna chewed on the inside of her lip in thought. "I'm sort of his girl-friend now."

"Did you bring it up or did he?"

"He did."

Trista sipped her tea in thought then said, "I think it was my fault."

"Huh?"

"I was really upset about Maureen not showing up for that deposition yesterday and I went over to talk to you, but you weren't there. I thought you might be over at his place. He asked me what was wrong and I broke down. He was really nice about it, though."

Jenna nodded. "He normally is nice, Trist."

"Anyway, Collin was there with him and it looked like I'd interrupted something important. Then he offered to help me find her, which I know will take up more of their time."

Jenna waited for the waitress to deposit their plates on the table and leave before she spoke. "He offered to help?"

"Yeah, I thought that was weird, too, but I guess Collin has a friend at the police department. He called me last night to tell me that since she'd been missing for more than forty-eight hours they were opening a missing persons file on her."

"Jackson did?"

"No, Collin. Why?"

Jenna shook her head. "I don't know. I guess I was hoping that he was preoccupied with that when I went over."

Trista set down the pickle she was munching on. "What's this really about, sweetie?"

Jenna debated telling Trista everything, but thought better of it. She couldn't tell her that she stole Daniel's badge and dropped it in a trash can for this guy that was going to kill Lana if she didn't. She couldn't tell Trista that driving away from that park, knowing it was over, made her feel like a weight was lifted from her shoulders. She couldn't tell Trista that all she wanted to do once she got home was feel Jackson's arms around her, making her feel safe again.

She couldn't tell Trista about any of it because she was warned not to and Jenna had no way of knowing if that awful person was sitting at the next table, waiting for her to slip up.

"I told you," she replied instead.

"You're lying to me, Jen. I know you far too well for you to put one over on me."

"I'm not."

"You're worried that he still hasn't told you he loves you, aren't you?"

Jenna supposed that sounded all right. "I guess," she lied.

"See Jen, I told you couldn't put one over on me," Trista said, triumphant, before she took a bite out of her sandwich.

I knocked on Jenna's door slightly past seven. I took Collin's words to heart. It was all for the best, but that didn't make it any easier. My heart didn't have an off switch the way hers did.

"Peace offering," I said, handing her a single stem red rose tied to her cell phone once she opened the door. "I took the liberty of programming my numbers in there so you'd be able to reach me anytime. Can I come in?"

She absently glanced down at her rumpled t-shirt and shorts before stepping aside. "Of course. Where did you find this? I've been looking all over for it today."

"You left it on my coffee table last night. I was going to return it to you this morning, but I left pretty early."

"I know. Four-thirty. You weren't kidding about having an early morning," she replied as she headed to the kitchen.

How the hell did she know about that?

"You were up?" Was there any chance my voice sounded as nonchalant as I hoped?

"I haven't been sleeping well. I got up at two to start working."

"You must be exhausted."

"A little, but I have good news."

You aren't working with a terrorist against me, I thought. Instead, I asked, "What's that?"

"It's done. My book's done. I just emailed it to Chet before you knocked."

I wrapped my arms around her in a hug. "That's great news, Jenna. I'm happy for you."

She pulled away from me and walked over to the refrigerator. After she rummaged around for a minute she said, "I guess."

I stared at her, trying to figure out what game she was playing.

"I thought you'd be a little happier about it than that. You seemed worried about it on Sunday."

"It's no big deal," she replied once she'd retrieved a soda and closed the refrigerator. That was strange. She normally didn't drink anything but water, tea and coffee – not that I could pretend that I really knew her. Maybe this was just her cover persona starting to slip.

"What the hell is the matter with you?"

As soon as the words left my mouth I knew they were a mistake. She spun around and looked at me, her eyes cold. Without speaking, she tried to walk past me, but I stopped her by placing a gentle had on her elbow.

"Fine. You. You, Jackson. You're what's wrong with me. Just let go of me and get out!"

I let her storm into her bedroom, where I heard the sound of the television being turned on. I didn't leave; I knew this game. I hadn't played since right before my divorce. I walked down the hall into her room and leaned against the doorframe. This was the part where she'd tell me I was emotionally unavailable. Guess I'm the same guy undercover that I am when my job is out on the table.

"I told you to leave," she said as she wiped the tears from her eyes.

"I know you did. I'll leave when you tell me why you hate me all of the sudden."

"I don't hate you. I love you."

Even for a terrorist, that was a low blow.

"You love me," I whispered.

"Yes and I can't deal with it right now."

I sat on the edge of the bed next to her. "You have to know that you aren't making sense right now."

"I know that. I've been having a horrible week so far and you aren't helping." Her voice broke. "I just want you to leave, Jackson...please."

"Jenna, please tell me what I did."

"Fine. This weekend was the most amazing few days of my entire life."

"Mine too," I admitted. It was true. It was...until I got the call about her last night.

"I thought everything was fine when you left here on Monday morning, but now it's like you don't even want to be around me. I can't read you and I don't know if I want to try anymore. I'm almost too worn out to care."

I thought about that for a moment before I spoke. "I wasn't upset with you last night and I'm sorry I took it out on you. I got some bad news about work right before you came over."

She snorted. "What, an accounting widget crisis?"

"They might transfer me back to D.C.," I lied, well, half-lied.

Her face softened. "But you just got here. Why now?"

"It's not definite yet. The acquisition isn't going as planned and I was warned they're looking for a scapegoat. If the client isn't happy with me, I'll get sent back."

"When will you know?" Jenna asked, voice quiet.

"Next week."

Jenna threw her arms around my neck in a fierce hug. "I'm so sorry, Jackson. I had no idea you were dealing with all that."

I smoothed her hair down her back. "You couldn't have known."

"You know I can write from anywhere, right?" she asked.

"You would want to come with me?"

She released my neck and pulled away enough to look me in the eye. "It's an option…if you want it to be."

Being so close to Jenna again felt good. She just said the one thing I would have killed to hear from her a few days ago. I made the conscious decision to push what I knew about her from my mind. She wasn't working with the enemy.

At least for tonight.

Thursday, October 9

Chad paced around his apartment aimlessly. It appeared from last night's events that his plan failed. Why wouldn't this guy give her up? His plan should've been foolproof.

Of course, he knew he'd be followed to the park. Chad allowed them to follow him because it served his purpose. After watching that other FBI guy put wire taps on Jenna's phones, he wanted them to know she was leaving something for him. The plan was for her little boyfriend to find out about it and think she was working with him. Success should have meant they wouldn't be in bed together when he'd tuned in.

Knowing that Jenna's phones were tapped gave Chad another idea. She'd served her purpose to the letter by getting him what he needed. Why shouldn't he expect her to do it again?

Chad knew his phone was tapped, but didn't care. It would be even more damning for her to get a call straight from his number. He smiled while dialing.

After a few rings Jenna picked up.

"Good morning, sweetness."

He took pleasure in the way she shot upright and glanced over as if to make sure the fed was still asleep.

"What do you want?" she whispered as she got out of bed and walked into the hallway with the cordless phone.

"Don't you think you should be nicer to me?"

He heard her shudder before answering. "Yes."

"I need you to get something else for me. Will that be a problem?"

"No." Her even tone of voice would play well on the FBI's recording of the call.

Chad enjoyed toying with her. She was so stupid that she was playing right along with him without even knowing it. He couldn't wait to let her know he was behind everything.

"Get paper."

After a moment, Jenna said, "Okay. I'm ready."

Chad rattled off a list of chemicals he needed and a few he wouldn't to throw off the FBI...not that they posed much challenge so far. When he was done, he asked, "Did you get all that?"

"Yes, but I don't know what half this stuff is."

"You don't need to." Chad gave her an address. "Go see Nathaniel and he'll get you everything you'll need."

"Okay," Jenna said.

"Go now."

"It's four in the morning."

"I know. I want you to make the drop by six. Same location as before."

"Okay."

"Don't forget to take your checkbook with you," Chad said before he hung up.

He knew he already paid for everything, but loved the look of panic that came across her face when he said it. He lingered over the sight of her dressing before calling Nathaniel.

When he was done and certain she left, he called Jenna's condo again. He wanted to make certain her FBI boyfriend knew she wasn't there.

Chapter 24

Once I was sure Jenna was gone, I went back to my condo to shower and dress. Within thirty minutes I was at headquarters. Collin met me there an hour later.

I woke up on the first ring because of my training, several rings before she stirred. I pretended to be asleep, but I heard her entire side of the conversation. Even without hearing the rest I'd been certain she was talking to Blackstone. Listening to the tape once confirmed my suspicion.

After I played the conversation for Collin, he got on his cell phone.

"It's confirmed, Jackson. She's already made the drop and is heading back our way. It's your call. We can make sure you beat her home if you want to make it look like you never left."

I shook my head. "No. I thought of that before I left. I put a note on her pillow telling her I woke up and decided to try to get a head start on work so I could meet her for dinner tonight."

"Good thinking. I guess...never mind," Collin said, shaking his head.

"What?"

"No. Never mind. It's a touchy subject."

I already knew what he was going to ask. "Go ahead."

"If you woke up with her, I'm assuming you stayed the night." He cleared his throat and looked uncomfortable. "I was just wondering how that went."

I pushed the files around on the table in front of me. "Okay, I guess."

"I'm starting to know that look. What happened?'

"She told me she loved me before she told me she would go with me if I got transferred back to D.C.," I said. When I realized it sounded like I'd confessed everything to her, I filled him in on the rest.

He let out a long, low whistle. "She's good."

"Yeah, I know." I sighed. "Can we not talk about this right now?"

"Sure. It's still early, but I can see if the boys in Psych are done with their analysis yet," Collin ventured.

"That sounds like a plan to me."

Jenna was disappointed to find Jackson missing when she returned home, but his note cheered her up some. She knew she needed more time to come up with a reason for leaving so early in the morning. Even after thinking about it the whole drive home the best she could come up with was that she'd gone to the gym, not that she belonged to one.

It was before seven when she got back, so she decided to try to get more sleep. Jenna was exhausted, but sleep didn't come easily for her. It occurred to her that this ordeal might never be over. She couldn't keep helping this person with whatever they were doing. She had to do something to stop it.

But what?

She could just picture going to Daniel and Elaine to tell them what she did. Jenna imagined they would be thrilled at the prospect of taking Lana and going into hiding while she went to the police. As she started to doze off, she'd wondered if the police would even believe her. She didn't believe it herself.

By eleven-thirty, she gave up on sleep and went to her computer. She read through what she'd written on her novel and decided she might spice it up a bit with some of the intrigue going on in her life. Jenna learned long ago that sometimes the most unbelievable situations could wind up a bestseller.

While she was writing, it occurred to Jenna that she could put it all down on paper. She could give it to someone to read and let them know it was a true story. She wouldn't even change the names. Her mystery man could control what she said, but would have no way of knowing what she wrote. It was all still fresh in her mind and she put every last detail into words before one o'clock.

As it was printing, Jenna debated who she could give it to. Collin had ties to the local police department, but it would look suspicious to anyone watching if she went to him. She could give it to Jackson or to Trista; she trusted them both to help her.

It had to be Trista. Jenna wasn't ready for Jackson to know about this. He led a normal life, much like she had before this started. How could he ever understand?

I was glad the profilers kept the same insane hours I did. They thought what Eddie said was crucial. As I'd expected, they said it fit the profile. They also felt it gave us a new direction to explore.

By midday, Collin and I were up to our eyeballs in paperwork.

"I can't believe we didn't think of this ourselves," Collin said bitterly, tossing another stack of paper into the trash. "We could have saved countless man hours."

I rubbed my temples. "At least we know now. I was starting to get worried we were running out of days and had no clue which terminal might be hit."

"Starting to get worried? I don't remember the last solid night's sleep I've had. At first, I wanted to be the hero and save the day. It hit me a few days ago that this case wasn't just about showing my boss how good I was. This is about hundreds, maybe even thousands of people who are going to die if I didn't come through."

"I know what you mean, Collin. It's cases like these that make me wish I'd never left the private sector."

"It's sure not helping that the damn TSA won't just take our word on this and close down the airport."

"I guess you can't expect a lot of professional courtesy between agencies when you only have a vague theory about where and when they'll strike. In their shoes, I probably wouldn't want to be the one responsible for shutting down a busy international airport for no reason either."

I watched Collin stand up. "I need a break from this. I'm going to try McNamara's office again and see if he's out of that meeting yet. We need him to run that query for us. What we're doing is taking too long."

I realized Collin was right after he left me alone with the mounds of paperwork. I didn't want to admit it to him, but I was furious I hadn't thought of this myself. We knew Blackstone had a troubled past. Why hadn't we considered his attack wasn't going to be on the airport itself, but on specific people who would be there? The profilers always impressed me with their insight, but I was floored when they put it together so quickly after hearing Eddie talk about the incident.

Blackstone was after the people who caused his grandmother's heart attack. It was so simple once I really thought about it. If only stopping him could be that easy.

Collin and I spent hours comparing the football roster to airline manifests, but we hadn't found a single match yet. Conveniently, McNamara was in a meeting all morning. We needed to know which flights they were on so that we could set our trap.

At this point, we didn't have anything solid on Blackstone. We could put him at the scene of the explosion in Houston, but we couldn't prove he caused it. The only credible person we had to testify was dead. Jenna was the only link I had left to him, but I doubted she would testify against him. Hell, she was probably in it as deep as he was. We had to catch him in the act if we had any shot of making the charges stick.

If only I knew what Jenna gave him at the first drop she'd made. It could be pivotal.

Trista looked up from her stack of filing when she heard the door open. She'd hoped it would be Maureen, but she'd hoped that every time the door to the law office opened over the last four days. Client complaints were piling up and the other partners of the firm were ready to vote Maureen out if she didn't have a damn good reason for abandoning her work the way she had.

She let out a sigh. It was just Jenna, probably ready to pour out some new meaningless tragedy to her. Trista loved her friend, but she didn't know how much more she could take right now. It was awful of her to even think, but she liked it better when Jenna was playing the hermit. There'd been less drama in both of their lives.

"Do you have a minute, Trista?" Jenna asked.

"Sure. What's up?"

Trista could hardly wait for her response.

"I need to give you something," Jenna said as she set a letter size envelope on Trista's cluttered desk.

"What's that?"

"I just finished part of my novel and I could use a second opinion."

"I'm swamped right now, but I promise I'll read it as soon as I get a chance."

"Okay, Trist. Please make sure that you do. It's really important to me," Jenna said before leaving. "There's a lot of truth to the fiction."

Trista shook her head and tossed the envelope into her inbox.

"Why is everything always life and death with her? Can't she see I'm busy right now?" Trista muttered to herself.

Jenna's behavior at dinner surprised me. Over the past few days, a fog settled around her, swallowing every shred of personality. But tonight she was alive. She was the woman I loved again.

Of course, maybe I imagined the fog because I was jaded by her. It was possible she was thinking about what was going to happen on Sunday and her adrenaline was kicking in. How could I not have figured this one out before I put my heart on the table? I knew every curve of her body, but I had no idea what was really in her mind.

By the end of meal, as we sipped our coffee, I was too intrigued to let it go.

"Why are you in such a good mood tonight?"

"Because I love you," she said, a touch too fast.

"That isn't it. You loved me last night too, but you didn't seem this happy."

"I beg to differ. I think there might have been a point or two that I was even happier."

"Why can't you stop being evasive and tell me the truth?"

She appeared to think about that while she sipped her coffee. "I don't really know. Let's just say I did something positive today that is going to make things a lot better."

I couldn't believe she had the nerve to look me in the eyes and call her affiliation with Blackstone something positive.

"Is that where you ran off to this morning?" She still had yet to try explaining that one to me.

"No, I had to go calm Elaine down."

This was sure to be good.

"What happened? Is everyone all right?"

"Oh, yeah, everyone's fine," She took another sip of her coffee, clearly stalling. "Daniel got came home really late and Elaine accused him of cheating on her. This has been going on since I lived with them. He had enough of the accusations and left. I was only there until Lana got up and I got her to school. Daniel was there when I got back, so I came home."

I knew for a fact Daniel and Elaine Whitman were asleep at that time of the morning.

"Is he having an affair?" I asked, hoping she wouldn't pick up that I already knew the answer from my tone.

"I've always thought so, but I don't know for sure. I think it's better I don't know. It would be too hard to sit at the table with him every Sunday if I knew for a fact he'd done that to my sister. How are you supposed to act around someone after they've done something so terrible?"

Still waiting for the answer on that one myself...

Jenna shook her head and added, "If you don't mind, I'd rather not talk about this anymore. I have something I need to ask you."

"Okay."

I felt like I was ready for anything she could throw my way.

"I want you to know it doesn't matter to me what your response is; it won't change anything for me, but I still need to know."

I nodded for her to continue.

"I heard what you said last Friday when you thought I was asleep. I haven't wanted to pester you about it, but I feel like we can be honest with each other. Did you mean it?"

There was no question as to what she was asking me about. I'd only said one thing, so I couldn't pretend I didn't know what she was talking about.

This was the one thing she could ask me that I wasn't prepared for. I meant it when I'd said it. Now things were so much more complicated. Even still...I loved her now, knowing I would have to put her in prison, knowing this could all be a game to her, I loved her.

"Yes," I said quietly.

She looked like she didn't expect my response. What was that in her eyes? Genuine feeling? Doubtful. More likely, she needed to confirm she still had me on the line at this stage of the game.

"Really? You do?"

"Yes," I said again.

Later that night, as I started to fall asleep with Jenna in my arms, I wondered if any of this was as real for her as it was for me.

Chapter 25

As soon as I saw the look on Collin's face, I knew my decision to stay in bed with Jenna longer than usual this morning was a poor one. At only a quarter till ten, it looked like we'd suffered some new setback. I braced myself for what was to come.

"Would you like to know why we haven't heard back from McNamara?"

Collin didn't wait for a response...or take a breath.

"He wasn't in a meeting. He's not even in the state. He had to attend a funeral for a co-worker in Denver yesterday. When's he coming back? We don't know because the airport is snowed in. Yeah. Snowed in. At the beginning of October. Some global warming."

"This isn't good news," I said, doing my damnedest to remain calm.

"No, it isn't. We can't monitor the entire airport for one man. Game over, don't pass go, don't collect your money because innocent people are going to die!"

Collin was on the verge of a nervous breakdown. I was maybe five minutes behind him. I shoved him into the first empty room I saw and shut the door behind us. There had to be more to this than I knew.

"We'll come up with a plan B and go to that. We still have forty-eight hours to narrow it down. You know he'll call his assistant. We'll let her know that he needs to call us the second she talks to him and..."

"I already did that. I told her exactly what I need-ed so we could save a step and he could call us once he had it," Collin interrupted, calmer now.

"I'll admit that I haven't worked with you that long, but you're too agitated by this. Is all this because of a setback, Collin?"

"Maureen's car was found in a ditch this morning, burnt to a crisp. No body."

"She could still be alive then. That's good news, right?"

"That isn't the point, Jackson. I'm a fucking FBI agent. I should have been able to protect her. I can't even keep one woman safe. What the hell good am I?"

"What happened to Maureen is not your fault. For all we know, she did this herself and skipped town for some reason. It's a longshot, but it's possible. Your atten-tion has been on this case where it belongs. You couldn't have done anything different and we both know that."

Collin nodded slowly. "Do me a favor and don't say anything about this. Trista's already upset from when I talked to her about it the other night. I don't want to worry her with this yet."

"Okay." An upset Trista might upset Jenna, mak-ing it even more difficult to get a read on her. "Are you ready to figure out what our plan B is?"

At five o'clock, Trista decided it was time to go home. All of the partners who weren't in court left for the weekend hours ago. It was just as well she leave, she'd done everything that needed to be done twice already.

She made sure her desk was cleared off. If Maureen didn't come back, Trista would need to make sure she was putting her best foot forward. There was always the hope that one of the partners could use her services. Otherwise, she'd be out of a job.

As Trista was about to turn out the lights and lock up, she remembered the earrings one of the partners had given her as an engagement gift were still in her desk. She'd wanted to wear them to the reunion the following evening, so she retrieved them from her drawer. Out of the corner of her eye she saw the envelope Jenna gave her the previous day peeking out from underneath a stack of legal briefs that needed to be sent to the county clerk's office on Monday.

Trista retrieved it from the stack and turned it around in her hands. Jenna was so insistent she read it; maybe she should take the time to read it now. Once she looked at her watch she realized she would be late meeting Blaine for dinner if she didn't hurry. Jenna's new story would have to wait. Traffic was always murder on Fridays.

It was well past eight o'clock before we had, what we hoped, was our plan B. We knew Blackstone could strike at any time on Sunday, so we'd have to be ready for him tomorrow. It was a long shot, but I thought our plan just might work.

We'd spent the better part of the day marking positions to station agents at every single gate of the airport. DFW was enormous, making our task no small feat. It would take far too much manpower to actually place someone at all of the places we'd selected, but it shouldn't come down to that if things worked out according to the plan.

McNamara was a dead end. He was still stuck in Denver. I had to give the guy credit, though. He tried to remote dial into the network from an airport terminal computer. When that didn't work, he made dozens of phone calls, only to find out the program that could do what we needed was wiped out by a computer virus earlier in the day. I had little doubt that Blackstone or maybe even Jenna was behind that one.

The last option he gave us was to call each airline individually for the information, but it could take until Christmas to cut through all of their red tape without a warrant or some kind of credible proof that this wasn't a hoax. And with what little information we had, getting a judge to sign off on what we needed didn't look good.

A call to the high school confirmed all the men we were looking for should be attending the reunion the following day. We decided we would find a way to isolate each of the men at the reunion and take them into protective custody. That was the fastest way we could come up with to get the information we needed from them. Then, we'd be looking at maybe a dozen different gates instead of the entire airport. At that point, Collin would make one phone call and the team waiting at the airport would go to the prearranged positions for that gate.

I got home around nine-thirty and found an envelope taped onto my door. Inside, I found a letter and key. The letter was simple and to the point. It read:

Come over when you get home. It doesn't matter how late. I love you. Jenna.

I didn't know what to expect, so I opened her door with caution. In fact, I was surprised the door was locked at all. The only time I remembered the door being locked since I met Jenna was the night I flipped the lock myself for privacy while I got her out of her robe. Had that really only been a week ago?

The condo was dark, which made me wish I was carrying my gun. Did she know I was onto her? Was this when she'd try to eliminate me?

I noticed the trail of rose petals on the floor leading down the hallway towards her bedroom. I guess she was still playing the girlfriend game on me.

The room was lit by at least thirty candles. Jenna was asleep in a skimpy blue silk robe I hadn't seen before. From the wax drippings on the candles I could tell she had been waiting for me for quite a while. It was such a beautiful gesture that I realized something. If everything was going to happen on Sunday, tomorrow night would be our last night together. That realization hit me harder than I'd expected. I'd heard it said before and never thought it was possible, but I could feel the exact instant my heart broke.

Why couldn't we both be who we said we were?

I kissed her softly on the lips and she stirred, the creamy skin of her breasts struggling underneath the blue silk, dark hair flowing like silk against the pillow.

"What's with all this? Are you trying to set your room on fire?"

She propped herself on her elbows and smiled up at me.

"It's Friday. You told me you'd know something about your transfer next week," she said. "I thought it was about time for me to start putting some friendly pressure on you."

I was taken aback by her statement. "Pressure for what?"

"I was serious about moving to D.C. with you. I'm hoping to pressure you into considering it."

"My God, I love you, Jenna," I said, loosening my tie and joining her on the bed.

I'd learned a long time ago that nothing about life was fair. My marriage was great for all of about a minute before Melissa figured out a way to steamroll over my heart. It shouldn't be any surprise to me that the first person I'd let into my battered heart would find out the best way to rip what was left to shreds. When the case was over, there would be regrets and there would be liquor – lots of liquor.

For just one more night, I couldn't bear to live in reality. I kissed every inch of her body, committing the silky feel of her skin, the sweet smell of her hair, and the way she looked at me like I was the only man alive to memory. If memories were going to be all I was left with, I wanted them to be good. Special. When it was all said and done, when I was back in my D.C. apartment, I knew I might never be able to trust another woman as long as I lived.

Even if I could...there would never be another Jenna.

As we made love, I pushed everything from my mind. She was playing a role and so was I. The people we pretended to be were happy. They were in love and their life together was just beginning. Kids, house, dopey white picket fence – they could have all of it. We, on the other hand, had nothing but pain in our future. The only thing that stood between happiness and heartache was tonight. Just tonight.

Jenna pulled me close. "I love you, Jackson. I love you so much...I can't stand the thought of not being with you every day."

"Me, either," I whispered to her. It was the God's honest truth, too.

Damn, I hated that bastard who was getting his white picket fence.

Chapter 26

The day went by far too fast for me. Collin and I agreed to meet one last time to go over our plan in the light of day. It held up to our scrutiny and we were satisfied we were doing the right thing. Several members of the clerical staff stayed all night, but still hadn't come up with anything. They had a stack of paperwork left to go through, but there was still a chance they could come up with something in time.

We decided I would oversee the team at the reunion and Collin would take the airport teams. I knew it would be difficult to hide what I was doing from Jenna, but I didn't have a choice in the matter. Besides, it was too late in the game to care if she made me. My team was prepared to take her into custody that evening if needed.

After meeting with our respective teams, Collin and I met one last time. It was getting late and I had to get going if I was going to be back in time to change clothes. We were ready for Blackstone.

We were ready for anything.

"I'm out of here, Collin. My cell's fully charged. Call me if anything happens, but remember that Jenna will be around."

"I'll let you know if there are any changes," he said, then added, "Don't be surprised if you see me on your way out. I'm going to stop by Trista's to let her know what's going on with Maureen."

I didn't know how Collin was doing it. Even though he'd been out with her only a handful of times, I got the impression he had genuine feelings for Maureen. If Jenna were missing, I don't know how I'd be able to function.

Then again, I'd probably have to arrest Jenna within the next twenty-four hours...

I successfully managed to avoid thinking about Jenna for the majority of the day, but when I saw her in the short, strappy black dress she was wearing to the reunion my mind flooded with everything I fought so hard to suppress. I made a conscious effort to block out the previous evening from my mind. Without a doubt, it was the single best night of my entire life. It wasn't easy to have something like that and know you would spend the rest of your life without it.

I actually thought I could trick myself into believing I'd come to terms with what I would have to do, but I realized now that I was a damn fool. How could I put the woman I loved with every ounce of my being behind bars?

At three-thirty this morning, I awoke in a cold sweat, sick over what I'd have to do to her. It occurred to me that I could tell her I was onto her, that I could give her the chance to get away, that we could still be happy together after this night. Of course, I also knew it was a desperate plan born out of the sense of hopelessness settled upon me. Banks would have me locked up before we made it out of Texas. The Mexican border was maybe a day's drive, but we'd be lucky to make it out of the metroplex.

"What?" Jenna asked, eyes wide with concern. She did a mini turn as if she were trying to see what was on her that was causing my frown. "Do I not look okay?" She craned her neck the other way for inspection. "I knew I should have shopped for my own dress instead of wearing the one Elaine picked out. I might have something else I can wear." She bit the inside of her lip. "Do I have time to change before we leave?"

"No," I answered, my voice calm despite my inner turmoil. I couldn't help grinning at her. Even if she was a terrorist, she was cute when she was nervous. "You look amazing. Are you ready to go?"

"Are you sure? I really look okay?" She glanced down at herself. "This dress is showing a lot more skin than I'd usually…"

"You've never looked better." I moved towards her and drew her into my arms, intoxicated by her scent. "We don't have to go to the reunion, you know."

What the hell was I saying? I had a team waiting for me.

"I know, but having you with me actually gives me something to show off."

"Me?" I pulled away to meet her eyes. "Jenna…" I shook my head. "You're a successful author with a law degree from Harvard. You have plenty to show off."

Her dark eyes glistened. "True…but you're the best thing to ever happen to me." She fussed with the knot of my tie. "Even though what little family I have left is right here, I'd follow you to the edge of civilization just to wake up in your arms."

I couldn't do this. Pretending I didn't love this woman was out of the question. Arresting her was impossible. It didn't matter what she'd done. She could change. I could change.

"Let's get out of here."

Her expression changed at the urgency in my voice. "Yeah, okay. I've got the reunion tickets in my purse."

"No. I mean, let's really get out of here. You're done with your book and my case...study on this company couldn't be going any worse. Let's just get in the car and drive. No set destination, no luggage."

"You want to go on a road trip? Now?" She stepped back out of my arms. "Is everything okay?"

"Everything's perfect." I stroked her cheek. "I have you." I pulled her lips to mine, kissing her with fervor, mouth begging in silence for her agreement. Resting my forehead against hers, I said, "I love you."

"Okay."

I nuzzled her neck with my nose and brushed my lips across her shoulder. "It's customary to say it back."

"No...well, of course I love you. I'm saying okay, let's go. No destination. No luggage. Just each other."

Trista scrutinized herself in the mirror and realized she forgot to put on her earrings. She opened her briefcase and saw the envelope from Jenna. She pulled it out with the earrings and placed it on the table. Once she was convinced the sparkle they gave her ears was just right, she opened the envelope and removed its contents.

She was interrupted by a knock on the door and set it back on her dining room table. Trista hoped it was Blaine at the door. He was delayed by some crisis at the club. Par for the course, really. Jenna and Jackson left an hour ago, but she wanted to wait for him. Now she regretted her decision.

"I wasn't expecting to see you, Collin. What can I do for you?"

"May I come in?" he asked.

"Of course." A realization came to Trista and she added, "This is bad, isn't it?"

Without waiting for an answer, she walked into the dining room and sank into a chair. Collin closed the door and joined her at the table. He cleared his throat before he spoke.

"I feel terrible about telling you this now, knowing where you're heading. They found Maureen's car in a ditch outside of town. Someone set it on fire, but she hasn't turned up yet. There's still hope she's alive, of course, but the best chance is within the first twenty-four to forty-eight hours," he said gently.

"And it's been a week," Trista added for him.

She was too in shock to cry. She had worked with Maureen for years; she was practically family. Maureen was the one who introduced Blaine to her. Trista put her head in her hands and stared into space.

That was when she noticed Collin's name on the top of what Jenna gave her to read, but that didn't make any sense to her. She scanned the first few paragraphs for some explanation and drew in a deep, shuddering breath. Her eyes grew wide and she wished she'd read it the moment Jenna gave it to her.

"Oh my God," she cried.

Collin took it from her and read it. Once the shock wore off, she sprang up to action, saying, "We have to call the police. Jenna's in danger."

"No, we don't," Collin said, voice firm.

"Are you crazy? Did you read that?"

"Yes, I did."

"You're being too calm about this. Jenna is in danger. We have to help her. Someone's forcing my best friend to do terrible things. They might even kill her if they found out she gave me this. Call your friend at the police station. Help her!"

Trista waited for Collin to respond. She watched as he looked at the ground and sighed. "Jackson and I are undercover FBI agents. Jackson is with her now, so she's fine. I guarantee he'll keep her safe."

Trista heard the words as they left his mouth, but they didn't register in her brain right away. She watched, dumbfounded, as he dialed his cell phone.

"This is McShae. Take the Whitmans into protective custody right now."

He dialed another number once he'd disconnected the first call.

"Mr. McNamara, I'm glad I caught you. This is Special Agent McShae. No sir, everything is still under control. I wanted to make certain you can still trace the employee we spoke about. Excellent. Please call me the moment you get something. Yes, that's the correct number. Thank you."

Trista looked around the room as though she'd never seen it before.

"Trista, I need you to pull yourself together now."

"What's going on? I don't understand. Jackson can protect her, but he's...wait. He just appeared in her life out of nowhere. So did you. What does the FBI want with her?"

"Jenna was under investigation, but this would help clear her if I can corroborate it."

"Investigation?"

"Caldwell will be relieved," Collin said as he dialed another number on his cell phone.

"Wait. Why was Jenna under investigation? What's going on?" Something occurred to her. "Jackson is undercover?" The realization of what was going on washed over her. Her best friend would be destroyed by this.

"For your own safety, I can't tell you more than you already know. I need you to get ready to go. It will raise suspicion if you aren't there. You can't let Jenna know anything is wrong. Jackson's cover cannot, under any circumstances, be blown tonight. Do you under-stand?"

Trista nodded. Her throat was far too dry to speak.

"Do you think you can do what I've asked?"

She nodded again, wordless. How could she face her best friend in the world knowing everything she believed was a lie? Jenna was in love with Jackson, yet he was only with her to investigate her.

How could that asshole do this to her?

Chapter 27

With the head start we had, Banks wouldn't know I ran off with Jenna until it was too late to catch us, but getting to a country without an extradition treaty posed a problem. Unless I found a way to smuggle Jenna out of the country, she needed a passport. Mine was always in the glove box. Even though I planned to tell her everything once we got where we were going, I couldn't risk raising her suspicion.

I tried to make my voice nonchalant. "What do you think about someplace sunny, tropical?"

"I like that idea. Florida or California?"

"Actually, I was thinking Mexico. Should we go back to the condo for your passport?"

"Um…" She opened her purse and rummaged for a moment. "Nope. I've got it right here."

She was walking around with her passport? Who does that? Who expects to leave the country on a moment's notice?

Federal agents.

International salespeople.

Criminals.

I couldn't do this. Pulling over onto the shoulder, I turned to Jenna. "This is a crazy idea, isn't it?"

"A little, yeah." She bit her lip. "I'm all for Mexico, but I'd sort of like to pack a few things first. Maybe we should stick with the reunion for now."

We were at the reunion for a half hour before my cell phone rang. Jenna was at my side, so I answered carefully.

"It's Collin. Two pieces of good news. One, the clerical staff came through and I'm getting my team into position. Two, Jenna isn't involved. She's clean."

I was stunned. "Are you certain?"

"Positive. I'll fill you in on the details later, but the short of it is I was given a piece of evidence to clear her and I just got it substantiated."

"This could be good news. I need to know how you know for sure."

"Is Jenna standing there with you?"

"Of course. Why?"

Collin hesitated. "Call me back when you're alone."

"Why?" I didn't understand why he wouldn't tell me.

"You won't want to be around anyone when I tell you," he answered before disconnecting.

After I hung up I turned to Jenna and said, "I'm sorry about that. I need to make another call that could last longer."

"Is everything all right?"

"Perfect, Jenna." I gave her a quick kiss, pulled away to gaze at her, then gave her a deeper kiss. "I'll be back in a few minutes."

As soon as I was out of her view, I sprinted to the hotel room my team was using as its mobile command center. I had to stop them from approaching anyone. We would be better served if they joined the other teams at the airport. Even though nothing should happen tonight, we'd agreed to man the terminal twenty-four hours in advance in case Blackstone showed up to set things up.

I called Collin the moment the last agent had cleared out of the room.

"Are you alone?"

"Yeah," I barked. "Stop wasting time and tell me how you cleared Jenna."

I listened as he relayed his visit with Trista to me. He didn't go into much detail about their conversation, but I hoped Trista could keep her mouth shut. Facing Jenna with the truth about me would be hard enough. It would be impossible to make her understand if her best friend got to her first.

When he paused, I asked, "How did you substantiate it?"

Collin cleared his throat. "Because Blackstone was at the reunion, we sent someone into his apartment. He, uh, found some tapes."

"Tapes? What does that have to do with this?"

"They were surveillance tapes. Of Jenna's apartment."

"He's been watching her!" I shouted into the phone, understanding why he wanted me alone when he told me.

"I had our man view the tape for Monday night and it turned out that everything Jenna said happened actually happened."

I slumped down into the desk chair. "What's going on with the rest of the tapes?"

"They've been taken in as evidence."

My throat was dry. "All of them?" Jenna might forgive me for my deception, but I doubted I'd ever get her to forgive me once she found out half the FBI had seen us having sex.

"I've had one of my tech pals assigned to handle the viewing. He'll be discreet about it. I can arrange for him to have you present when he views certain rooms."

"What certain rooms?"

Collin cleared his throat again. "The rooms that, um...you know...where the two of you...uh..."

I'd always prided myself in being a man who wasn't often embarrassed, but that was out of the question in this situation. I was hard pressed to think of a room in which I hadn't practically ripped off her clothes. "That would be all of them." I paused and blew out a breath. "I don't want to hold up the investigation. Just make sure that this guy understands...Jenna would be destroyed if she knew..."

"You can trust me on this one, Jackson. You just make sure Blackstone doesn't head back here until we've finished replacing the tapes with dummies."

I disconnected the call and buried my head in my hands. Once I was reasonably certain I'd be able to face Jenna again, I left the room. I'd spotted Blackstone the moment we arrived and I'd been itching to take him down then. Now that I knew what he'd done, I just hoped I'd get five minutes alone with him before he lawyered up. He tried to set up Jenna, to make me doubt her, and I had no intention of letting him get away with that.

But he was already gone.

The agent assigned to tail him had lost him while I was on the phone with Collin. He could be anywhere by now. I called Collin back and broke the news. Losing Blackstone so close to zero hour...this was a setback we could ill afford.

Now, I just had to figure out how I could go back to Jenna and pretend everything was still fine.

Chad laughed at how easy it was to elude the agent following him. He'd learned to drive on these roads and knew just how to get away. The agent probably reached the dead end before he realized he was no longer following the correct car.

Fulfillment of his revenge was close now. So much had been put into the planning that Chad was on autopilot. Unstoppable, really.

Once he reached his destination, he pulled over. He slipped into his coveralls and grabbed the bag. The FBI might know who he was, but they would never be able to figure out his plan until it was too late. It was too ingenious.

It was the fuel. They would never think to check for contaminated fuel. Even if they did, it was unlikely they'd notice his nasty little creation until it was too late. It would remain dormant in the fuel until after takeoff. Once enough of the fuel burned, the chemicals would produce a highly toxic gas that would seep into the cockpit, killing the pilots. With no one to fly the plane, every man, woman, and child on board would die.

Chad learned on the Internet that after the appropriate amount a fuel was determined for a particular flight, the airlines would mark the container it was in with the flight number to avoid confusion. It still baffled him that one could find out those kinds of details on the web, but he wasn't complaining. His task was reduced by Monday Night Football. Apparently, all of his enemies would be on the same flight tomorrow to attend Monday's game.

Chad enjoyed the irony. The very game that brought those scoundrels together against him, the game they loved with all their life, would bring them together to die.

"I just got a call from McNamara. Blackstone is in the offsite fuel storage hanger. This is going down tonight. You need to get here. Now," Collin said.

"I'll be there as soon as I can," I said, disconnecting the call.

Jenna gave me a worried look.

"I'm sorry, honey, but I have to go. There's an emergency at work."

Trista shot me a look. "You're leaving? Now."

I was the only one who understood the implications of her tone. "If there was any way for me to stay here, I would."

"But...I thought you were supposed to be here all night. With Jenna."

Jenna shook her head at the blonde. "Lay off, Trist. It's really not that big a deal. Things are intense with the merger right now."

"Right. The merger."

What the fuck did she think she was doing? Was she trying to blow my cover?

I turned to Blaine. "Would you mind taking Jenna home for me? I'm not sure how long this is going to take."

"No problem. We have to start packing Trista's condo tomorrow anyway, so we're staying at her place tonight."

"Thank you." I exchanged a meaningful glance with Trista. I just needed her to keep her mouth shut for the rest of the night. Once I dealt with Blackstone, I could come clean with Jenna.

I pulled Jenna to the side. "I am sorry about this."

"It's okay. I know you'll make it up to me when you get home."

"Indeed I will."

I gave Jenna a kiss and ran out of the building to my SUV.

Fifteen minutes later, I was on the scene amidst a sea of law enforcement personnel. I wondered if we had a standoff in progress. Once I saw the look on Collin's face, I knew we weren't that lucky.

"He's gone."

I didn't want to believe the words I heard him speak. "How did he get away?"

"In all of our planning, we never thought about the fuel. None of the teams were close enough. He was gone when we got here."

"Fuck," I screamed into the air. "We were so close."

"We have isolated and contained the contaminated fuel. We're locking down every mode of transportation out of the city and the nearby highways are being shut down as we speak."

I shook my head in frustration. "He can still get out. Every town has a black market for people-smuggling. He'll have to meet one of them somewhere." I took off my tie and unfastened the button at my collar. Stuffing the tie in my jacket pocket, I added, "We'll get him when the deal takes place. He either leaves this town in handcuffs or a body bag."

We spent the next few hours getting our teams regrouped. The metroplex was too large to handle alone. We had to call in local law enforcement, which felt like it took forever to mobilize. Once I was certain everyone knew the area they were covering, I pulled Collin aside.

"Go home."

"I can't do that, Jackson."

"Look, there's the very real chance this won't be over tonight. One of us needs to get some rest to be ready for tomorrow."

"You should go home, too," Collin snapped. "Every available agent is on this right now. Jenna could still be in danger."

He could be right. We found Foster and Rodriguez and left them in charge. We both left as the media started to arrive. I was grateful for the timing. I didn't want Jenna to find out I was with the FBI while she was watching the news.

It was after midnight when I arrived home. I was opening the door to the building when my cell phone rang. I knew that I shouldn't have left the scene. I closed the door to take the call outside. I didn't want my conversation to echo through the common area to anyone.

"He was at my apartment," Collin said, his voice void of emotion.

"How can you be sure?"

"He left Maureen's head in a cooler on my doorstep. I'm going after this bastard and when I find him...Jackson, I'm going to kill him."

"Collin, don't do anything stupid. Collin? Collin? Dammit!"

It was too late. He had already hung up. I was about to go back to my car to find him when I noticed movement coming from the other side of the glass entry door. A closer look revealed the movement was near my door.

Jenna was sitting in front of my door with a large envelope. It looked like she had been crying for hours. I decided Collin would have to take care of Collin right now.

I just hoped he wouldn't do anything stupid.

Chapter 28

"I did something bad," Jenna said as I approached.

I helped her up and got her inside my condo. She was shaking so badly I had to practically carry her to the couch for her to sit down. I sat next to her and tried to put my arms around her to comfort her, but she pushed me away.

"What happened to you, Jenna?"

"I heard about what happened at the airport on the news." Her voice was emotionless when she spoke.

I didn't know how, but I'd been made. This was not the way I wanted to explain things to her. "Jenna, I..."

She cut me off. "I think I'm to blame for it." She handed me the envelope containing pictures of Lana and a typed page. Once I'd looked at it, she told me everything she had been through over the past week, including the letter she'd left with Trista for Collin.

So this was what Collin was talking about. I felt stupid for ever believing Jenna could...I'd never seen anyone as upset as she was right now and I could only imagine how hard this weighed on her Monday – and every day since. Fuck. I knew something wasn't right about the conversation we recorded between her and Blackstone.

"Why didn't you tell me sooner? I could have tried to help you."

She met my eyes for a moment before looking away. "I don't think there's a woman alive who'd want to dump this on her new boyfriend. You have such a normal life…I couldn't even imagine trying to tell you about this. I couldn't image what you would think of me. If you knew…I wouldn't blame you for breaking things off with me, but…I already knew I was in love with you. I could almost handle having to keep what was going on a secret, but I couldn't bear losing you on top of it." Her eyes met mine. "I'm in this too deep with you. I can't lose you, Jackson. I can't."

"You won't lose me, Jenna. I'm not going anywhere unless you tell me to go. I'm also in this too deep."

After she was done telling me, she finally let me put my arms around her. She collapsed against me and my heart broke for her. I kissed the top of her head and smoothed her hair down in an attempt to calm her. She went through absolute hell and, all the while, I was pissed off she played me. I felt lower than I ever imagined possible.

How could I ever have doubted her?

She sobbed for several more minutes before falling asleep. I was about to doze off when my cell phone rang. I glanced at her as I picked it up, but she didn't stir.

"I found him, Jackson. He's at Blaine's Rain," Collin said wildly.

"Did you call for backup?"

"No. I want to kill him myself."

This was not what I needed right now. We had the location of the man for whom we were searching, and my partner had flipped his lid. I had to get there before he got himself killed. "Okay, but at least wait until I get there."

"You'd better hurry. I can't promise anything."

After I hung up, I eased Jenna off of me and down onto the couch. I found a blanket and laid it over her. Giving her a kiss on the forehead, I went to stop Collin from making a huge mistake.

All the highways in Grand Prairie, Arlington, Irving, and Dallas were shut down, but the Addison toll road was ignored. Of course, Chad was long gone before they thought to do anything. He could anticipate everything now before it happened.

The FBI agent was easy to lure to the club. Chad saw him long before he let the guy notice him. Getting him alone in the alley was a piece of cake. Leave a door open and watch the lab rat run through for a pellet. But he didn't get a reward, just the sharp point of a hunting knife. Plunging it deep into his back was much more satisfying than he dreamed possible; a definite step up from dogs and cats.

He grabbed the cell phone from him and smashed it on the ground. "You can't stop me now. No one can. Once I pick up my wife, we'll vanish together and be happy. Forever."

Then he slit the guy's throat and watched him bleed, kneeling to get a better look at the life gushing from him. He wanted to see the life drain from his eyes, but he couldn't stay. Some things were more important.

There would be other opportunities for that...

Once he reached the condo, he was delighted to see that the other agent's car was missing. Killing the man who dared defile his sweet Jenna was a satisfying thought, but that would take up precious time; time that he didn't have. Chad slipped into the building and picked her lock with ease, but she wasn't there. He walked across the hall to pick another lock.

He stood over a sleeping Jenna for a long moment before shaking her awake. Just as he hoped, she was groggy and disoriented.

"Come on, Jenna we have to go. Now."

She sat up, fast, worried. "What are you doing here, Chad?" She looked around and rubbed her hands over her face. "Where am...oh. Where's Jackson?"

"Jackson sent me. We have to go. It's Lana."

Chad enjoyed the look of panic that flashed through her eyes before she got to her feet and followed him to the van he started using as his mobile base of operations that night. He also enjoyed the way her dress clung to her and revealed enough of her skin to remind him of how great she looked naked on the video. The anticipation of tearing it off her to get an up close and personal look was maddening.

Not yet, he thought to himself. The fed could come back and he didn't want any interruptions once things got started. He'd waited years for this night and nothing was going to get in his way now.

Not even Jenna.

Once she settled in beside him, he handed her a cup of coffee to help wake her up. He started the engine after she gulped down much of the bitter liquid. It wouldn't be long now before he would have everything he always wanted.

Chad would have what was rightfully his.

I was too late. Jenna was gone when I got back. Blackstone beat me to her.

"Think, dammit," I shouted into space.

Blackstone was unstable and Jenna was with him. I tried her cell phone only to hear it ringing from inside her condo. Her door was locked when I tried it. Why did she choose now, of all times, to start locking her door? I dismissed the thought of picking the lock. That would take away precious time I knew I didn't have.

I kicked it in.

The condo was dark. Her kitten glared at me with terrified eyes, obviously trying to be invisible by remaining motionless. That was something I hadn't planned for. Jenna would be furious if I let her cats out. I picked up the door and put it back up as best I could.

"What the hell am I doing?" I had to figure out where he would take her. He had to know nowhere was safe for him.

I paced back and forth from my door to hers until I heard the sounds of her downstairs neighbor opening their door. Retreating to my condo, I picked up where I left off and paced from room to room for several minutes. The situation was becoming desperate and all I could do was think that Jenna was with a madman who I couldn't stop. My God, he murdered Collin, Maureen, the people in that office building. He would have killed a plane full of people if we hadn't stopped it. Jenna was going to be his next victim if I didn't hurry, but I couldn't think through the wave of sheer panic I was experiencing.

God only knew what he would do to her. He was obsessed with her – with the woman I loved. Images, violent images, filled my brain and clouded my vision. It didn't take a genius to guess what he wanted from her and he wouldn't be able to accept her rejection of him. He'd try to take what he wanted anyway, then he'd take revenge on her...like Collin. A wave of nausea washed over me at the very thought of Jenna broken and bleeding at his hands. I couldn't let this monster hurt her. If he touched one hair on her head, I would rip him from limb to limb with my bare hands.

I wasn't an agent right now. I was a desperate man in love. A man on the edge.

No, I was a man wasting time.

I racked my brain for any next step that would seem rational to him, but I knew Blackstone was insane. I forced myself to stop thinking like a man terrified for the woman he loved and to start thinking like an agent. My training would have to take over or all was lost. Although Blackstone's actions appeared to be random, I realized what I already knew.

Every single act of violence he committed was because of Jenna or his grandmother, because of his twisted love for them. I knew he would take Jenna to his grandmother's house. He was crazy enough to think that could work.

I ripped into my files and found her address, ignoring the sea of paperwork left on the floor in my wake. The maps I had printed of the city were a frustrating waste of time, but I didn't know my way around the area without it. Collin usually drove.

And with the traffic jams currently still unwinding from shutting down the major highways, the car's GPS would be useless if I had to find a side street quickly.

The quickest way to get there would be to take the Tollway to 190 and head west until I got to I-35...Damn these people had too many highways. I hate Texas. Jenna was going to have to move to D.C. where the people who designed roadways weren't on meth.

I was too frustrated to remember all that, so I grabbed my printed area maps and raced out to my blazer.

"Hold on, Jenna. I'm coming for you." I prayed I'd make it in time. "I want my fucking picket fence."

Chapter 29

"Where are we going, Chad? What's going on?" Jenna asked once she cleared the sleep from her head.

"You'll see. How was the coffee?"

"Fine, I guess. Where did you get it? It tasted like it had lemon in it."

"You're imagining things. I love you, Jenna."

She put up her hand to stop him. "We've been through this already. I value your friendship, but...I'm with Jackson."

Chad retrieved something from the floorboard and handed it to her.

"You need to rethink that. Take a look at this."

Jenna looked at the tiny monitor and saw Jackson on the phone. This was happening in her condo. After she heard his conversation, she watched herself come onto the screen. This happened last Friday night. She didn't understand any of it.

Especially the conversation.

Why was he talking to his sister about Chad? Why would his sister care about him?

"What is this, Chad?"

"You've been used, Jenna. Your boyfriend is with the FBI. He's only been hanging around you to get to me."

Jenna stared at him, but didn't say anything. No way that was true. Jackson told her he loved her. He wouldn't make that up. Would he? To get to Chad? That was insane.

"I don't understand...he wouldn't use me."

Chad smirked. "Really? He spent the last week investigating you."

Jenna was shocked. "Why would he do that?"

"Because I made him think you were my accomplice."

"Your accomplice in what?" Jenna had a sinking feeling in the pit of stomach that she already knew the answer to that.

"It's all over the news by now. My plan was flawless...Why can't you just tell me that you love me?"

"Because I don't."

Jenna watched as darkness swept across his face, transforming it to something wholly evil. He pulled the van onto the shoulder and stopped. They were at the end of construction on 190 and there wasn't another car around for miles for some reason. She knew she should be afraid.

"How can you keep saying that to me? We're supposed to be engaged."

Jenna shook her head in confusion. "What are you talking about?"

"You promised at graduation that we would get married in ten years. It's been ten years and I'm here for you now."

Chad's voice was cold when he spoke and Jenna detected a note of hostility in his voice she never noticed before. She never believed he would take that seriously. Was it possible he'd held onto his crush for the last decade?

"Chad," Jenna began softly, hoping to calm him, "I didn't think you were serious about that. We were always friends, but that was as far as it went. I've never been in love with you."

"Mouthy bitch!" He backhanded her across the face. "I don't remember you being such a fucking slut! What the hell happened to you in Boston? I shouldn't have let you go away to college."

Jenna opened the door and fled the car. She was on an overpass and didn't think she would be able to out-run him in her heels or barefoot. He laughed from behind her, a sickening, evil laugh.

"How do you think it felt to watch you try to fuck the guy right after you rejected me?"

Jenna turned slowly. "You've been watching me?"

Of course he had. How else did he get the record-ing of Jackson from last Friday?

"I saw it all, Jenna. I heard everything you said to each other. I saw you with him in bed, the shower, the floor, the couch...everywhere!" He cleared his throat. "It's a good thing the last guy got himself killed before I found out you were engaged. I would have killed you both be-fore I let you marry another man."

Jenna scanned the roadway, looking for means of escape.

"Go ahead, run, it doesn't matter. The lemon you tasted in your coffee was the Cardenolide Glycosides I added."

Jenna's heart skipped. "The what?"

"You'll be dead soon enough, so I'll put it in easy words for your slut mind. It's a substance found in the sap of the Oleander plant, but I've altered its chemical structure to make it more potent. Your heart should stop soon, but don't worry, sweetness, you'll lose conscious-ness before that happens anyway. Probably."

Nonsensical fragments began merging in her head. What she saw on the news at the airport was

Chad's handiwork. Jackson didn't freak out when she told him because he already knew. Everything. If he was FBI, so was Collin.

Now Trista's strange behavior at the reunion made sense. He must have told her they were FBI when she gave him the letter about the threats to Lana. How could Trista know about Jackson and make it through the evening without telling her?

Jackson's odd behavior made sense when all the missing pieces snapped into place. His cold treatment of her didn't start until after she delivered Daniel's security badge. This whole time he was sleeping with her while he thought...She didn't know what he thought.

Had he only gone to bed with her to get information about a case?

Or was that just a perk?

Jenna watched as Chad retrieved a vile containing a bluish liquid from his pocket before he continued, "I took the liberty of bringing the antidote, but I don't think you'll need it. I bet you wish you said you loved me now."

Before Jenna could respond, she saw the gleam of approaching headlights. She waved her arms like a wild woman in an attempt to stop the SUV, but it was moving too fast and sped past her. Her one hope was gone now. Chad, one of her closest friends from her teenage years, was going to kill her.

I'm going to die, Jenna thought to herself. I'm going to die and he's going to get away with it.

Jenna mustered all her resolve and turned back to Chad. Hatred burned in his eyes and she knew she couldn't let him win. She chose her words with caution and took a careful step towards him.

"You sent me the pictures of my niece, didn't you, Chad?"

He smiled a mirthless smile. "I thought your Harvard education would have figured it out sooner, love. I suppose you were busy being used by a man who doesn't love you."

His words hit Jenna with the force of an avalanche. She was used like a pawn between the two of them, but Jenna knew by the sudden pain in her chest she would never get the chance to find out why Jackson did that to her. Instead, she rallied all of her remaining strength and took another step forward.

"Would I be so much better off with you, Chad? At least Jackson never tried to kill me."

Chad snickered. "Really, Jenna? Really? I know his partner wasn't dead when I left him. I'm sure he was able to tell Jackson I was coming for you before he died. If he loves you so much, where is he?"

"Collin's dead," Jenna whispered as she took another step towards him. Her chest felt like it was ready to explode but her mind was clear. It hadn't been so long ago that she studied the law and she knew what she had to do.

Jackson may have used her, but she was in love with him in spite of it. Jenna clung onto her love, hoping it would give her enough strength to reach the monster a few steps away. If I'm going to die on this overpass tonight, she thought, I will give Jackson all of the evidence he needs to convict Chad for my murder.

She just had to get close enough to get his skin embedded under her fingernails and forensics could do the rest.

I didn't realize until I already exited 190 and was a few miles away on another highway that Jenna was the frantic woman waving her arms from the stalled van I passed. It would take too long to exit and get back to them and I knew I could already be too late. I glanced in my mirrors to make sure no one else was on the road before I slammed on my brakes and U-turned. Traffic was nonexistent on my drive up until this point, probably because of the roadblocks. I prayed my luck would hold long enough to get me back to Jenna.

I found them on the side of the road where I passed them minutes before. It looked like Jenna was moving towards him as I slammed on my brakes. I drew my gun and approached slowly. I couldn't tell what was in his hands, but I didn't want to take any chances.

"Whatever you're doing, Blackstone, I promise you need to stop right now," I said to him. "Jenna, come over here by me."

She looked at me as if in shock, but didn't move. The sight of me standing there with a gun in my hands couldn't be the most comforting sight to her. There would be a time for an explanation of what I was doing, but that time couldn't be now. Blackstone tossed the vile at the ground where it shattered.

He grinned at me. "That was your girlfriend's only chance to live."

"Don't play with me."

"That was the antidote to the poison I gave her and I'm the only man who can recreate it now," he yelled to me, smug.

I flicked a finger over the safety, just to be sure.

"You're bluffing," I shouted back.

I watched as he removed something from a sheath on his hip. Once the light hit it, I realized it was a hunting knife. A sticky red substance glistened on the blade and I knew I had all the proof I would need to take him in. He murdered a federal agent and hadn't even tried to hide it.

He took a menacing step towards Jenna, a grin on his face. "Maybe we shouldn't wait for the poison to take effect. What do you think, agent? Maybe you'd like to watch me slit her throat the way I did your partner. I think you should get to see her bleed."

"Jenna, come over here. You've got to move now."

Instead, she stood, unblinking, watching the scene unfold.

"Oh, you don't think she trusts you right now, do you?" He flourished the knife. "Face it. You killed her. Not me. The three of us wouldn't be here right now if you hadn't gotten in the way of our happiness."

"She was never yours."

"Maybe. She was never yours either. My Jenna wouldn't give you the time of day if she knew what you really were."

"I'm not your anything," Jenna said, barely a whisper.

"Bitch!" Blackstone pounced on her, grabbing her by the wrist to yank her closer. While she was still off balance, he backhanded her hard enough to make her stumble, but he didn't let her fall. Instead, he pulled her in front of him as a human shield.

He grinned at me and licked her cheek. "I would have had fun with you. Now I'm going to have a different kind of fun."

"Let. Her. Go."

"Not a chance." He ran the knife across her skin from her neck to the valley between her breasts. "Heart or neck?"

"Excuse me?" I didn't have the shot. I had to keep him talking until I did.

"Would you prefer I put my knife into her heart or her neck?"

I'd prefer he move a few inches to the left so I could get a shot, but he wasn't waiting for me to answer.

"This guy, Jenna? All the assholes in the world and you needed to fuck this guy?" He moved the blade to her right shoulder and slit the straps. His free hand slid across her hip and pulled at her skirt, hiking it up a few inches. "Let's see if I can make you scream the same way he did."

"Don't touch me."

Her speech seemed slurred. This was going bad fast. I inched forward.

"Don't you fucking move!" He dug the blade's point into the skin at the top of her breast, creating a thin line of crimson. "You've already ruined her for me. Don't think I won't enjoy opening her up for you."

"Take it easy, Blackstone. I was just shifting my weight."

"So am I." His hand crept from her hip the dress's hem. "God, you smell good." His lips grazed her ear. "I can almost pretend you don't smell like him."

Jenna met my eyes, lids drooping. "Chad, I don't love him. Needed him to make you jealous." She drew a shuddering breath. "It's always been you, Chad. Always."

What the fuck?

The knife wavered in his hand. "But you said…"

"Was a game…stupid, silly game." She twisted against him, moving slightly to the right. "Kiss me before I die…"

Without hesitation, I put a bullet between his eyes. I clicked the safety on and rushed to Jenna. There was no time to explain who I really was or what I was doing. Her time was running out.

I placed my hands on her shoulders, trying to keep her with me. "Do you know what he gave you?"

"Oleander," she whispered, collapsing unconscious into my arms.

I had no idea what Oleander was besides the name of a chick flick I didn't see, but the ER staff knew what they were dealing with. They promised to do what they could and took me into the waiting area. I called on the way in to have her family released from protective custody. They had a right to be here with her now.

More right than I did.

They arrived with Trista and Blaine a few minutes after I did. I told them everything I knew about her condition, but kept the details of the situation vague. Trista's eyes shot daggers at me as I spoke.

She slapped me. "You unimaginable asshole! This is your fault. Collin told me you would protect her!"

"What are you talking about, honey?" Blaine asked in an attempt to calm her.

Trista turned to them. "Jackson is with the FBI. He's been lying to all of us since he got here. So has his pal, Collin. Is he off doing your paperwork while you sit up here and pretend to give a shit about Jenna?"

"He's dead. Blackstone took him out before he got to Jenna."

Trista didn't blink. "He killed Maureen, too...didn't he?"

I nodded and Trista turned away, shaking her head.

Elaine looked at me in horror. "Is this true, Jackson?"

I closed my eyes. "I'm afraid it is."

She opened her mouth and no words came out. Her face was expressive as her mind caught up with what Trista already knew about me. I braced myself, waiting for the onslaught of anger she would unleash once she found the words.

"But...Jenna loves you."

"I know. I love her."

"Oh, just shut up." Trista advanced on me. "This is your fault. All of it."

"Trista..."

"Maybe if you'd spent a little more time working on your case instead of screwing around with Jenna while you investigated her then this wouldn't have happened."

"I know."

Everyone was quiet after that. I don't know how much time passed and I didn't care; time was meaningless to me. I rubbed my temples, willing time to stop and move in reverse, but of course, that was impossible.

If only I had been straight with Jenna in the beginning. If only I thought to place a team at the fuel hanger. If only I stopped the first time I passed them. If only…

I looked up at the clock, but the numbers didn't make sense to me. The hands of the clock floated over spinning numbers. I blinked several times to clear my vision and realized tears welled in my eyes.

When Melissa left me, I thought I knew sorrow, but now I realized I had been a damned fool then and I was a damned fool now. If Jenna died…God only knows what Blackstone told her about me. I held my head in my hands and prayed for one more chance to let Jenna know how I really felt about her.

She couldn't die.

"Mrs. Whitman?" a doctor asked as he approached our group.

"Yes, that's me." Her voice was frantic.

"We were able to control the toxin. Your sister is going to be just fine. She's awake now and is asking for you."

"Can I see her?" I asked quickly, rising to my feet.

The doctor raised his hands to stop me. "Right now, she only wants to see her sister. She's still very weak and she can't take a lot of excitement."

Elaine left with the doctor and no one said anything for a long time. I noticed the angry glances Trista and Daniel kept sending my way, but I knew they were justified in their anger. Even Daniel. The man was a lot of things, but I came into his house, played with his daughter, ate dinner at his table and lied my ass off about everything. Mercifully, Blaine broke the silence.

"Well, you certainly had me fooled, Jackson. I never would have pegged you for FBI."

I didn't respond. Elaine returned a few minutes later. Her eyes were cold. Whatever Blackstone told Jenna about me, her sister didn't like it.

"Jenna would like to know if your wife really died, Jackson." Her voice held no emotion.

"No," I answered quietly. "My ex-wife lives in Virginia with my ex-partner."

Elaine crossed her arms over her chest. "Then Jenna would like for you to leave now."

Shit. I knew that slip was going to bite me in the ass one of these days. I woke up almost every morning since I said it wondering when it would catch up with me. Of all the ways I imagined, of all the ways things could end between me and Jenna...Not like this.

"I need to talk to her."

"You can have a different agent question her or debrief her or whatever you call it. But she will not talk to you. She doesn't want to see you and I'm not letting you get anywhere near her. If I was smart, I would have told her to run for the hills to get away from you instead of encouraging it."

"Elaine, this isn't about the case. It's about us."

"There is no us between you and my sister. You used her."

"It's really not like that." I wouldn't be able to make her understand. I didn't have the words to explain how I felt about Jenna. "If I go...Will you at least give her a message for me? Will you let her know that not all of it was part of my job? Will you tell her it was real?"

"No. I've let you hurt my sister enough for a lifetime."

"It's not like...No. I'm not leaving here until Jenna knows that I'm in love with her, really in love with her."

"You need to leave," Trista shouted, drawing the attention of an orderly near the nurses' station.

"I'm not going anywhere. I'll tell her myself and then I'll leave when she tells me to, but she needs to know how I feel about her."

A security officer came into view. "Everything okay here?"

Trista shot me a look. "No. This man is harassing us."

"Sir, I think it's time to go."

"No." I shoved past him in the direction of the patient rooms. "Jenna! Jenna! I love you!"

"Rudy, call the cops and page the other security officers."

Blaine stepped in. "That won't be necessary. He's leaving." He placed a hand on my shoulder. "You're not making things better."

I let him guide me out of the waiting room. "It's not like I can make things worse."

"You may deal with bad guys, but you don't know the meaning of making things worse until you antagonize Trista and Elaine." He waited for the sliding glass doors to close behind us and added, "I'll tell her, Jackson."

"Oh, God, thank you."

"You shouldn't count on it doing any good. Don't get your hopes up." He gave me a serious look. "You don't have any allies in this."

"I know. I just...I need to know I tried. I need to know I didn't lose her without a fight."

He nodded. "I would feel the same if it were Trista." Blaine moved through the automatic doors and turned back to me. "I'm sorry about your partner. He seemed like an okay guy. Maureen really liked him. She told me the last time I saw her." The doors closed between us, severing my last line of communication to Jenna.

Chapter 30

I spent the next week tying up the loose ends of the case and completing the necessary paperwork. I was cleared to return home on Friday, but I wanted to attend Collin's funeral. Though I only knew him a short time, he became a friend to me. He was like family, really. Almost like an annoying younger brother.

A brother whose age I didn't even know.

His family was pleasant, considering the circumstances. Apparently, Collin ran his mouth about work to them and they knew all about me. His older brother shook my hand and told me he heard about the way I dealt with his brother's murderer. His parents acknowledged me and were whisked away by the priest.

I remained at the fresh grave long after everyone else left. I owed him an apology, but couldn't find the words. That night, I made more mistakes than just my behavior at the hospital. I tried to split my focus between the job and Jenna from the moment I fell in love with her. Without fail, I chose wrong every time. When I should have chosen my girlfriend, I chose to be an agent and investigate her. When I needed to be an agent and go after Blackstone with Collin, I chose to be a boyfriend.

In the end, I was neither good agent nor good boyfriend. If I was at the club with Collin, Blackstone wouldn't have the opportunity to kill him and would be in custody before he got to Jenna.

I was near the back of the cemetery when his twin sister approached me. Déjà vu didn't even come close to meeting her. She looked just like Collin, just like someone put him in a dress and stuck a long red wig on his head. And made him hot...incredibly hot.

"So, you're Jackson. It's good to meet the man who made my brother try to be a better agent," she said, lighting a cigarette and walking to the shade of a nearby tree.

"Your brother was a fine agent without my influence."

She blew out a stream of smoke and smiled. "Nice of you to say, considering the circumstances, but I think we both know what my brother was." She cocked an eyebrow. "And what he wasn't."

I wasn't sure how she wanted me to respond to that. "Collin was instrumental in stopping a major catastrophe."

"Somehow I doubt he was able to stop chasing skirts long enough to realize that there *was* a catastrophe to avoid." She dropped her cigarette onto the dew-damp grass and mashed it with a long, pointed heel. "Besides, Collin was too busy being jealous of you. He placed an emergency call to me while I was in the middle of a stakeout to complain how he didn't get to be the primary undercover guy. That's just how he said it – primary undercover guy." She walked over to me and fussed with my tie. "I can see why you were primary. I'm sure you were more than effective." She dropped the tie and her look grew serious. "So, what are you going to do about the girl?"

I took a step back. "Excuse me?"

Her lips curved into another smile. "You know, the mark? You're in love with her right? Collin said you were. I can't imagine she was too thrilled about being played."

"I'm not going to stand here and talk to you about this." I started to walk away, but realized I had no idea what that would accomplish. Turning to face her, I asked, "What do you think I should do?"

She shrugged. "Camp out in front of her door until she trips over you or talks to you. Either way, you'll get a reaction."

"I'm supposed to fly back to D.C. today."

"And? You've broken some rules and you've played some things by the book. What do you have to show for any of it, Caldwell? A broken heart and some frequent flier miles." She shook her head. "Take a chance."

"And if she laughs in my face, calls the cops on me, tells me she never wants to see me again...Then what?"

Again, she shrugged. "Is that really so much worse than spending the rest of your life wondering what she might have said?" She glanced over her shoulder. "I have to go. Look me up if you're ever in New York."

She started to walk away. "But I didn't catch your name."

She glanced back at me, an easy grin on her lips. "Probably a good thing. I wouldn't want to tempt you." She continued walking, waving her hand. "Call your girlfriend. Work things out."

"And if I can't?" I called after her, not expecting a response.

She spun around. "Then come to Manhattan. Look for Kyly in the phonebook."

She was gone.

I stayed in the cemetery for a while after she left. Kyly McShae, huh. If I didn't know better, I would think she was hitting on me at her brother's funeral. Of course, it didn't matter to me one way or the other if she was. Only one woman existed in the world to me and she would probably slam the door in my face as soon as I knocked. Come to think of it, I doubted she would even answer the door.

I checked my watch. I still had some time before I needed to check in for my flight and I already finished packing my belongings; a crew was coming this afternoon for the standard issue stuff.

What the hell? It's not like I could lose Jenna again. She was already gone.

I called the hospital every day to see how Jenna was, but she never accepted my calls. After spending a week under observation, I learned she was released. My emotions were still raw from the funeral, so I should have stopped to collect myself before going over to her condo and pounding on the door. But that would require rational thought; something I didn't have, something I hadn't had since Jenna collapsed into my arms, dying.

When she didn't answer, I kept on knocking. "Come on, Jenna. I know you're in there."

"Actually, she's not," Trista said as she approached from the stairs. "It seems some nutcase busted down her door."

I turned to face her. "You and I both know why I did that."

"Yeah. We both know you were just doing your job. The whole time. Why don't you go back to your life and leave Jenna to pick up the pieces of hers?"

I sighed. "I need to talk to her before I can go. When will she be back?"

She regarded me with ice in her turquoise eyes. "She has no intention of coming back until I've confirmed you've moved out."

"Fine. I'll go and bang on her sister's door until she comes out."

Trista shook her head. "She's not there either. We knew you would think of that, what with all of your FBI training."

"Trista," I pleaded, "I have to talk to her before I go. Just tell me where she is. Hell, come with me and supervise if that's what it will take for you to tell me."

"I think you've hurt her enough for one lifetime, don't you, Jackson? Wait. Is that even your real name?"

"It's my name. You have to believe I never meant to hurt her. I swear to you, Trista. I tried not to get involved with her, but how could I not fall in love with her? She's everything to me. I can't control what she feels, or if she hates me, but I can let her know it was real – all of it. I have to let her know how much I love her before I can walk away and pretend she didn't change my whole world."

Trista's expression softened. "Do you mean that?"

"Yes."

"Every word of it?"

"Yes. Please help me, Trista," I begged.

She bit her lip to buy time. "She's at her sister's house."

"I thought you said she wasn't there?"

"I lied. We thought hiding her in plain sight while Blaine used her credit cards on the other side of the metroplex would be the easiest thing to do."

I hugged her. "Thank you. Thank you, Trista."

I took off down the stairs.

"I can't guarantee she'll see you," she called after me.

I knew that, but I had to try.

*****

"You have some nerve showing up here like this," Daniel said the moment he opened the door.

"My flight is in a few hours. I need to see her before I go."

"It's all right, Daniel," Jenna said, walking up behind him. "I'll take care of this myself."

"I'll be in the kitchen if you need me," he replied before he left.

Her eyes were cold when she looked at me...when she looked through me. "What do you want, Agent Caldwell?"

Once I saw her, I wanted to hold her, but I restrained myself. That would be the quickest way to get the door slammed in my face. Even though she looked like she'd gotten about as much sleep as I had – which wasn't saying a lot – she was still the most beautiful woman I'd ever seen. I wanted to make her understand everything I felt in my heart. I wanted her to know everything I could never find the words to say.

"Well?" she asked impatiently.

"I love you, Jenna."

She shuddered. Then she did the one thing I never expected. She punched me square in the jaw. "No, you don't! You used me and even worse, you used the memory of my dead fiancé to get to me."

She had one hell of a punch. "I swear to you, Jenna, I didn't know about that until the second you told me."

"Stop lying to me, Jackson!"

"I'm not. You said it yourself; the relationship was kept secret. It wasn't in any of the intelligence we had on you. I'll let you read the files if you want."

"You are some piece of work...read the files...they've probably already been doctored." She fought to remain calm. "Why should I believe you?"

I looked her in the eye. "I may have lied about what I did for a living and why I was here, but I swear to God that everything between us was the truth."

"You lie for a living."

"Look, it may have been my job to come here, to become a part of your life, but you should know that I don't regret meeting you. I tried to keep everything plutonic between us to keep things from getting complicated."

"So this is my fault now?" She shook her head and blew out a breath. "What is this? I just kept on tossing myself at you and you eventually thought it might be fun? Was it pity?"

"No, Jenna, it was all me. I wanted you the second I laid eyes on you, but I didn't want to hurt you so I tried to get close to you as a friend. I thought I could handle just being friends with you. I was wrong. Once I realized how amazing you were, I couldn't stay away from you. I tried to tell myself I had to stop things with you before they went too far, but how could I not be with you, make love to you, fall in love with you?"

I watched as Jenna put her hands over face and ran them through her hair. It looked like she was about to cry. The last thing I wanted was to cause her more tears. I wondered if anything I said got through to her.

"How can I believe a word you say, Jackson? You told me your wife was dead to make me feel sorry for you."

I sighed. "No, the person I was supposed to be when I was undercover was never married. When we were talking, I let her name slip and I had to tell you something."

"But not the truth," she said bitterly.

"If you really want to know, Melissa left me for my last partner. Frankly, it's easier to pretend she's dead than to face the truth that I was the one who was dead inside. I built this wall around my heart after that to keep it from breaking again, but you changed all of that."

Jenna looked away.

"I have two sisters; one older, one younger. When I was growing up, I would always hear my father tell them that whatever heartbreak they were going through would be okay. He said that the sun would still come up and set the following day and that the world would go on despite their pain. No offense to my father, he's an intelligent man, but he never would have said that if he'd met you even once."

I took her hand in mine and tapped it on my chest.

"You're in here now. You broke through the wall I built and you'll be in my heart until the day I die. Longer. Without you in my life, the sun doesn't rise and set for me. My world doesn't work unless you're in it."

I watched as a single tear slid down Jenna's cheek. Then another.

"I want so much to believe you, Jackson, but I don't know how."

"You know in your heart I'm telling you the truth, just listen to it."

She was silent. I pulled her into my arms and kissed her, hoping she could feel the truth in my kiss since I couldn't get through to her with words. Of all the miracles I've ever been blessed with in my life, the most cherished was that she kissed me back. It wasn't a stiff kiss and it didn't feel like a good-bye kiss. Jenna wrapped her arms around my neck and kissed me with everything she had. It was a perfect moment in time.

Until her body grew rigid and she pulled away.

Her soulful eyes were full of mixed emotions. There was confusion, anger, love…There was also the silent plea for me to say something, anything, that would repair the damage I'd done. Still keeping her in my arms, I fought to find the words to do the impossible.

"You wanted me to tell you the truth, Jenna, so here it is, as best as I can tell it. I love you. I love you more than I've ever loved anyone else and I love you more than I'll possibly love again."

Tears streamed down her cheeks. "Jackson...I don't know..." Her voice trailed off.

"Tell me you don't love me and I'll leave. If you truly don't love me, if this entire love affair between us was all in my head, then I won't make any trouble for you. You'll never have to think of me again." It was an awful possibility. I took a steadying breath to continue. "But if you can't look me in the eye and tell me you don't love me...I'm not going anywhere. If you need to sleep on it, if you need more time to think...I don't care how long it takes for you to decide. I don't care what I have to do to prove to you that you're it for me. I'll wait right here on this doorstep for you forever if that's what it takes."

Jenna stared at me for a long moment. "I don't know how I'm supposed to respond. I don't know where we're supposed to go from here."

I hugged her close. "Tell me that you love me, Jenna. We have the rest of our lives to work out the details." I pulled back enough to look into her eyes. "Do you love me?"

"Love you, Jackson? I don't even know who you are. I don't know that I can ever forgive you. What did you really expect to accomplish by coming here?" she asked, shoving my arms off her.

My heart sank and I looked at the ground. "I guess I wanted to tell you goodbye then."

Shattered, I turned around to walk out of her life. I paused after a few steps. "It was real, Jenna. All of it."

She remained silent. The only thing in my life that felt right was gone and I had only myself to blame. When I heard the door slam at my back, my heart died.

It was really over.

Epilogue

I decided it was time to start packing. The movers would be here the day after tomorrow to collect my things. It wasn't too late to back out, but I'd worked too hard for it to do that now, even though it wasn't what I wanted anymore.

My homecoming was bittersweet. Banks kept me buried under a steady stream of paperwork and I was actually grateful for the distraction. I wanted to tell myself I had moved on, that it didn't hurt anymore, but the dull ache in my chest was still present every day. It had been two months since I last saw Jenna, yet every morning she was still the first thing in my mind; her face haunting me whenever I closed my eyes.

Work provided no solace, but was the only distraction I had. Even on the good days, Jenna's face was everywhere. A few weeks ago I actually woke up not thinking of her. It gave me hope that maybe I could go on without her. Of course, I now knew that to be impossible. When I picked up my dry cleaning that afternoon, a small picture fell out of my wallet onto the counter. It was one of the snapshots that Lana had wanted at the zoo.

The picture seemed harmless enough at the time and I put it back in my wallet. It didn't hit me at first, but I later realized that was the day we first made love. I thought about burning it a few times. Someone told me once that it was a therapeutic way to obtain closure...probably my younger sister. I needed closure – desperately. I could still remember the way her lips felt on mine that night. I could still remember how her body responded to my every caress. The best part of making love with her was the way she would look into my eyes and say my name as though I were the only man in the world.

She was the only woman in the world...

It was foolish of me to believe for even a moment that I could really have someone like her in my life. I'd even fooled myself into thinking I deserved someone like her. I'm an FBI agent. When all is said and done, I give everything I have to the job and have nothing left for anyone else. Even if things went differently on that porch, if she told me she loved me, if we were able to work things out, then I still wouldn't be able to give Jenna the sort of life she deserved.

Her fiancé was a cop and she better than anyone else understood the danger that came along with the job. Even if by some miracle she took me back then it still wouldn't be fair to her. She'd spend the rest of her life jumping when the phone rang or someone knocked on the door, wondering if the worst had happened to me.

That was no way for anyone to live.

All I had done from the moment I laid eyes on her was hurt her. It was never intentional, but I'd hurt her all the same. My last image of her was that of tears streaming down her face and pain in her eyes – pain I had caused just by being there. I couldn't stand for that to be the one memory that stuck. Jenna looked happy in the picture from the zoo and I couldn't bear to part with it, so now I had a constant reminder in my wallet of the happiness I would never again have. Hell, maybe I never really had it at all. Maybe it was never mine to have.

I spent most of my time at the office on autopilot and, despite the fact that time crept by, the first few months at work flew by only to stand still again. Banks told me the *good* news early last week. I was being transferred to Financial Crimes, just like I always wanted. As I once suspected, the field trip to Dallas was in part to determine if I was ready to move on. I passed their little test with flying colors. Unfortunately, it came with a hefty price. I was also being relocated to the Dallas field office.

I knew I should be thrilled to be getting the job I'd coveted for years, but I was too numb to care. My first thought was that it would be great to live near Jenna again, as though there was any hope for us. Now, I was consumed by the knowledge that I could run into her at any time and she would stare through me like I didn't exist. Of course, I *didn't* exist to her, not anymore. The only thing left between us was a few thousand miles.

Soon I wouldn't even have that.

A knock at the door interrupted my thoughts. I blinked several times after I opened the door, not trusting my eyes. At first I thought I might be dreaming because it was a reoccurring dream of mine.

Jenna was standing in front of me.

"What are you doing here?" I asked, stunned that she was there and dismayed that I hadn't thought of a better greeting.

"I thought it was only fitting to deliver you the manuscript for my novel in person. You did inspire it, after all."

She handed me a bound stack of papers and walked past me into the apartment. It occurred to me after that I should have invited her in, but the synapses in my brain didn't seem to be functioning. I turned my attention to the papers in my hand and could tell what it was about by looking at the title. The Agent Next Door. Cute.

"You can't publish the details of a case without..."

"...the express written permission from the Bureau," she interrupted. "I've had verbal approval for the last month, but your boss signed off on it this morning to make it official. Charming woman."

"You know Banks?"

I couldn't believe that after imagining this moment for the last two months that all I could think of was to ask her if she knew my boss. There were so many things I wanted to tell her, so many things I had even practiced saying. Why couldn't I just say them? It wasn't as though I could make things between us worse than they already were. I had nothing left to lose.

"She was at my farewell book signing this afternoon. Her children are huge fans of mine."

I didn't know she was married; much less that she was a mom.

"Sherry and I had an interesting conversation." She paused and regarded me with hostile caution. "What happened to the tapes, Jackson?"

I hadn't even thought about the tapes since leaving Dallas. After everything was reviewed, the tape containing material information was logged into evidence. They turned the rest over to me.

"I burned them."

Jenna looked skeptical. "You burned them?"

I looked away. "Making a sex tape with your girlfriend is one thing, but it didn't feel right to keep them since neither of us knew they were being made." I turned back to her. "I didn't think you'd want them. I destroyed them so they wouldn't end up on the Internet."

She let out a sigh of relief. "Thank you for doing that."

"I figured it was the least I could do," I said, looking down at my feet. "You look good."

"After a week on the beach, I'd better." A slight smile touched her face. "Trista and Blaine eloped in Bermuda. I had to leave straight from there to get to my first book signing appearance in time."

"Good for them. Blaine seems like a good man."

"He is." She bit her lip. "He, uh, pulled me aside to tell me what you said that night at the hospital."

"Well...he said he would."

There were a few moments of awkward silence. "I hear you're relocating to Dallas."

"Yes."

I didn't know what else to say to her. I hadn't heard from her since the day I left Dallas. I'd picked up the phone no fewer than a hundred times, but I could never make my fingers dial her number. I'd even gone so far as to do enough snooping to get her email address. I could fill a book with the number of e-mails I'd written to her and never sent.

Jenna standing in front of me now was everything I had wanted, yet at the same time, it wasn't. In the dreams, I pulled her into my arms and kissed her. Her response varied every time I had it. Sometimes she had kissed me back; sometimes she slapped me and left. Either way, I was left with same hollowness I felt every day.

The oddness of one of her earlier statements struck me. "Wait. Did you say your farewell book signing? You aren't writing anymore?"

"Not children's books, anyway. What you have in your hands will hit bookstores in the spring. That will determine if I stay with it. I'll be plenty busy in the meantime. I passed the Bar last week."

"Why?" I didn't understand why she was telling me any of this, but I didn't care. All that mattered was that she was here with me. A part of me didn't care if we spent hours making small talk as long as it kept her near me. I hated the idea of her leaving far more than I hated making idle chitchat.

Hell, she could sit down and read the phonebook to me if she wanted to.

"Law gets in your blood and Trista needed some-one to work for once she got back from her honeymoon. I start in the Collin County Prosecutor's Office after the first of the year."

Sure, because why wouldn't she go to work in the one county in the state that would remind me of my dead partner?

"Okay," I said softly. "Why are you telling me this?"

"You're moving to my town and I wanted to set the ground rules."

"That's a good idea. In your new line of work, we're bound to cross paths. I meant it when I said I wouldn't make trouble for you. I don't want my transfer to make things any more difficult than they have to be. For either of us."

"Exactly. Don't ever lie to me again."

"Done," I said. "And?"

With our history, I knew that couldn't be all of it. I prepared myself for the laundry list that was sure to come.

"And...I've missed you, Jackson."

I shook my head in disbelief. "What?"

"Don't misunderstand; I'm still angry with you for lying to me. I may never be able to forgive you for all of the lies. After you left, I thought about what you said some more and I realized you hadn't lied to me about what was important though." She paused and picked at an imaginary piece of lint on her coat. "I understand that you didn't lie about loving me. Even when you thought I was part of some diabolical plot, I know you weren't fak-ing your feelings for me." Her lips curled into a half-smile.

"Actually, your spontaneous road trip to Mexico idea makes more sense now."

My mind was racing. "What are you saying, Jenna?"

"I'm saying that maybe when you get settled in Dallas, you can call me. We can't pick up where we left off since I don't know who you are, but maybe we can try to start over." She glanced at her watch and frowned. "I have to go. My flight home leaves soon. I...guess I'll see you around."

Jenna placed her hand on the doorknob and paused. She looked back at me and I saw that same loving look in her eyes I'd seen before it all fell apart. Even though her face was expressionless, her eyes told me she was still in love with me. I wanted to pull her into my arms and never let go.

Her voice was broken when she spoke. "Jackson..."

I didn't know what I was waiting for. This was her way of making a move without actually having to make one. Dammit, why wouldn't my legs move and take me to her? Why didn't I say something that would help instead of what I said?

"Yes?"

Jenna's eyes glistened with the tears I knew she was too proud to cry in front of me. "Uh...Merry Christmas, Jackson."

I watched her leave and stared at where she had stood for a moment. It must have taken a lot for Jenna to come see me. She must have realized she could easily come and go and I'd never know she was in town. Her explanation as to why she stopped by made sense when she said it, but it felt more like a ruse as the words played over and over in my head. That was when it hit me; I let her get away once before, but I didn't have to make the same mistake twice. If she had even five minutes to spare before her flight then I was going to spend every second of that time with her.

I grabbed my coat and chased after her. She didn't have any luggage with her so that told me she must have a cab waiting. I made it to the street just in time to see her reaching for the door to a cab.

"Jenna! Wait!"

Her eyes met mine and she froze. The tears she was so careful to conceal were now free. I hurried to close the distance between us before I awoke from this dream and she was gone.

"What are you doing, Jackson?"

I captured her mouth with mine and kissed her the way I'd imagined every day for the last two months. When I broke the kiss, I held her close and whispered in her ear, "Don't go. Not yet."

"I have to go...or...I'll miss my flight."

I pulled back and looked into her eyes. "Then miss it, Jenna. I'm heading that way the day after tomorrow. Stay here with me and I'll take you home." When I noticed the apprehension on her face, I added, "I'll sleep on the couch. I just want time to talk."

"I can't. Tomorrow's Christmas. My family is expecting me."

"Tell them you had a change of plans. They'll understand."

Jenna shook her head. "My family hates you, Jackson. They won't understand."

The cab driver stuck his head out the window. "Are you getting in or what, lady? I don't got all day."

I opened the door and grabbed her luggage. "No. She isn't getting in."

"Jackson...what are you doing? I have to go."

I paid the cab driver. "Let me drive you to the airport."

She bit her lip. "I don't know..."

"Please, Jenna." I walked the short distance to my car and placed her bags in the backseat. I turned back to her. "I just want a few more minutes with you before you go. Besides, you're not going to find another cab in this weather in time to get to the airport."

Wordless, she got in and fastened her seatbelt. I followed suit and turned to face her. "You should know something before I start the car."

She looked worried. "What?"

"You should know that you don't need to look so worried. I'm a highly trained federal agent. You have a much better chance of getting to the airport in one piece with me behind the wheel than you would with a random cabbie."

"I've seen your driving, Jackson. Are you planning to go the wrong way on anymore highways?"

I started the engine and grinned. "Naw. I only do that when I'm trying to rescue a pretty girl."

"And?"

I saw her smile out of the corner of my eye. "I'm off duty tonight. The only pretty girl I want to talk about is sitting next to me and she doesn't need rescuing."

"No, I'm good right now. But...I did. I know that. He was going to kill me if you hadn't..."

"I couldn't let that happen. No power on this earth could stop me from getting there in time."

Jenna was quiet after that. We made good time on the way to the airport – too good. I carried her bags for her all the way to the gate, mildly surprising her when I flashed my badge to get past a security checkpoint.

"Isn't that an abuse of power or something?" she asked once we were past the final security guard.

"Probably, but it was worth it."

When she was about to board the plane, I mustered the courage to ask her the one question I needed answered before I could say goodbye to her again. I touched her elbow to stop her from leaving. "Jenna..."

She turned to face me. "Jackson?"

"I need to know. Do you still love me?"

"No," she said, her voice soft. "I'm still in love with this man who spent the whole day at the zoo with me and pretended to be a flamingo with my niece. I should get over him before I let myself fall in love with anyone else."

I touched her face. "That was me, Jenna."

She met my gaze. "I don't know if that was the real you or not. It's still hard to separate fact from fiction." She took a breath. "I need time."

I brushed my lips over hers in a tender kiss. "You may not believe it yet, but I love you, Jenna. I'll give you all the time you need."

She picked up her bags and turned to go, but stopped short, turning back to face me. "You know something, Caldwell? You may not be the same man I thought I knew, but I think I like the man you are."

Without another word, Jenna turned and boarded the plane. I stayed in the terminal for a long time after the plane took off. She liked the man I was, huh? It wasn't a declaration of love, far from it, but it was a start.

The day after tomorrow I would be back in Dallas, for good this time. That gave me little more than forty-eight hours to figure out what I was supposed to do next. I didn't have the faintest idea how I was going to turn like into love. Even though I'd done it once before, it was different this time. I couldn't mess this up. Not again. This time I was playing for keeps.

Sure, I'd been in love before. Hell, I'd even been married for a while, but that couldn't count since she'd bailed on the marriage. This time I was actually in love with a woman I could spend forever with.

It was my first time and I knew I'd never forget the way it felt.

The End

Sydney Katt has been writing books for as long as she could string words into sentences. Today, her books are more complex and feature romance, murder and mayhem, all subjects her grade school teachers frowned upon.

Happily married since before the beginning of time, Sydney and her husband live in the Dallas area, where three demanding cats rule their lives. When they aren't slaying video game dragons, the five of them keep a watchful eye for the first signs of the Zombie Apocalypse.

For more information about Sydney's adventures in Dallas, new book projects and upcoming releases, visit www.authorsydneykatt.com if you dare.

NEED MORE SYDNEY KATT?

Turn the page for a preview of

The Shattered Alliance
Undercover Series Book 2

Available May 2013

Prologue

Love is a fickle bitch. That's right. I said it. Some-one had to.

It's not that I have anything against love, per se. I just...it's complicated. Suffice it to say, she and I have met and parted ways. A few times. Each time, she sucker punched me then kicked me while I was down.

In retrospect, all those little things I took for granted pop into crystal focus. All those tiny details I didn't care enough to see at the time reveal themselves to me as what they really were: pivotal moments. These are the insignificant pieces of life – picking up dry cleaning, smiling at a stranger in the coffee shop, answering the phone.

But here's the thing...life and death don't bow down to a simple trip to the cleaners. The fate of the world doesn't hang in the balance of a ringing phone.

Actually, that's a lie. Answering that one phone call a few weeks ago set a chain of events into motion that I could no more avoid than I could possibly hope to stop. Sending that call to voicemail would save my life.

The choice I made to answer it is what killed me. I know that now.

Answering that call killed the one I love most in the world, even if I didn't know it at the time.

Despite it all, I can't blame love for this. I'm the fool who ran blindly into that bank, thinking my eyes were open because I could see. Unfortunately, love chose this unique moment in time to restart our turbulent affair. Now things are...difficult, to say the least. Getting the love I've waited a lifetime for right now is cruel. How long did I get to revel in it? A few days?

Fickle bitch.

Does love realize that dying now is an unfathomable fate? Three weeks ago, I could be standing in this bank, staring down the barrel of his gun, and I wouldn't so much as blinked. The end of my life was little more than the bitter matching bookend to what started this whole mess those years ago. But now...

Now I have so much to lose. I have everything to lose.

Funny, I always thought my life would flash in front of my eyes during my last moments, not a contemplation on the nature of love. There's something ironic about that. Or is it something else? I never paid much attention to all those grammar lessons back in school.

Too late to figure it out now. He's done grandstanding. He's pulling the trigger.

Well, Love, I guess I'll meet you in hell...